NO LONGER HUMAN

Placido climbed out of the car, reached for the unit's radio. He thumbed the Send button. "Dispatch and any and all units in Fourth Precinct, we have a blue-on-blue incident. Two are dead, one dying and the shooters are still at large, so please send us a goddamned ambulance and some coverage—"

Hands grabbed his ankles. Screaming, he jumped back, but the grip on his legs yanked him off his feet. White hands, coated with slimy white fur. He fell hard on his ass and found himself staring as something inhuman crawled out from under the car and climbed up his legs.

Something in a cop's uniform.

Placido frantically crabbed backward on his elbows, kicking the melting white mess in what he took to be its face. Its jaw came off like hinges out of rotten wood. Bloated bladders swelling out of its misshapen skull popped and splattered white foam everywhere. Its features slid off to reveal the grinning skull underneath, but still it kept coming. . . .

Other *Leisure* books by John Skipp and Cody Goodfellow:

JAKE'S WAKE

By John Skipp:

THE LONG LAST CALL

By John Skipp and Craig Spector:

THE BRIDGE

"In *Spore* [...] mas-
terwork [...] and
visceral [...] efore
and man [...] *Living
Dead* and the down and dirty drug-dealing grittiness of
HBO's *The Wire*."

—John Joseph Adams, bestselling editor of
Wastelands and *The Living Dead*

"*Spore* is infectious. Let it seduce you with its drug-fueled
mayhem, powerful imagery, engagingly complicated people,
and extremely fun plot—with zombies as you've never seen
them before. Enter a Los Angeles so well rendered that you
can feel your lungs filling with smog, and check out this
brand-new powder. Just one taste and you're hooked."

—Amelia Beamer, author of *The Loving Dead*

"An ever-escalating symphony of violence, cruelty and
gore."

—Monica S. Kuebler, *Rue Morgue* on *Jake's Wake*

"Skipp and Goodfellow have the ability to hit the reader,
and hit him hard. . . . I loved it."

—Peter Tennant, *Black Static* on *Jake's Wake*

"Skipp and Goodfellow get inside your brain, and they
know just where to detonate the explosives for maximum
effect."

—Christopher Golden, author of
The Boys Are Back in Town

"Don't call the nurse, call the hearse. Here come Skipp and
Goodfellow with a pair of sharpened undertaker's shovels
and a new novel called *Jake's Wake*. You want some fire
and even more brimstone, step right up . . . but watch out.
These boys are about bad business and bad intentions. No
one's going to rest in peace around here."

—Norman Partridge, author of *Dark Harvest*

"Like thunder and lightning, Skipp and Goodfellow are two singularly powerful forces that make one dynamic, masterful combination."
—Brian Keene, author of A *Gathering of Crows*

PRAISE FOR *NEW YORK TIMES* BESTSELLING AUTHOR JOHN SKIPP AND *THE LONG LAST CALL!*

"Readers with a taste for . . . blood and guts . . . will enjoy Skipp's latest excursion into Splatterpunk. . . . Think Stephen King's *Needful Things* meets *From Dusk to Dawn*."
—*Publishers Weekly*

"A mind boggling jolt to the brain. . . . Unforgettable and addictive."
—Stuart Gordon, director of *Re-Animator*

"One thing is for certain: John Skipp ain't lost his touch. One of the founding fathers of Splatterpunk has produced a gruesome, zippy little number that does anything but ratchet things down. . . . The book hurtles along at a bullet train's pace, and Skipp has that golden ability to draw the reader further along in the story than he or she may wish to."
—*Fangoria*

"Just try to put this frenetic novel down, we dare you."
—*Rue Morgue*

"John Skipp is a badass."
—Dread Central

CRITICS PRAISE CODY GOODFELLOW!

"A new and original author. Goodfellow's descriptive passages leap off the page, his dialogue snaps and crackles."
—Jack Olsen, author of
Son: A Psychopath and His Victims

"Goodfellow is one of those writers whose voice sweeps you away like the undertow of a tsunami, and once you're in, he's got you pinned."
—Michael A. Arnzen, author of *Grave Markings*

SPORE

John Skipp
and
Cody Goodfellow

Dorchester
Publishing

DORCHESTER PUBLISHING

December 2010

Published by

Dorchester Publishing Co., Inc.
200 Madison Avenue
New York, NY 10016

ISBN 13: 978-1-4285-1134-7
E-ISBN: 978-1-4285-0974-0

The "DP" logo is the property of Dorchester Publishing Co., Inc.

Printed in the United States of America.

Visit us online at www.dorchesterpub.com.

ACKNOWLEDGMENTS

Skipp and Goodfellow would like to thank the following places and things for representing so much of what's to love about Los Angeles, thereby balancing out all the far less lovable parts:

Little Ongpin, Freak Beat Records, Earth 2 Comics, Joe Peep's, Big Tommy's, Kung Pao Bistro, Noodle Planet, Tree People, White Oak Dog Park, Cinespia at Hollywood Forever Cemetery, The Vista, The Cineramadome, New Beverly Cinema, Video Club of L.A., Sanamluang Cafe, Dark Delicacies, Golden Apple, Iliad Books, Wacko's/The Soap Plant/La Luz de Jesus, Skylight Books, Copy Hub, Cass Paley's swimming pool, Marc and Rebecca's Thanksgiving Orphan's Feasts, KCRW, Amoeba Records, The El Rey Theater, the Eagle Rock Coffee Table Bistro, Taco Spot, The Oinkster, Lemongrass Cafe, M.O.C.A., the Getty, Meltdown, The Bucket, Griffith Park, Bronson Caves, the Los Feliz Farmer's Market, Yuca's, Neverending Panel, Samuel French, Mystery & Imagination (a.k.a. Bookfellows), The Best Fish Taco in Ensensada, the open fields and winding roads adjoining Hamilton/Skipp Manor, Earthquake Weather on Dubstep.fm and the Museum of Jurassic Technology.

And, as always, our families and friends.

SPORE

PROLOGUE

Crossing the Bridge

Los Angeles was a drug, and it wasn't a good one.

It made assholes out of people who were supposed to be your friends.

When Tommy Rubini finally screamed "YOU ALL SUCK!" and threw his mic to the floor, jumped off the stage, and stormed out of the loft party, his crappy band was still slamming away behind him. They were so hammered that they were probably barely even aware he was leaving. They certainly couldn't remember how to play the goddamn songs.

He half hoped someone would follow him out, tell him he'd done the right thing. He didn't want to be stopped—nothing and no one could convince him to stay another minute—but he hoped that at least *someone* would notice, even if no one cared.

They noticed, all right, as he plowed through their ranks. In fact, some of them were actually applauding as he passed. As if to say, "Yeah! HIT THE ROAD, MOTHERFUCKER!"

It was the first and only applause he'd gotten all night.

Anger got him off the stage, but shame took him the rest of the way out the door. That, and the eyes that followed him, mocking, as if suddenly *he* was the asshole.

Then Nando laughed into the other mic and yelled, "Yeah? *You WALK home*, pendejo!"

That was when the fear set in.

Tommy slammed the door behind him, and the volume cut abruptly in half. But the applause roughly doubled, and the band kicked in hard, as if to signal they were *glad* that he was gone, like a great weight had been lifted from their shoulders.

Suddenly, they almost sounded good.

It was a hideous moment of truth.

He had to ask himself: did he honestly suck that bad? Even he, the only one who *wasn't* hammered, and was actually giving his all? Sure, he'd missed some notes—how could you even *find* the notes, when those guys were so monstrously out of tune—but it wasn't like he wasn't trying. He'd been screaming his ass off for fifteen minutes, trying to get everybody to feel the depth of his hard-core alienation and pain.

But it was just a joke to them.

And by extension, so was he.

Tommy Rubini was tall and thin, a pasty eighteen-year-old straight-edge punk rock scarecrow. He wore tight red jeans cuffed above his high-top sneakers, a baggy gray hoodie two shades darkened by his sweat.

As soon as he was old enough, he had run off to L.A. to become somebody. It had seemed like the right thing to do. But it was almost too horrifying to contemplate, now, just how stupid that decision had been.

Downtown Los Angeles, in the middle of the night.

You could die out here, he thought to himself.

Down the stairs, the fluorescent lights flickered an epileptic rhythm that two hipsters with glow sticks danced to, striving to outdo each other with retarded pop-lock maneuvers. They burst out laughing as he passed. Maybe they saw the show.

Nobody came after him as he turned out of the Brewery complex parking lot, huge fences topped with razor wire, and walked onto First Street with a heart full of dread.

You could die out here. It was like a mantra now. *Somebody could shoot or stab your ass—for money you don't even have, or for no good reason—right here on the street. And they might not find you for days.*

Or—and this thought made him angry again—*you could wait here and beg like a little bitch for someone to give you a ride. Maybe Nando, the last guy on earth who belongs behind the fucking wheel of a car.*

You'd be better off shooting yourself in the head, and getting it over with.

Bleakly, Tommy weighed his options. If he could figure out the spaghetti of overpasses and bridges between here and Union Station, he could catch the Red Line to Hollywood and be home before his worthless bandmates.

Or . . .

He still had his dad's credit card. If the bastard hadn't canceled it, he could buy a one-way Amtrak ticket back to Albuquerque instead. What with tomorrow being Thanksgiving, they might even be glad to see him. Embracing his failure with open arms.

Tommy had run away a year ago last week, dumping high school and family and everything else in his stupid race to self-determination, if not actual fame. The Straight Razors (ha!) was his fourth shitty band since he got to L.A. And they weren't even the worst.

Would they wonder and worry in the morning, when they found his futon undisturbed? Or would they just divide his paltry pile of stuff and place a Craigslist ad for a new lead singer? The way they were carrying on tonight, they probably already filled the vacancy at the party. Fucking jerks.

Framed in those terms, he had no choice but to keep going. Better to die with his pride intact. If this was his moment of truth, then so be it.

And down the road he went: one step after another, each one more willful than the last, hunching down into his hoodie in the hope that no one would see how pale and frail and terrified he actually was.

Cold streetlight glow carved rusty orange halos out of the darkness, illuminating nothing. A dry, chilly Santa Ana wind blew down the avenue, but the night was still freakishly clammy for November. Unwholesome warmth seemed to bleed out of the ground itself, as if everything out here was just a little bit radioactive.

The ugly, blank buildings that crowded the buckled sidewalk were colorless brick boxes, anonymous or scabbed with illegible, ancient signage, most of the doorways boarded or bricked up. There was no sign of anyone else on the street, for blocks in either direction.

You could die out here.

The farther he got from the party, the quieter and more unearthly it became, with just the echoing buzz of freeway traffic bouncing off the walls from far away. As desolate as anywhere in New Mexico, this sub-basement of Los Angeles only drove home the emptiness of the rest of it.

Packed with people who wouldn't piss on you if you caught fire, L.A. was easily the loneliest place he'd ever known.

Skipping over the giant cockroaches basking on the sidewalk—many of which, he discovered the hard way, could fly—Tommy felt like a bug himself, scurrying in a colossal gutter.

And the ugliness flooded him, the clear sensation of doom that had dogged him all his life.

All of which raised that third, most beguiling option.

You could die out here.

And that would be the end of that.

As he rounded the bend, and the road arced up before him, the ugly brown buildings came to an end.

At the mouth of the great bridge, looming suddenly before him.

*   *   *

For Tommy, it was like wandering out of a nightmare and into the back lot of a dream.

He *knew* this place: the lampposts shaped like old-fashioned gas jets, lending a theatrical amber glow to the ornate molded stonework and the triumphal arches set at intervals over the gently soaring span. He knew it from a hundred TV shows and movies, with a shuddering, ghostly déjà vu that transcended never having set foot here before, much less on what was arguably the worst night of his life.

What business did this beautiful bridge have out here, in this industrial hellhole? In movies, the view was always a splendid skyline; but in truth, it looked out on a panorama of eyesores: rail yards, warehouses, prisons, and the Los Angeles River itself, a vast concrete bed for a pitiful ribbon of ooze that was less than knee-deep, and less than half water.

Tommy stopped at midspan and leaned on the railing, looking up at the moon. Would he miss it? Of course. Would it miss him? Not at all. Life would go on, empty and full of shit as ever.

He wished he hadn't left his journal in Nando's van. Not that he had anything left to say.

A car honked at him as it crossed the bridge, stereo screeching like a siren; and he clearly heard the passenger scream, "DO IT, YOU PUSSY!"

The wind sucked the warmth out of him, turning the sweat and stink of his failure into a shivery, icy hair shirt.

Another car passed, slowed down to look him over. Jesus, they probably thought he was a hustler.

He turned and looked down into the riverbed. It would sure as shit freak that pervert out if he just hopped the railing and threw himself over. But who else would notice? His parents would grieve, but they wouldn't beat themselves up about it. None of the bullying dicks and tiny-minded skanks who used to pick on him in school would give a shit. His untimely end would probably just tell them they were right to live like desert sheep, grazing and breeding and getting sheared every year.

The riverbed would make for a pretty squalid death scene, anyway. The slopes of the concrete spillway were built to withstand a river the size of the Colorado at mid-spring, but they mostly made the world's greatest canvas for graffiti. Spiky tags and convoluted signatures crowded every square foot of concrete, many big enough to be visible from space. But nothing you could call a picture. Nothing but indecipherable dog-piss autographs.

No, he couldn't feature throwing himself off this bridge. The fall probably wouldn't kill him, for one. The slime on the banks of the black creek was so thick he might not even hurt himself.

He leaned farther, moved to a kind of reverence by the stark strangeness of the landscape, so that he almost slipped and tumbled over the railing.

That was when he saw the body.

It was almost directly beneath him, splayed out on the bed of shiny slime that reflected a broken mosaic of the moon.

When the body sat up and waved at him, he very nearly shit himself.

"HEY!" it called out. "How's your night goin'?"

Tommy jumped away from the railing like it was electrified, started hauling ass the rest of the way across the bridge. Peeking over the railing, he saw the shadowy figure leap across the river, fall and slide laughing on its ass in the scum. "Hey, buddy, wait up!"

That was all he needed, to be stalked by the sewer-dwelling homeless. Suddenly, the bridge was very, very long, and the echoing laughter of the thing in the river splashing off the concrete spillway walls seemed very, very close.

Tommy reached the far end of the bridge before he looked over the edge again. Nobody down there, and no sound but the hum of the streetlights and his own panicked breath.

The riverbed walls were slotted with gaping storm drains like civil defense bunkers. The freak must've ducked into one of them. Or maybe it was hunkered down under the bridge, like a troll lying in wait for unwary billy goats.

Tommy felt very silly now, but his relief was real. All solidarity with the downtrodden aside, there was no telling what someone with nothing to lose might be capable of.

He turned to walk on, his heart a snowball in his throat, thinking *wow, that sure put things in perspective . . .*

And the river-dweller slithered over the railing at the end of the bridge, and onto the sidewalk before him.

"I *know* you heard me calling you," it said.

Tommy fell back, gripped the rail to keep from falling. The thing from the river stepped closer, still dripping oil-slick blackness. It had something in one hand, which it kept cagily behind its back.

The stink brought tears to Tommy's eyes, but he forced himself to smile as he stumbled in retreat.

"Sorry, sir . . . I'm just in a hurry. Gotta catch up with my friends."

"'SIR'?" The river-man laughed like it was hawking up a flotilla of phlegm. "Aw, ain't you got a beautiful voice. Lousy liar, though."

It was impossible to tell if the fucker was black or white or what. Its eyes popped out through the slime, teeth white as a game show host's. "I know what you were thinking about doing back there. Ain't got a friend in the world. Just like all of us used to be."

"I got lots of friends." Tommy pulled a lateral move, slipped by the guy's reaching hand, and passed him, continuing briskly west.

At the end of the bridge, the street resumed its straight course, through a maze of alleys and dead-end streets lined with blind sheet-metal security doors. Not another soul in sight, except for a few sleepers in cardboard cocoons in the few unbarred doorways.

The muck-man's braying voice and slapping footsteps echoed down the avenue, threatening to wake them. "Hey, man, slow down! I wanna talk to you!"

Over his shoulder, Tommy hissed, "Listen, I hardly got money for the subway, okay? I'm sorry, but I can't help you . . ."

And suddenly, he felt the sonofabitch *so close behind him* that he whirled instinctively: fists up, ready to fight.

The reeking shape slid to a halt, sounding hurt. "Did I ask you for anything, buddy? I don't want your money. I don't *need* your money."

From behind its back, it held up a briefcase. Even in the washed-out streetlight, its shiny leather and intricate locks looked absurdly out of place in its mud-caked shit-mitten. "Right before you got all class-conscious on me, I was about to offer you something."

Tommy's hands opened up, sticky with sweat. He stuffed them into the pouch pocket of his hoodie. "I'm good, dude. Thanks. I don't need anything."

"I got something that'll take the edge off, or put it on, are you feeling me? I got what everybody in this shitty old life needs, more than anything."

Still backing away, Tommy asked, "What's that?"

"*More lives.* You can be somebody else. Be *everybody* else. Fuck the Internet, man. By tomorrow, this whole city's gonna be wired—"

Tommy pulled his hands back out and showed the guy the big black X's tattooed on the backs of them. "I'm straight-edge, asshole. Leave me alone before I go call a cop."

"Cops never come around here," it said, still pacing behind him. "Not after dark . . ."

The words shot ice water through his bones.

But they didn't turn out to be true.

Sudden headlights flared up behind him, and the shadowy streetscape drowned in red, white, and blue. Tommy yelped in Pavlovian terror at the squealing tires and piercing digital war-whoop of an LAPD squad car, screeching right up in their faces.

"STOP AND DROP WHERE YOU ARE, SHIT-HEADS." Through the speakers, it was unbearably loud.

Tommy turned and froze, with his hands on his head. "I'm just minding my own business, Officer—"

"I SAID DOWN, FUCKSTICK. KISS IT, OR YOU WILL GET YOUR SHIT PUSHED IN BY CARING PRO-FESSIONALS TONIGHT."

Tommy lay down in the street, cheek flush with the Taco Bell detritus on the pavement. He knew he should be somehow relieved, but that wasn't how he felt. He couldn't see if the muck-man had also hit the pavement. He was almost afraid to look.

A black cop came over with her gun pointed at him. Her burly shadow stretched halfway to the next corner.

"What's your fucking problem tonight, kid?"

"Nothing! I was just walking to the train—"

"Honky, please. We saw you score off your new best friend. Are you carrying any needles or weapons, or anything that might—"

The other cop shouted, "Hey, Rita, come look at *this* happy horseshit!"

"Please just search me! I'm clean, Officer! I swear to God. I was trying to get away from that guy—"

"Shut up and stay put." Her anger sounded almost motherly. Like a mother with a gun. "After tonight, you're damned lucky we didn't just shoot you where you stood."

Jesus, had *everyone* heard about his show?

Officer Rita stomped back over to where her partner stood, less than ten feet away, towering over Tommy's new best friend. Obscured by the blinding wash of the headlights, the whole scene played in painful shadow-puppet silhouette.

Tommy cautiously shifted his position for a better view. He didn't want to see. He *had* to.

The cops flanked the muck-man, who was down on his knees. One showed the briefcase to the other. They opened it and looked inside.

The muck-man started laughing.

The male cop asked the guy something Tommy couldn't hear; but before he could answer, he drew his nightstick and brought it down across the side of the poor fucker's head like he was trying to drive a golf ball to Mexico.

Something flew out of the violently whipping head and sprayed the cop in the eyes and mouth. It left a floating haze in the air, like a nimbus being blown across the head-light glare by the Santa Anas, yet thick enough to linger.

Tommy stayed down, but scuttled back instinctively. "Omigod!" he yelped under his breath.

The lady cop—Officer Rita—slammed the briefcase shut and kicked the guy in the chest till he crumpled on the pavement. The male cop stepped on his crotch and tuned up his head a few more times.

And then they went fucking crazy.

Tommy had seen the Rodney King video in high school government class. But he had never witnessed a true act of police brutality up close like this. So close he could smell it, know the animal terror that sheep must feel when the wolves move in.

He wanted to run. He wanted to stop them. He wanted to scream "FASCIST!" or cry out for help.

But what he did was just lie there, all but paralyzed, piss-ing himself as he inched his way backward, getting out of the direct headlight beam . . .

. . . just as Officer Rita brought her club down . . .

. . . and Tommy saw, with sudden crystal clarity, the cy-lindrical rod sinking into the yielding soft crown of the skull like an overripe melon. Something bright and wet and anything but red sprayed out like a fire extinguisher, into her face.

"BURT!" she screamed and wiped it away, as her partner moved in for the kill.

All around them, the miasma hovered: a shimmering halo of glistening mist that seemed to plume volcanically from the river-man's head.

And then all of them froze.

Just *froze*, for a long moment.

As if time had stood still.

And then—impossibly—they all started laughing.

Tommy blinked and looked around, thinking *what the fuck* so loud it almost came out of his mouth. Were there hidden cameras? Were they still making *Fear Factor*? Had he just been Punk'd? Was there a special *Punk'd* spin-off for nobody losers?

The three of them turned to face him, still laughing: the cops on their feet, the muck-man on his knees. They all seemed to be in on the same joke together, that much was for certain.

Then the muck-man's laughing face slid off, landing in his own lap as his skull buckled and sluiced like a cracked egg.

Tommy screamed, still on the ground, less than ten feet away.

In the time it took for the body to fall, the cops were almost on him.

At the very last moment, Tommy scrambled for his footing, was nearly to his hands and knees when someone grabbed him by the hood and yanked him backward to the pavement.

Then he was on his ass and shoulder blades, screaming and sobbing, as they dropped to pin him down. Foamy white slime dripped from their smiling faces; and a bitter, biting stench rolled off them, like moldy bread left in a car in summertime.

"*Shhh,*" said Officer Rita, eyes wild and shiny wet.

"AUGH!"

"It's all good," said Officer Burt. "We're cool, man. Everything's cool."

All at once, the briefcase was on his chest. Tommy struggled and screamed, but he was going nowhere. The cops leaned closer, popping the clasps and holding him fast. The smell got stronger, but also somehow sweeter.

"We like to party, too," they said.

And opened the briefcase in his face.

He had nowhere else to look. Shining inside, reflecting the piss yellow streetlight and the silvery moon glow back in his unbelieving eyes, fat plastic bags of white powder filled the case up to the rim. Enough to buy a nice place on the Westside, or send some clown to a federal pen until the day he died . . .

"Oh, God," he moaned, as Officer Rita opened one of the Ziploc bags, and Officer Burt pinned his arms above his head. "NO!"

"We just want to share this with you," they said.

Both of them. In unison.

The plastic bag closed over his face in a sloppy, suffocating kiss. He tried to hold his breath, but one of them punched him in the stomach.

His next breath was made of white powder.

And strangely, it wasn't so bad . . .

It stung like a motherfucker as he choked it down, but the pain was like the quickening opening licks of a runaway hard-core song: power, chaos, and fury lifting him out of himself as his brain danced away on the rush like a dervish.

And oh shit, that was just the beginning.

With every racing heartbeat, his blood and brain seemed to rush through an expanding circuit that already spanned half the city: a network of illuminated souls, an ocean of memories and emotions that he tapped into as they shared this transforming ecstasy with him.

Tommy swam on his back in the street, going, "*Whoooooa!*" while the cops just knelt over him, laughing and kissing each other deeply. He wanted to laugh, too, but the sensations just kept coming.

And with them, the realization that he'd been wrong all his life.

Everyone cared. Everyone, like it or not, was connected. Or they would be, soon.

And he need never be lonely again.

When they hauled him to his feet, he was already reaching for the bag. Giggling like kids, they pressed it into his shaking hand, held it to his nose so he could inhale another blizzard.

It started all over again, but this time, he was expecting it. And when they joined him, it was in more ways than one.

Then they all just stood there in the street for a long time, laughing. Until they polished off the bag.

"We got shit to do," Officer Burt finally cut in. "But we want you to have a real nice night, buddy. Here."

He handed Tommy four big, floppy baggies from the briefcase.

Tommy stuffed them into his pouch pocket and started to chatter. He had so many questions. He wanted to tell them how he felt, though he could tell from the frenzied glee in their eyes that they felt precisely the same way.

He didn't want to leave, but they patted him on the back and sent him on his way, the squad car rolling off to spread the word.

Alone then, but never alone again, Tommy sprinted to the corner and turned onto Alameda. The huge sandstone fortress of the county jail loomed on his left; across the freeway overpass, he saw the art deco cathedral of Union Station.

Cars cruised or blasted past, buzzing with potential connections. No longer did they seem like the hostile, spitting face of the city, but other isolated, unlit souls. A million friends he hadn't met, yet. He could almost taste those other lives flying by.

And the last thing he wanted was to go home.

A silver BMW pulled up to the curb. A balding head, stained deep copper from a spray-on tanning agent, leaned out the window. "Hey, guy, you need a ride?"

Tommy came up to the car, looking around for more cops. "Where you headed?"

"Going to a party in the Hollywood Hills," the older guy said as he checked Tommy out. "You, uh . . . got a little milk mustache."

Tommy peeked at himself in the car's mirror and giggled. White stuff dangled in little snot-strings from his nose, and his eyes ran like they were melting. He'd never felt half so good in his life.

The guy in the car was dirtier, in his way, than the guy from the river. But Tommy had something he needed to share. He popped open the door and slid into a white leather seat, skid-marking it with the oily traces of his journey.

"Oh shit, kid! What the fuck is *that*?"

Tommy shrugged. "You wouldn't believe me if I told you. But you better believe this."

He showed the driver one of the bags from his pocket.

The BMW took off across the bridge and peeled out as it swerved onto the 101 on-ramp.

Even with the windows rolled up and the music blasting, anyone who listened for it could hear how long and hard they laughed.

It was as if they'd known each other all their lives.

PART ONE

King Kooker and the Kitchen Queen

ONE

Trixie Wright had a way with knives, a knack for rapid cutting that was almost uncanny. Right now she was chopping an on-ion so fast that the sulphuric acid fumes barely had time to reach her eyes: the blade doing a piercing, staccato chik-chik-chik *against the Pyrex cutting board, like Rory's foot playing hell-bent rockabilly on his battered kick drum, only at roughly double time.*

"*Whew!*" she whistled, briskly scooping the onions di-rectly into the heated pan, which sizzled as oil met onion, unleashing a smell almost too good to be true.

"*Goddamn!*" said Joel, clumsily assembling the salad be-hind her in the warm, cramped kitchen. "Forgive me, Kitchen Ninja, for I am slow!"

"Greenhorn." Trixie grinned, blinked back the whisper of a tear, set down the cutting board, and moved briskly toward the mushrooms. "How many of these do you want?"

"Umm . . . I'm not a big fungus fan, myself."

"Really?" Still assessing the young newbie in her kitchen at this year's L.A. Orphan's Thanksgiving Feast. Huang's latest catch.

"I don't know. Mushrooms just kind of creep me out." He shuddered convincingly, but his pot-bleary blue eyes looked suddenly daunted. "Is that wrong?"

"Mmm. Just depends on how you look at it." She emp-tied the carton of baby brown Bajas onto the cutting board, picked a plump one out, and chopped it straight down the middle. "Take this guy, for instance."

Laughter erupted from the living room beyond: a half dozen giddy people, enjoying themselves. The rest were in the backyard, or Rory's garage, where the thumping live jam showed no sign of abating.

But Joel's eyes were on the mushroom, which flopped to either side like a bisected cockhead. Its halves suddenly resembled a pair of big-nosed, sad-eyed aliens, with filament striations moping down either side of the bell.

"Meet Slicey and Dicey," she said.

Joel laughed. "Awww!"

"They're your little friends from the fungoid kingdom."

"They look sad!"

"That's because they don't think you like them."

"Oh, I like you!" he informed the mushroom segments. "I just don't want to eat you!"

"That's okay," Trixie said, in a cartoon voice. *"Maybe someone will want to eat us . . ."*

"Of course they will!"

"We'll be the crown on your mashed potatoes, beneath a veil of gravy, if you'll have us . . ." Trixie continued.

And then *chik-chik-chik*, one second later, they were a dozen faceless chunks.

"Noooooo!"

"See?" Trixie said, in her normal voice again. "When in doubt, anthropomorphize."

Joel shrugged. "Now I *really* don't wanna eat 'em!"

"Oh, well." And with that, she proceeded to liberate the rest of the mushrooms from their earthly form.

Trixie Wright was tall and slender, with a natural feminine strength and grace that never let you forget what a woman she was, even if she was replacing your carburetor or helping you lug a bed up a flight of stairs. She had skin the color of sun-bleached cocoa and wavy dark chocolate hair, plush lips, and slightly canted almond eyes, reflecting her mixed Kenyan/Brazilian/Filipino heritage.

For all of that, she was third-generation American, at least on her father's side. And she had come to L.A.—like most of the orphans here today—to re-create herself in one of the most mutant-friendly territories on earth.

The people she and Rory had invited to their home were not orphans in the technical sense. They all had families. But those families were far away *on purpose*: which is to say they had moved away either because they couldn't *stand* their fucking families, or because they couldn't find what they needed in their places of birth.

Los Angeles was a mecca for such souls, be they artists, hedonists, social climbers, saints, sinners, or any oddball variation thereof. Most of them came for what they hoped was their slice of the pie called Success, hoping against hope there was a slice with their name on it, and that nobody else had already swallowed it whole.

As such, Los Angeles was brutal.

But Trixie had found—fairly early on—that the Los Angeles she loved was not the heavily entrenched citadel of Hollywood power and fame. The Los Angeles she loved was the *secret L.A.*: the one that grew between the cracks in the official L.A., where genuine people with their hearts still intact tried to become something truly special, without selling out or giving in to their own weakest impulses.

These were the friends—the true friends—that she sought. And they were there, if you knew how to look. Discernment was the heart of engagement.

Finding really good people.

In the heart of Crazytown.

Out in Rory Long's garage, it was louder than sin, hotter than hell, and fragrant as the devil's cologne: a wicked potpourri of cigarettes, sweat, medicinal kush, and deep-frying turkey from the big King Kooker in the back corner, by the lube rack.

It was a three-car, professional auto shop—Long's Auto Repair, in point of fact—on the corner of Fernwood and Hyperion, in beautiful Silver Lake, California. Just one of dozens of garages clustered on that strip of Hyperion, and far from the most successful. Zoning regulations had packed them together like sardines, so guys like Rory had to make do with the ancient trickle-down hypothesis: if the big boys got too busy, you hoped their cast-off clients might just trickle down to you.

But today was Thanksgiving, so the shop was closed for business. Instead of changing out mufflers and spark plugs and brakes, he was banging the fuck out of his antique drum kit. Jamming with old pals, for no reason but fun. Taking his mind off his troubles, the best way he knew how.

They were wailin' on one of Dan Dutton's old originals, "Thanks for the Canker," at full polkabilly speed, everyone jumping up and down for the thrill-packed final chorus:

"Thanks for the canker!
Be careful not to squeeeeeeeeze!
Thanks for the canker!
I WANTED THAT DISEASE!"

That was when Bing launched into his solo: a barrage of virtuoso electric fiddle madness so superb that it galvanized them all into overdrive, Rory speeding up the tempo without even trying.

All of the rest were garage band veterans—Dan on guitar, Fran on bass, himself on his rattletrap five-piece set—but Bing was for real. A professional jazz violinist, who nearly forty years back had played with fucking Frank Zappa. Had played with some of the greatest musicians who ever lived.

Rory'd met Bing three years ago, on the night that he and Trixie moved onto this corner, scoring the two-headed rental coup of a lifetime. A house they both loved, adjoining a garage that Rory loved? Both available, at the same time? At a point when they both had miraculously achieved decent credit?

It had seemed like one of those messages from God that you ignore at your own peril. So they'd jumped on and almost instantly closed both deals, consolidating home life and work in one fell swoop. And quite properly feeling like the luckiest bastards on earth.

So once the moving vans were emptied, and they were up to their tits in boxes, it had been time to order some pizza. There were eight friends to feed, and Trixie was beat. And it was, after all, the moving-day food of choice.

Forty minutes later, the doorbell rang, and Rory was the guy who answered. He had fifty bucks already in hand, ready to speed this transaction along.

The guy with the pizzas looked strangely familiar, though Rory knew they had never met before. He was in his late fifties—not a typical delivery boy—with wavy graying locks above a distinctive Fu Manchu mustache.

And it was Dan who walked up, goggle-eyed with awe, saying, "Omigod, you're the great Bing Fusoli."

And watching the mingling of pride and shame in Bing's eyes—at being recognized for who he was, while wearing his stupid pizza delivery shirt—was one of the most cut-to-the-heart-of-it L.A. moments that Rory had ever known.

So now every Thanksgiving, the great Bing Fusoli knew where he was welcome to feast among friends. An orphan no longer.

And God*damn*, that boy could play: taking the crescendo of the song up to the fucking stratosphere as Rory hammered his snare drum like a madman, just trying to keep up . . .

. . . until he *broke through the snare head*, at the moment of triumph . . .

. . . and the King Kooker's buzzer cut through the sudden silence, welling up with the happy applause.

"THANK YOU, LADIES AND GENTLEMEN!" hollered Dan through the mic. "NOW LET'S EAT!"

It was turkey time at last.

Two

Rory Long and Trixie Wright didn't have a banquet table per se. Theirs was not a fancy place, though it felt like a home, and a warm one at that. Even with all the Mexican skull art on the walls.

But because she did catering from her rolling truck kitchen—when she wasn't serving fine portable cuisine on the streets of L.A.—they simply cleared the rest of the furniture out of the living room, and set up some long plastic catering tables. Enough for twenty, with folding chairs to match.

Those tables were now dangerously overloaded, and surrounded by people well on their way to being overstuffed themselves.

When they called it a feast, they were not just boasting. Even in these tough economic times—this was the first year, for example, that Trixie had to forgo her legendary turducken—the cumulative weight of everybody kickin' in just a little bit extra made for a staggering smorgasbord.

Rory's deep-fried turkey was the centerpiece: so moist and juiciliscious it was almost obscene. This freed up the ovens and a whole lot of time, letting Trixie go to town on almost everything else. Oyster dressing that was just like a dream. Cajun dressing that raised sweat on your brow. A traditional corn bread dressing that would bring tears of joy to the most finicky Midwestern grandmother. All surrounded by her famous garlic mashed potatoes, incomparable brown gravy, lush vegetable sautés, and sweet silver corn on the cob.

That was just the in-house fare. When Renee flew in from Vermont yesterday, she'd gone straight from Burbank Airport to Porto's Bakery on Hollywood Way for fresh loaves of French bread and their signature meat-stuffed potato balls. It was a miracle the latter had survived last night in the fridge, because they were sooooo gooood.

Josh's salad, though mushroom free, more than made up for it with oodles of arugula, diced carrots, red cabbage, and perfect cherry tomatoes. Huang's curried cranberry sauce also raised quite a stir.

And as always, Fran's white-trash green beans in French onion soup with those crispy fried onions on top were completely irresistible. No apologies required or accepted.

Altogether, it was pretty much as good as life gets.

Which made giving thanks unusually easy to do.

Unless, of course, you were Richie, and stuck in jail like a dumbass. But Rory didn't wanna think about that just yet. Plenty of time for that later, when the annual ten o'clock holiday phone call came.

But until then . . .

"Hey, baby? Pass me that oyster dressing, would'ja?"

"Mmmm." Trixie was in a food trance, blissing out on the waves of flavor. The creeper weed and a couple glasses of wine probably weren't hurting either.

"Aw, Trix," said Renee, beside her at the table. "You're exhausted, aren't you? Here." She passed the dressing to Rory, winking.

Renee was a fascinating counterpoint to Trixie, in that she was lovely in almost exactly the opposite ways. Her lips were thin. Her skin was pale. Her eyes were small behind oversize spectacles. Her hair was straight and wispy. Her curves were slight. She tended toward the abstract and intellectual, whereas Trixie thought almost entirely in practical terms.

They were like two halves of the same megawoman, which was exactly how they felt about each other; and when Renee bailed on Los Angeles last year, it had almost killed them both.

"I'm not exhausted, exactly," Trixie sighed. "More like . . . happy."

"Here's to *happy*!" chirped Huang, from down the table. He was second-generation Chinese American, flamboyantly gay, set-dresser for an NBC sitcom slated to be canceled at the end of the year.

"TO HAPPY!" Everyone raised their glasses, and the toast went around the room.

"If we're toasting," said Joel, who leaned in to kiss Huang on the cheek, "I want to thank Huang for being the sexiest man ever." Everybody laughed.

"You better believe it . . ." Goosing Josh under the table.

"WOO! And Rory and Trixie and, well, *everybody here* for making me feel welcome, even though I've never met you before!"

"TO FEELING WELCOME!" And the glasses went up again.

"Here, here!" yelled Bing.

"There, there!" yelled Dan.

"Where, where?" yelled Stan.

"Right here!" yelled Fran, pointing at baby Edie, who was nursing at her breast.

"TO EDIE!"

"Fuck! I need a refill!"

"Don't say fuck in front of my baby!"

"TO SAYING FUCK IN FRONT OF YOUR BABY!" And everybody drained their glasses on that one, laughing.

Then the bottles of wine went around again, and the pitchers of juice and ice water for those abstaining. Baby Edie continued to suckle, almost entirely unperturbed. Baby Edie was less than three months old, and couldn't speak English for shit.

"I have a toast," said Manuel, from the far end of the tables. He was looking at Rory as he said it.

"Go ahead," Rory sighed. "I already know where this is going."

Manuel nodded, leaned forward with his elbows on the table. He was older than Edie, slightly younger than Josh, and Rory's only employee at the garage: sending money back to his family in Mexico City when he could, which, these days, was almost never. Rory knew he had cousins in L.A., and knew Manuel really didn't want to work with them.

"To all the people who couldn't be here with us today," he said. "For whatever reason."

"FOR WHATEVER REASON," a few wags intoned.

"I don't think that's the toast."

"No," said Manuel, shaking his head and grinning like a good sport should.

"Oh, all right." Everyone raising their glasses.

"TO ABSENT FRIENDS AND FAMILY."

And with the clinking came the melancholic shroud.

"I miss Bernie and Marc and Rebecca," said Dan.

"And Naomi and Ivor and Dawn," added Stan.

"Has anyone heard from Sam and John, or Tom and Julie . . . ?"

"I miss hanging out with you guys," gushed Renee, leaning in to hug Trixie, who fired a helpless painful grin at Rory before settling into the hug.

"I miss you, too."

"But I made it."

"Yes, you did."

And then they both started crying.

"Well, thanks for sucking all the air out of the room," said Rory to Manuel. "Good job, man. Well done."

And though he was saying it as if it were a joke, there was no mistaking Rory's temper. Its pilot light had just ignited.

"It had to be said." This from Dan, who knew Rory as well as anyone. They'd been in bands together, which was almost harder than being married.

"I know. I know. It's just—"

Dan said, "It's a tough time, and everybody knows it. So let's get it out of our system, okay? And then"—flashing his great infectious smile—"the rhubarb pie!"

"Oh, fuck!" Rory laughed, felt his temperature lower as perspective kicked in. "I can't believe I totally forgot about the rhubarb pie! *Feel your feelings, everybody!*"

"TO RHUBARB PIE!" A robust clinking, as the vibe veered back toward fun again.

"What's rhubarb pie?" asked Joel.

THREE

By 9:52, according to Trixie's watch, everybody was pretty much incapacitated by gluttony and joy. Fran and Dan and Huang had blacked out entirely (on the couch, the floor, and a comfy chair, respectively); and little Edie had clearly sucked enough secondhand tryptophan to deck her out in the traveling playpen, quite possibly for the night.

Trixie knew the Thanksgiving drill. She already had a fresh pot of coffee brewing. In about an hour, the pall of logyness would begin to lift. People would rise and rally to face the road, the journey home; and nobody too tired or high would be allowed to leave the premises.

The Orphan's Slumber Party was as traditional as the Orphan's Feast—in fact, was its natural sequel—so blankets and pillows and sheets were already stacked up and ready for deployment.

Trixie was a one-woman Army Corps of Engineers, in that respect. She planned. She implemented.

And even better, she knew how to adapt at a moment's notice.

"So Fran and I get the f-fold-out couch, right?" mumbled Stan, who was wobbling as he walked. He already knew the answer. He was just asking out of drunkenness—a confirmation for his reptile brain—and to somehow justify the fact that he was still standing.

"Once the crowd clears out," Trixie told him, "the living

room's all yours. Unless Dan and Huang can't make it. In which case, the couch is *still* all yours."

"Yur'ra goddess," Stan muttered, draped around her in a lethargic zomboid hug. Sober, he was strictly a handshake guy; but once he got loaded, he couldn't hug you enough.

"I love you, too," she assured him, patting his back, glad he was too worn-out to slightly embarrass them both by popping a boner. Oh, that Stan.

Stan and Fran and Edie lived in Santa Barbara now, where Stan taught economics and Fran taught Edie how to be less neurotic than their parents. So far, so good.

They'd both been raised by Israeli expatriates with almost unbearably serious minds. They'd both moved to L.A. to cut themselves loose from the weight of history their parents still carried.

And that was where they'd met—at a Jane's Addiction concert—introduced by Rory and Trixie, who had also just started to date.

These were the kinds of moments that bonded people together. The surprises that cut through history, and showed us who we really were.

"Okay," Trixie said, peeling loose. "I'm going out back now for a smoke. You can come if you want."

"Oh, I can't do that," he said, comically officious, then stage-whispered, *"We've got a baby."*

"Yeah, I heard about that!" she whispered back, and ducked past him into the kitchen. Her domain.

They'd gotten as far as stacking the dishes, soaking the couple of pots and pans that needed it. Now she was just waiting for her own second wind, biting back her personal addiction to taking care of business first.

"Stay," she admonished the dishes, as if they were pets that might wander off and piss in somebody's slippers. Then she poured herself just a little more merlot, before pushing past the screen door and down the three steps to the yard.

Bing was lighting Josh's cigarette. Those were the first faces she saw. She smiled at them, and they smiled back as she passed, but the ones she sought were just beyond. Evidently smoking a bowl.

Rory was a head taller than she, slim and sunburned from hard work. His dark brown hair flopped down over his eyes, but the lighter's glow made a rakish beacon of his face as he roasted a bowl.

He looked like a hoodlum from an old movie in his pegged jeans and his emerald green vintage bowling shirt, but it was as close as he'd get to formal wear. The shirt was from the Fontana Bowl's Cold Rollers, with Rory's name embroidered on it—all he inherited, aside from the shirt, from his grandfather.

"Can I have some of that?" she asked, stepping between Rory and Renee in a way that included them both without touching either one.

Renee stepped back, even though she now held the bowl, letting Rory swoop in with two lungfuls of herb that he breathed into Trixie's open mouth as the two of them met in a kiss.

"Wow, you're like *a bong with benefits!*" laughed Renee, as Trixie disengaged and exhaled a full plume.

"Just weed, though," said Rory. "I'm done with everything else."

"I noticed you weren't drinking."

"You noticed correctly."

"You've been *sooooo* good," Trixie murmured, leaning back in to kiss him again.

Kissing Rory was her favorite thing, in a world full of things that she truly loved to do. There were reasons for this, chief among them being that kissing was the most intimate act on earth.

Cooking was great. Fucking was great. Laughing was great. Conversation was great. Persistence was great. And God was great.

But kissing Rory—even after all they'd been through, or particularly *because* of all they'd been through—was the one act in all of creation that bonded her closest to love.

It didn't hurt that he was a great kisser.

And that he truly loved her, too.

Behind them, Renee started violently coughing. Trixie was the first to laugh, right into Rory's mouth. Their lips disengaged just in time to keep from clacking teeth together, as they happily met eyes.

"Awwww. Somebody wants attention," Rory noted, cackling.

"You could have just cleared your throat really loud," Trixie added.

"Yeah, but—KAFF KAFF KAFF—" Renee struggled to say, "This gets you *waaaaay higher!*"

And before they could debate that inarguable truth, the phone in the kitchen rang.

"Oh, hell," said Rory. "What time is it?"

It was ten o'clock on the nose.

Four

Rory sprinted across the yard, was up the back steps by the third ring. Every holiday season, Richie called from some exotic location as far as he could get from L.A. This year, he was right here in town, but he wouldn't have the luxury of calling back a second time.

Rory rushed through the door, swatting a stacked plastic colander out of the way of the wireless, and grabbed the handset before the fourth ring finished brrrringing.

"Yo," he said.

"Who won this year?"

It took Rory less than a second to know what his brother meant. The vegetarian tofurkey alternative at their feasts was a sore subject that his brother never failed to bring up. "King Kooker's ahead by three plates, but it's looking tight."

"Hungry, hungry hippies."

"I saved you a leg and a boob, and the crunchy stuffing."

"Great, great . . . so, you got a full house right now?"

"Yeah, but most of them are almost passed out . . . What's up?"

"I dunno, I'm just thinking . . . ah, shit. I wasn't going anywhere this year . . . You know, it was always Gretchen's idea to go somewhere for the holidays, and my first year stag . . ."

"You would've found something to do. But look at you now . . . How's jail turkey?"

"Reconstituted Thanksgiving loaf. It tastes exactly like

everything else here. I shouldn't bitch, though. It's all good. I'm not even in the real county lockup."

"No shit."

"Yeah, there's an annex for low-threat inmates."

"They don't know you too well, do they?"

"It's shitty, but they keep all the civilians away from the lifers and the gangs, so I'm just waiting."

"Your lawyer's gonna sort this shit out, right?"

"It's complicated, man. Political." Rory waited for him to go on, but he just breathed.

The arraignment hearing was on Tuesday. Richie ordered his friends and family to stay away. He'd take them all to dinner at The Palms when he posted bail. But bail was denied, and they took him back. He didn't want to talk about it, Rory could tell. The heavy slow breathing pushed Rory, as always, toward what Richie wanted.

"So, how's the shop?"

"Still open. You need brakes or mufflers?"

"Those assholes across the street still there?"

"Yeah." Autovision did paint and body work on top of regular maintenance.

"You were any kind of serious about success, you'd burn them out."

"I guess I don't care that much, then. What's eating you, man? Aside from your cell mate, of course."

"Ha. If you only knew . . . Anyway, remember when we used to work for the King Snake?"

Rory chuckled. "Is he your cell mate?"

"I wish. No, dummy. When we first got paroled, he set us up, you remember that?"

Rory did, indeed. They got caught with a '72 Corvette Stingray that was on Jerry King's hot list. Riverside sheriff's deputies knew Richie and his kid brother weren't just joyriding, but they refused to roll over on the Snake, just on principle, and a healthy fear of the stories they'd heard. When Richie got out of county and Rory came out of

CYA, they each got the thousand they would've gotten for the car, and a polite request to stay the fuck out of the King Snake's path.

"*Jerry tried to go legit after that,*" Richie said. "*They chewed him up. Long as he was ripping off other rednecks, they let him be, but when he tried to go straight, they never let him forget what he was, and it killed him.*"

"Richie, you're freaking yourself out. What's your point, man?"

"*I was just thinking about all those guys we knew and where they ended up. None of them wanted to do anything more than what we did as kids. Remember working for Minimum Wade? Or Tonny Malreaux?*"

Rory smiled at the memory of Malreaux. Minimum Wade, not so much. "Those guys had shit for brains. You're going to come out of this fine." *Whatever it is*, he didn't add.

"*I wasn't thinking about me, Rory. I was worrying about you.*"

Rory looked around the kitchen—Trixie's headquarters—seeing it for the first time. He'd been facing the wall, picturing Richie at a pay phone in jail, maybe with a line of angry convicts waiting to use it after he got done. But he'd felt his brother looking at him. "I'm doing okay, Rich. Really."

"*Sure?*"

"Staying out of jail." A long, stale breath later, he added, "Sorry."

"*No skin. But seriously, I know you guys are hurting, and I want to help you out. Let me do something for you.*"

The other shoe dropped out of the phone and hit Rory in the face. "Aw, Christ. I can't drive tonight, man. I'm thrashed, the house is a sty, and we got people sleeping on our fucking countertops. Trixie'd kick my ass."

"*I know it's a lot to ask, but I'm not exactly in a position to interview new people.*"

"Use one of your old ones."

"I need somebody I can trust, who knows what they're doing. This is delicate."

The talk of the King Snake took on many new wrinkles of meaning. "You remember what we both said when we got out of jail?"

"Yeah, I remember."

Rory waited. Make him say it.

"Never again. And up until last week, I made good on it . . ."

"I didn't say I'd never get caught again. I said I'd never do stupid shit that would get me thrown in jail again."

Richie didn't say, *but you did something very stupid and went in for hard state time, for no good reason at all.*

"Nothing the least bit hinky. I swear. I don't want any company in here."

"I didn't say I'd do it, anyway. What would I have to do?"

"Drive this guy and his party to wherever they want to go."

"Someplace extra special, naturally."

"If they wanted to be seen, they'd call a stretch limo."

"I fucking hate those things."

"I know you do. Three hours, unless they want to hire you longer, on holiday clock."

"Three hours plus these fuckers own me."

" 'Come on, man. How much y'all charge?' " His pitch-perfect imitation of Tonny Malreaux's dopey Creole drawl set Rory off laughing. The ugly, ignorant bastard insisted that any woman would drop trou, if the price was right, and deadpan asked any woman he aimed to nail straight up what it'd cost him, just like his daddy did his mama.

Rory laughed at the memory and at the image of his brother hunched over a prison phone, trying to crack him up. After a while, he tried to put a fuck-you figure in the air, but he found himself saying, "Three hundred an hour would be decent—"

"Two thousand, if you stay with them till they want to go home."

Rory whistled. Anywhere else, such money would scream illegality, but here, people laid out that much coin for convenience and security every day. "Where's home?"

"House in the Hollywood Hills, off Lookout Mountain."

"I don't have a black suit, or a stupid hat."

"No problem. Wear whatever you want. Pick up the car at the garage."

"Hold on, fucker. I didn't say I'd do it yet. You never told me who you were driving when you got pinched."

"Ha. Nobody you know."

"You took the possession rap for whoever you were driving?"

"That's insulting, man. You know me better than that."

"That's what I thought. But I'm not falling on anybody's sword for two thousand dollars."

"Like I said. I'm not looking to get anybody in trouble. Any trouble that could happen, by tomorrow, would just be background noise. Listen, I can have somebody else do it, but I don't know anybody else who would have any use for my old garage gear . . ."

"What?"

"My lawyer told me to strip the garage until the divorce is finalized. I got a bunch of shit I don't use. I could give it to you."

"If I drive your rich pricks around all night on Thanksgiving."

"Hell no, what do you take me for? I'm not an extortionist. Come over and look over the stock. I got lift racks and a smog tester and a bunch of sprayers and color-matching shit. It's all gotta go, and I'd rather you have it than it get counted against me in the settlement."

"She was always into all the wrong things about people, man."

"I know. I should've seen it, but you think people will grow, and you try to help them grow the right way, if you can . . . It's weird, how twisted up you get in the moment, you know? Of

course you know. But if you do it, you can have our Henkel knife set."

"That's stupid. What the hell are those?"

"They're fancy. I paid a fortune for them. Forty-nine knives. Trixie could fillet a whale with them."

"She'll fillet me if I walk out on her tonight."

"She'll fillet you with the new knives after you've paid all the bills, if she's as smart as I think she is. Come on, help me out."

"How about a new drum kit?"

"Can't help you. But I'll throw in a set of steel mixing bowls, if you act now on this special offer. You know I'm not using them." Richie never, ever ate at home. When Rory asked him once how a sex-change operation worked, his brother told him they made you cook your own food every day for a year, and your dick dropped off.

"Jesus, all right. When?"

"Union Station, in an hour. Listen, Rory—"

"Yeah?"

"Nothing. The car's at my garage. It's the old Lincoln, so it doesn't have a GPS."

"Good. I fucking hate those things."

"I know, man. Thanks for doing this. It's not going to be a big deal to you, but it's a huge deal to me."

"Okay. I'll see you on Saturday, if you're not on lock-down, or whatever."

"Yeah, looking forward to it. Hey, somebody else wants to use the phone, so I got to go, but thanks again, okay?"

"Sure, Richie. Happy Thanksgiving."

"You too, man." He didn't hang up right away, and Rory almost disconnected when Richie spoke up. *"Don't be afraid, little brother. Don't be afraid to do what it takes to make it."*

Click.

"Goddamn it," muttered Rory, to no one but himself.

FIVE

Trixie knew there was a problem, just watching him walk back down the stairs. It was all in his physicality. Where his cocky little swagger had been relaxed and natural not ten minutes before, it now looked like a psychic pep talk his body was giving to itself.

A little tense. A little forced.

"Goddamn you, Richie," she muttered to herself.

"Oh, no." Renee already had her sympathy mask in place.

"I'll be back," she said, already moving toward the gate where Rory's lot and their backyard met. She waved to Rory, who veered toward her, clearly gearing up for something.

"Spit it out," she said.

So he told her. Two grand for three hours of work. The smog tester, which would involve some extra wrangling with the state, but which would more than pay for itself in a matter of weeks. He'd been needing to go there. She'd said so herself.

"And what kind of knives?"

"I don't remember. Hankeys?"

"Henkels? Oh, those are good. You know I love those things."

"So—"

"So nothing," she said. "You already committed, right?"

"I did."

"So I'm a little pissed off. And slightly grateful."

"Of course."

"But mostly, I'm scared. Is it okay to say that?"

He sighed, eyes averted. "Yeah."

"If it gets ugly, you know what to do."

"Get the fuck out."

"Please, baby."

"Come straight home to you."

"That's all I'm asking." Leaning into him now. Needing to hold him. "Just promise me."

"I promise you," he said, wrapping his arms tight around her. "I have my priorities straight."

"Don't snort the coke."

"I won't."

"Don't altercate."

"Last thing I want is a fucking problem."

"Baby?" she said, pulling back to face him squarely, looking him straight in the eye.

"You know I love you."

"That's not what I'm asking," she said, helplessly grinning and kissing him deep.

Rory pulled back a little before he settled in. She took note of it, as she took note of everything.

But then the kiss got good, got sincere, Rory relaxing into it, demonstrating that it was not just a token gesture.

She rode it for all it was worth. Like it was the last kiss in the world. Though that thought itself was crazy.

"Be careful," she whispered between his lips.

But, of course, things were never quite as simple as that.

PART TWO

A Long Family History

Six

Anyone who knew Rory Long could and would warn you about him. Even his mother would tell you, *that boy'll give you the shirt off his back . . . but don't you cross him.*

Growing up at the racetrack, Richie and Rory were their daddy's creatures. When he could get away with it, he took Richie in the customized Mercury Cougar Eliminator that he raced Friday nights at the Fontana Speedway. It didn't make him luckier, but he didn't crash with a passenger, and totaled the Cougar by himself. To his mother's everlasting disgrace, Rory's first word was "Mama," but he was talking to Daddy's car.

When his teeth came in, Rory wouldn't go to sleep unless Daddy took him out for a night drive. The Long home was happy in a way that few of their neighbors could claim. They loved cars, and they knew what they were going to be when they never grew up.

Dad got sent up when Richie was eight and Rory six. To hear the Riverside DA tell it, Dad's night drives made him the number-one crystal meth courier in the Inland Empire. Mom immediately divorced him, and moved to a trailer park in San Diego. The boys took it hard.

When she remarried two years later, the boys also enjoyed a brief honeymoon. Their bedroom in James's house was bigger than the whole single-wide, and they had a pool. Richie kept his little brother in check.

Rory's temper had already begun to overshadow any

chances he had for a decent life. Banned from a Sav-On for hogging the Batmobile ride outside the drugstore, Rory came back and shot out three windows with his brother's BB gun.

Richie took his brother aside after the cops brought him home. He couldn't just go around hitting anyone who crossed him. That way was no end of trouble; *you'll have to go to live with Daddy.* That didn't sound so bad, but Rory wanted to make his big brother proud. And Richie made it a little better by sharing two of the Hot Wheels cars he'd swiped from the store during Rory's rampage.

That was the first time James spanked Rory. Though he said he regretted having to discipline the boys, he'd prepared for it. He'd bought a squash paddle sometime after the boys moved in, and he'd christened it, like almost everything else he owned. It was dubbed THE CORRECTOR, in a high-relief red sticker printed out on one of those label makers that you'd have to dial each character and squeeze, like a gun. On the back, James had printed out another high-relief label that the paddle left imprinted in welts on the ass cheeks of any sassafrasing ne'er-do-well under his roof: CORRECTED.

Richie and the Corrector were bosom chums, but Rory had not yet made its acquaintance. He already hated James like poison, ever since he realized their stepdad would be sleeping with their mom. *Why didn't you fight back?* Rory always asked. *Why didn't you take it away, and feed it to him?*

The day he shot up the Sav-On, Richie knew Rory would not sit still for the spanking. Before James got back from his job at the engineering company, Richie needed to show his little brother that there were other ways of getting revenge. You had to know whom you were really angry at, and you had to make them throw the first punch . . . if possible, at themselves.

James Stavridis loved three things in life more than anything else: his car, his record collection, and his wine.

Most weekends, he'd get crocked on fancy French cough syrup and spin his Elton John, Warren Zevon, Randy Newman, and Average White Band records until the boys fell asleep listening to his rambling cultural lectures. Hippies and disco fucked up everything, he told them a thousand times, but the rest went way over their heads. He used the word *flamin'* as a superlative, which caused no end of confusion: "Listen to that solo, kid, those guys're *flamin'*!" Most times, it was just a game, trying to keep a straight face around James. Laughing at James when he was lecturing was a spanking offense.

James's car was a Porsche 944, and neither of the boys had ever so much as breathed a whiff of the fresh-to-death air of its black leather interior. Over half the garage was already taken up by his home office and the washer-dryer combo, so he had rebuilt the garage to fit the car. A tennis ball on a nylon cord attached to the garage door opener lowered down to meet the Porsche's windshield when the door opened, to eliminate any chance of scratching the precious car's pearly silver paint job.

Any handy fellow could have managed such a trick, but James was a professional fucking engineer, so he'd gone and added a second nylon cord, which stretched from the garage into the house through a hole in the wall above the interior door, across the dining room ceiling to the kitchen, where it dangled a sign that lowered into view when the garage door opened. THE BOSS IS HOME, it said, and underneath, (GET BUSY!).

Richie gave Rory a big Slurpee cup of deep red juice to drink. "Gulp it down," he said. "It'll make it easier."

"I'm gonna kick his ass," Rory blurted out. "This smells funny." The juice was sour and made him gag, but he did as his brother told him. Before he'd half finished it, he'd already stopped sniffling, and started giggling.

That was when James came home. The dreaded sign came down into view and Richie tipped the cup so Rory bolted it down. Rory saw the sign and laughed so hard that wine shot out his nostrils.

Richie had taken the dust jacket from James's LP copy of *Caribou*, the most unbearably fruity album in his library. Upon this portentous canvas, Richie had pasted a picture from one of the stroke books James kept in the alligator-hide briefcase under his desk. A big-boobed lady feeling herself up in a shower, but she had James's awkwardly grinning face pasted over her own. With his bullet-shaped head, acne scars, unibrow and bushy black hair, the model had become the undoing of everything that made James into a worthy enemy. But Richie had further embellished his collage with the label maker, adding the caption, THE BITCH IS BACK . . . ASSUME THE POSITION.

Rory was still laughing his drunken ass off when James closed the garage door and stormed into the living room, already check-swinging the Corrector.

"What the fuck are you laughing at, Lee Harvey Cocksucker?" James could slap together an epithet on the fly with the best of them. That, and spanking (which he manfully called *flogging*) and how to iron his boxer shorts was all he really learned from the navy.

Richie tried to stop him. "James, the cops and the fuh— the man from the store, they already hit him a lot."

"I don't want to hear it. Assume the position."

Rory laughed even harder.

"What's with you, bucko? Is he . . . Jesus H. Christ, is he *drunk?*"

Tossing Richie aside, James rolled Rory over onto his belly. Bending the squirming boy over the ottoman and taking down his Toughskins jeans, he administered a stiff ten-stroke flogging. The superimposed CORRECTED legends were a scary red blur across Rory's butt. The poor kid really had no choice but to throw up all over James's scratchy tweed Barcalounger.

Just then, the garage door opened. Mom was outside with

her car filled of groceries, and she opened the garage so the boys could come out and help unload.

The defaced Elton John album dropped into view just as James was coming to grips with the pool of wine-stinking puke on his favorite chair.

Mom rushed in to find James whaling on Richie and Rory with the Corrector. Her youngest crawled up to her with his pants around his knees, his ass red as a beet, and red vomit streaming from his lips. "He made us, Mom. He *made* us do it!"

And for better or worse, she believed him.

"What in the hell has gotten into you, James?"

"Your no-good fucking boys. Your little turd-burglars shot up a store today, Marsha. And they ransacked my property and got drunk to celebrate, and . . . goddamn it!"

Just then, he took another good look at the defaced album sleeve, and flew into a rage all over again. Roaring, he crossed the room and ripped it down, and, in so doing, taught Rory a valuable lesson about anger.

As any halfway competent engineer should have realized, the thing to do would have been to grab the dust jacket . . . but in his rage, James seized the cord itself, and yanked it down.

The steel eyebolt screwed into the ceiling ripped out in a puff of drywall, while the cord snapped taut, then went slack and drooped across the dining room. A ghastly shriek of tormented metal came from the garage, as the Genie garage door opener motor was ripped out of its flimsy aluminum cradle on the ceiling.

Even Rory finally stopped laughing, and you could have heard a pin drop, if not for the endless racket of the garage door opener falling on the roof of James's Porsche.

PART THREE

A World of Shit

SEVEN

On the way to Richie's to pick up the car, Rory drummed on the wheel, nervously murdering the slinky, syncopated trap-and-snare rhythm on the Stray Cats disk playing in the stereo.

Tension is bad in a driver, but it sure beats drowsiness. As the dregs of the pot and tryptophan in his system urged him to nod off, he felt the welcome steel-eyed alertness that getting behind the wheel always instilled in him.

But he could not get into the pocket of the road, though he hit all the lights going up Los Feliz and over the 5 into Atwater, where he traded his '70 Dodge Challenger for one of Richie's livery service lead-sleds.

New enough to be stuffed with idiot lights and redundant gadgets, but old enough that the Armor All–shiny seats were real Corinthian leather, and the hood ornament was an upright targeting sight, not a plaque. More importantly, it didn't have one of those big digital GPS screens showing a scrolling map view in the dashboard. He fucking hated those things.

And blessedly, it wasn't a stretch. Rory had been stuck before with one of Richie's two stretch limos, which only a master driver could navigate through a Burger King drive-through.

Rory had worked L.A. as a wildcat cabbie for two years when he got out of Avenal, and knew every wrinkle of every road in the city. And if he didn't need the GPS, he sure as shit didn't need a satellite tracking his every move. With tracking devices in every car, why keep paying cops?

At the last minute, he remembered the rider on the passengers' contract, and went into Richie's garage fridge for two flats of Arrowhead bottled water. Dropping them on the drive-train ridge between the foot wells in the back, he figured they could negotiate them, if they had to have them.

First clue tonight could be a hassle; lots of water could mean thirsty people, but nothing made people thirstier than drugs. Given the choice between tweakers chewing his ears off and ravers on ecstasy turning his car into a petting zoo, he inwardly hoped for good old-fashioned drunks, but he looked up at the almost-full moon and said, *surprise me.*

The 101 was fairly clear, but he kept racing the monster Lincoln Continental ahead of the flow of traffic, even as his drumming barreled ahead of the song's tempo.

This wasn't right—he could feel it, even as he headed straight into it—but like Trixie always said, he just couldn't say no to Richie. Nobody could, really, except her.

As he tried not to fly down the 5 past Griffith Park, he thought about the way their fortunes had changed since he quit working with Richie. In the last eight years, while Rory struggled to keep his garage open, Richie had diversified into a little empire.

Putting the skills that got them arrested to work, Richie started a mobile locksmith business when he first came to L.A., and somehow made the right connections before he could get squashed.

From these humble beginnings, he had built his garage into a hybrid towing and limo service. But what brought in the real money, and what made him think he was invisible, was the special livery service he offered.

While the goods and passengers he ferried around town for premium rates paid handsomely to travel incognito, they were not quite illegal. More than a few political heavy hitters had used Richie to shuttle their significant others around under the media's noses, and he was on call with two studios and a record label to collect their wayward human unit-shifters before they humiliated their corporate patrons in front of the paparazzi, or killed themselves on the road.

Richie swore he was not doing anything illegal anymore. But he was saying it from a pay phone in jail. It was personal, Richie said, not business. He had money and a good lawyer, but he was in lockup pending a hearing. He had a gaggle of drivers on salary and more on call, but he hit up Rory.

His reason had stung him in places he thought were dead to pain. *I know you need the money . . . I need you to do this. Because you're my brother.*

He caught himself flying past traffic in the slow lane, and reined in the massive luxury sedan. Floating on a cushion, the Lincoln's suspension responded much better than it should have, but the chassis felt like a bank vault on wheels. The car had been extensively customized to handle like a smaller vehicle in evasive situations, and the doors were reinforced with quarter-inch armor plates.

Don't be afraid, little brother. Don't be afraid to do what it takes to make it.

As Elysian Park embraced the highway in its manicured golf course parody of nature, the road cluttered up with a herd of drunks, hugging one another's asses and trying to see straight enough to get home. Rory climbed up through them, cutting across four lanes to ride the left shoulder, letting his impatience take the lead.

Pick up a guy downtown, and take him where he wants to go. Keep it cool.

Rory could be cool. And they did need the money.

He knee-jerk braked as he passed a parked police car flashing its warning lights as two cops gave a drunk driver a field sobriety test at the Pasadena Avenue underpass.

Guy must be some kind of asshole to get the rough treatment they were dishing out. One cop had an arm around the guy's neck, while the other tried to make him breathe into a bag or something.

Rory checked his rearview for cops.

An old Chevy pickup with two households' worth of furniture piled in the back under a blanket whipped by in the fast lane as he passed under Broadway. A chair fell off the stack as the truck swerved around Rory and danced itself to bits across the pavement.

The Lincoln smothered the debris, but the smooth, corduroy grooves of the highway gave way to buckled, mismatched planks of concrete slapped together with hot patch. He bounced out of his seat as the huge car soared over the North Main Bridge.

This was one of the most heavily used stretches of freeway in the world, and only spit and miracles held it together. The heat and friction of four thousand cars per hour seemed to melt the roadway every day, and it was only half-healed.

With the long holiday weekend and the proximity of the monolithic LAPD central HQ, downtown threatened to be crawling with cops, but the sheer density and variety of traffic all but made him invisible.

His car was one of thousands of anonymous, expensive automobiles abroad in the city tonight, discreetly taking important people to important places this fine Thanksgiving night. He'd have to be doing something pretty stupid to attract attention.

Something like whatever Richie was doing last week.

Rory turned onto the "northbound" 101 and took the deeply confused Hollywood Freeway west to Alameda. Swinging off the highway and hugging the right lane of the massive off-ramp, he ogled the buff marble fortress of the L.A. County lockup looming over the freeway.

The place looked too sleek and stylized for its own good,

as if the Justice League stashed its superpowered enemies there. Almost a temple to wrongdoing, it made Rory nervous just driving by it, filled him with the kind of rank fear that only a two-time jailbird can experience.

Something that big had to be hungry for trouble, real or imaginary, to justify itself. Little fish like Richie didn't rate the fortress, and were incarcerated in some new privatized lockup overlooking the river.

Rory's first state sentence was for grand theft auto and narcotics possession. A wake-up call, but it could've been worse. He was running his dad's old route, moving crank from San Diego to Fontana and Yuma, and stealing cars for Minimum Wade on the side. Three years at Avenal, but Rory got out in eighteen months.

Following in Richie's footsteps, he went straight. Tried to, anyway. Still using speed, he ran double-shifts cabdriving. He lost his temper when some lady with a cat on a leash blocked the crosswalk, and some asshole in a BMW honked at him. Honked a long, loud blast that went right up Rory's ass, then rolled into his back bumper.

He barely remembered climbing out of the cab, going up to the guy's car and punching him. The guy was used to pushing people around, and didn't even expect such a violation of his space, let alone his face. He called Rory a "cocksucking troglodyte" and looked down his nose at Rory's fist, taking the blow in the throat.

Rory crushed the guy's trachea. Airport police saved his life. Rory got clubbed to a pulp and went to the county's Fortress of Justice for two months until his aggravated assault ticket got punched. Five years. Rory got a better lawyer than he deserved, and got out after three.

Since then, he'd gotten a lot better than he deserved, at everything.

Turning onto Alameda, he heard the frantic brassy banter of a mariachi band spilling out of Olivera Street's bandstand plaza and into his armored sedan. A slack-jawed redneck slouched on the corner with a cardboard sign: WHY LIE? I NEED BEER.

Turning into the Union Station parking lot, Rory had to smile at the palatial mission facade of the big old train station. Colored floodlights saturated the central tower in candy hues that cycled through a spectrum as he waited for the traffic cop at the entrance to sort out the jumble of confused drivers picking up, dropping off, and trying to park.

A loose mob of shell-shocked train travelers waited at the curb. He had a rough description of the guy he was looking for, but he didn't need it.

A trio of beautiful ladies in short black silk dresses like runaways from a music-video shoot commanded his appreciative eye, returned his smile with a wave and a wink. Two of them were twins, and the third, while no threat to Trixie, made him think *maybe this job won't suck, after all.*

And then a lanky stork of a kid stepped up in front of them and glared at the Lincoln as if he were holding a big sign with Rory's name on it. His hooded eyes reflected the low beams like chrome rivets, but no question he was looking right at Rory, and saying, *Me. I'm the guy.*

For the money, Rory knew there would be no answers to questions he asked aloud, but his mind buzzed with big bubbles of *what-the-fuck.* Who was this fucking kid?

Tall enough to play basketball, he had a long head with close-cropped hair and pinched, acne-raddled features that aged him badly. Narrow shoulders and a skinny chest concealed in a baggy hooded sweatshirt with the logo of some emo-core band Rory had studiously ignored: Breaking the Chain Letter. Grubby red jeans, fingerless black gloves, and some sort of fake Doc Martens made of hemp completed the ensemble. The kid smiled and skipped off the curb toward the Lincoln, and the trio of stunners followed him, towing big rolling suitcases and overnight bags on their shoulders.

The kid knocked on the roof as he walked around the car. Rory buzzed the window down. "You Tommy?"

The kid just nodded.

Rory shifted into park, killed the engine, and hopped out, came around to open the back door. Two of the ladies piled into the back, smiling but silent. Working girls for sure, but Rory didn't know anyone who could afford to throw down for this kind of tail.

The kid helped him throw the suitcases in the trunk. Each suitcase was a half-size black Samsonite hardcase, but they might have been filled with bricks. They had Amtrak tags on them, but they weren't dog-eared, like the luggage on every Amtrak train was, when it got sorted by the throwers.

"I wasn't told where you're headed tonight." Rory slammed the trunk and followed the kid around to the open door. The third girl got into the front passenger seat.

"I'll direct you as we go. We have a few stops to make, and then we'll come back down here. Just be cool. Are you feeling me?"

"No problem . . . sir." Rory knew what the role required, but he wasn't wearing a chauffeur's hat, and he wasn't angling for a fat tip from this smug, lanky kid, who might be a first-round NBA draft pick if he bothered to work out.

The vibe he got off this kid had Rory despising him and his hoochie harem before he closed the door and got behind the wheel, trying to ignore the mocha-colored virago beside him. The kid and his girlfriends were so high they couldn't feel their faces, and it made Rory a lot madder than it should have. Because underneath—and in spite of everything he had to be grateful for—he was jealous of them.

Those days were long gone, and he was a better man for it.

Tommy leaned over the seat back and passed him a Post-It note. "Here first," he said.

Rory did a double take between the road and the note as Tommy stuck it to his hand. A Boyle Heights address, in a bad place.

Someone behind the Lincoln honked a hurry-up at him. The man he used to be could never let the challenge go unanswered, but that guy was dead.

"Yes, sir," he said, and slid the car onto Alameda, headed north. Tommy broke out the bottled waters and passed them around. Everyone but Rory had one.

Watching the road and its clutter of potential threats like tumbling lottery balls, Rory eyed his passengers in the rearview. Tommy sat behind Rory, so all Rory could scope was the kid's unlovely silhouette, tilted to look out the triple-tinted window.

The girls beside him held their chunky, expensive purses on their laps and stared straight ahead, like machines waiting for coins or credit cards to bring them to life. Their smiles ticked and twitched, like they were talking to themselves.

All of them had the same glaze of fake excitement, like airbrushed highlights in the eyes of department store mannequins.

The girl beside him absently sang in a tiny, childlike singsong that got on Rory's nerves, because he had to strain to make sense of it. She was singing the names of the cross streets, but she was three or four blocks ahead. Her coy grin, always waiting for him whenever he looked at her—like she thought she knew him better than he knew himself—made him wish he was somewhere else.

And then there was the smell.

At first, it was only a bitter organic tang in the air, like wet laundry left too long in the washer. A few of Rory and Trixie's friends were hard-core vegans, and took the green-living thing to the extreme of refusing to use any real detergents or soap. Nice people, but sweet Jesus, they stank. A diet free of animal products changed one's B.O., but it didn't make them less of an animal themselves, and their clothes were rich ecosystems full of stinky biodiversity.

Trixie bought a bread box last summer, but donated it only a month later. Far from keeping the bread fresh, it seemed to incubate the mold; a fresh loaf of hearty sourdough would turn into a mushy mess of warring yellow, black, and white mold cultures inside of three days, the bag swelled up like a balloon with gas from the accelerated decay.

Within minutes of leaving the train station, the Lincoln's soothing chemical aroma of solvents and leather swiftly began to smell like that bread box.

Rory cranked up the A/C, opened his window a bit. "Could you turn that off, please?" the girl beside him asked. "It's murder on my sinuses."

I'll bet something is, he thought, but killed the A/C. He reached for the stereo before thinking to ask Tommy if he had any musical preferences.

"Oh, whatever's cool with you," the kid said. "We like everything, right?"

"It's all good," said the twins.

Boyle Heights was the high-water mark where the tidal waves of gentrification that roared through downtown L.A. in the '90s had crashed and rolled back, leaving a funky jigsaw puzzle of fortified yuppie condos, frightful apartment projects, and the odd vintage bungalow backwater where, bars on windows aside, nothing much had changed since Eisenhower was president.

Latino gang tags covered the real estate, but bigger gangs held the titles. Rory heard from friends that many of the new loan companies scarfing up the bad paper from the subprime collapse were Mafia and Triad fronts. If they could clean up the neighborhoods, people would probably welcome them.

Boyle Heights has good streets and bad streets. Manitou was a bad street. Most of the houses were barred or boarded up. The street numbers were guesswork, but there was no mistaking the place in question. It was a duplex with a garage in front, much like his own place, but the garage looked to have gone out of business ages ago.

"Pop the trunk," Tommy mumbled, and jumped out. The twins followed him around to the back, but the one beside him just kicked off her heels, crossed her sleek, lovely legs, and told him, "Sit tight, boy. They'll only be a few minutes. Maybe longer . . ."

Rory watched Tommy and the twins cross the street and approach a gate opening on the side of the garage. The kid waved to a security camera, and the gate buzzed to let them in.

"You're not going in with your friends?" he asked.

A wayward curl of her auburn bob hid her eyes, but her wicked grin was the stuff *Penthouse Forum* letters are made of. "I'd rather kick it out here with you."

Rory tweaked the stereo to a classic rock station and splayed his hands on the wheel so his wedding band caught the greenish aquarium glow of the streetlights.

"My name's Vanessa." She took a silver case out of her purse.

"Um," he replied.

"Your name's Rory."

"Yup," he said.

The mural on the roll-down steel doors and cinder block walls of the garage kept luring his eye and trapping it. At first, the whole of it was just a huge, complex signature, a jumble of alphabetical shapes embellished and warped by a ghetto Dalí with a thousand Krylon cans into a mind-maze of jeweled facets and hidden faces that unfolded deeper layers of complexity until it suddenly shoved him out.

His eyes did a spit-take as he realized the whole mural was a massive biomechanical face with continents for skin and tectonic plates for bones, and dull, inscrutable god-eyes judging him unworthy to know who was really in charge out here.

"Rory, you want some of this?"

Reluctantly, he looked at her, and it was so much worse than he feared.

She had a little sterling silver tray out on her lap, and was busily chopping up a small mound of white powder with a credit card.

"That is a really stupid thing to be doing right now," he said.

"But you want one, right?" Her tiny, talented hand expertly teased the fluffy white stuff into a quartet of fat lines, the length of her pinkie. "You look like you could use one."

Rory bit his lip and took his hands off the wheel, but couldn't decide where to put them. He could use more than one, and that was no lie, but admitting the truth hardly set him free. "I never touch the shit."

Flicking her hair back so her eyes, bright gold in the light reflected off the tray, finally pinned him. One of her pupils looked like the business end of a telescope. The other was so tiny the light got in a photon at a time. "You never *did*, or you never *do*?"

"I used to have a problem, but I'm over it." Sure, he was well past the bad old days when he used, and he never had much use for coke, anyway. For a white-trash wetback growing up in Fontana and San Diego, white powder meant crystal meth, and after a crank binge, coke was like substituting kerosene for rocket fuel.

And he was well and truly shut off crank. He didn't need it, now—never craved it, hardly ever thought of it at all, except when the news brought it up. He had a wonderful wife and a damned good life, and drumming and driving to fill those holes in himself that used to leave him insecure and violent, craving the certainty, the sense of invincibility and certitude that speed could give him.

Any other day or night, he could laugh at that shit or take it and dump it out the window, and know he'd done this crazy chick a favor. But tonight was draining him dry, and the old holes were open and leaking. To have that certainty on demand, to have everything lined up and pointing in the same direction, even if it was the worst one, was too much temptation.

And she smiled like she knew exactly what he was going through. Savoring his frustration, sucking it up like just another drug.

"You might want to finish up and put that away. Cops could come through here any minute."

"Cops never come through here at night. Not looking for trouble."

She took a rolled-up C-note and slalomed through all four lines in a couple of seconds. Her head rolled back and tears streamed from her eyes, but she didn't cough or gag, like most people who snorted coke did. She just trembled a little, her breathing coming fast and deep, as if she were floating out of her body.

Then she snapped out of it and put the tray away. "You might change your mind later, and that's okay. It's going to be a long night."

Rory hesitated, searching for the most diplomatic reply, but the twins climbed into the car. Tommy had a cheap Coach knockoff bag on his shoulder, swaybacked with dense weight. Rory popped the trunk and Tommy slammed it a moment later, climbed in sans bag. He reached over the seat and pasted a Post-It note on Vanessa's cleavage. Rory looked sidelong at it and shuddered.

Watts.

Eight

By 12:45, the kitchen was clean, and the last of the traveling orphans had finally hit the road. That left Trixie and Renee as the last ones standing, with the clan of Fran and Stan blissfully snoring in the living room dark.

But Trixie was anything but relaxed. Just sitting around talking would make her insane. She had to have something to do with her hands. So . . .

"You're going to do *what?*" Renee asked, half-incredulous.

"You don't have to come if you don't want to," Trixie told her.

"Oh, I'm coming all right, grease monkey. I need to see this with my own eyes. You sure Rory's not gonna mind?"

"I let him cook the turkey, didn't I?"

"Yeah—"

"So why would he mind if I changed out some brakes?"

"I guess I just didn't realize the skills were so interchangeable," Renee continued, trying to keep pace with her long-legged friend.

They were walking through the backyard now, to the open gate leading to the back of Rory's lot. The beauty of the adjoining properties was that they became one big one when the gate was open. It was always like owning—or more to the point, tenuously renting—an estate.

"It's all about attention to detail," Trixie said. "If you know how to do it, you just do it. If you don't, you either learn how or leave it alone."

"Or leave it up to people like Rory or, I guess, *you.*" Laughing. "Which is what I do every single time."

"But who do I go to when I want to write an angry letter to the editor? Or try to express myself in a delicate situation, where I don't know what to say?"

Renee raised her hand, grinning. "Okay. Point taken."

"I just wish I knew what to say sometimes . . ." Trixie let it trail off, punctuated by a sigh.

The back of Rory's garage was wide-open, all three doors up to expose its innards. As they passed through the gate, they went from lawn to parking lot pavement, where three cars in need of work patiently waited for attention.

The musicians had taken their amps and instruments, leaving only Rory's rumpled drum set in bay number three. He had cleared the cars out, so the lift was empty. It looked like a little airplane hangar full of tools and devices, anal-retentively organized.

The doors at the front were all shut, forming a wall before them as they advanced inside. "It still smells like turkey," Renee noted. "Mmmmm."

"That's the King Kooker." Trixie pointed to their left, far enough from the walls to constitute relative outdoorsiness. It looked like an aluminum Crock-Pot, up on its own pedestal, with a propane tank snuggled up beside it. "Guess Rory didn't dispose of the oil."

"That has to be the unhealthiest turkey I've ever eaten."

"I know. But *God,* was it good."

"What would happen if I turned it back on?"

"It wouldn't grow another turkey."

Renee cackled. "I know that! But would it hurt anything?"

"It would burn through some propane. Other than that, it would just—"

"Make the place smell like Thanksgiving?"

Trixie nodded, thoughtful. "I see where you're going with this."

"Like a turkey incense burner."

Both of them grinned.

"Aw, what the hell," said Trixie, walking over to flip the switch. "If it makes you happy."

"It makes me very happy!"

"Done and done."

The switches for the front garage doors were up front, where they belonged. Trixie went there, hit one, watched door number one rattle noisily up. Inch by dirty, unlit inch, the long, empty ribbon of Hyperion Boulevard appeared before her.

"Where are you going?" Renee called from behind.

"Just locking up," said Trixie, moving into the front lot, where Dan's Sentra and Renee's Rent-a-Mini Cooper were still parked to either side. They'd left the front gate open, to allow their guests safe, uncomplicated parking. But it was time to shut it down.

Unfortunately, the remote on the front gate was acting up, which meant that it had to be rolled out manually, even before you got to the padlock action.

To her left, Fernwood was a sleepy green oasis. To her right, Hyperion was most definitely not. Funny how a hundred feet in either direction meant the difference between privacy and publicity, suburban and urban, peacefully homey and woefully homeless. Although at the moment, both were almost entirely silent and still.

Occasional lights twinkled from porches and windows all up and down the Silver Lake hills. Most everyone had wound down for the night, but there were always the night owls and stragglers.

She wondered how many of them were at home with their loved ones, preparing to fall asleep in one another's arms, and how many were still up out of worry, or loneliness, or fear. Wishing for the person who was not there with them. Thinking and thinking. Thinking too much.

"It's nice out," said Renee, behind her, startling her out of her reverie.

"Yeah," said Trixie.

And promptly burst into tears.

"Awww," cooed Renee, enfolding her in a sisterly hug.

"GODDAMN IT!"

"It's okay. It's okay—"

"I'm so STUPID!"

"You're not stupid. You're a million miles from stupid—"

"Then why did I let him go?"

Renee hugged her harder, lending emphasis to what she was about to say.

"Because you trust him."

Trixie nodded her head, sniffled hard, looked for words she couldn't find.

"Because you finally trust him," Renee continued. "And he's earned it. And *you've* earned it. You've both worked so hard . . ."

Now Trixie was nodding her head, too. Nodding and sobbing. "I know . . ."

"He's working to bring you money, so you don't need to worry. That's all he's trying to do."

"I know."

"And that is a good thing. So . . . what has you so scared?"

Now the words came easily. "I don't trust Richie."

Up Hyperion Boulevard came the sound of an engine racing. A suddenly singular sound, in that canyon of emptiness.

"Nobody trusts Richie," Renee assured her.

"You'd be surprised," Trixie countered, gathering strength. "He has the knack. I mean, he's helped us out before. Sometimes, whatever he's doing comes up at just the right time. And it makes all the difference. I can't argue with that."

"But—"

"But you just never know with Richie. He sells the good stuff and the bad stuff exactly the same way. You know?

He's a salesman. He doesn't give a shit what he's selling, just so long as it gets sold."

On Hyperion, the noise was getting closer. It sounded like a van with a shit transmission and the idle set way too high.

And from the crazy dog-lady's RV—parked across the street on Fernwood—every one of her dozen dogs began to bark.

It was an eruption of the sort you'd expect when a coyote wandered down from the hills. Startling in its suddenness. Jarring as a car alarm.

And as distant dogs responded—all up and down the hills—headlights careened into view, high beams cutting a swath above the pavement that striped the walls of the buildings across Hyperion . . .

. . . and the screech of brakes proceeded the van that now fishtailed into view, directly before them . . .

. . . screeching to an abrupt halt, with the words ST. AL-FONSO'S DAY CARE emblazoned across its length . . .

. . . and as Trixie turned to gauge the distance between herself and the wide-open gate—too far to run to in time—the van screeched back into motion.

Wheeling into Rory's parking lot.

"Oh, fuck," she said, with the lights in her eyes.

NINE

At USC, they used to tell incoming freshmen that initiates to the local Crips franchise had to jump a Trojan to make their bones and become a made thug. Extra merit badges were dished out for rapes, murder, and permanent disfigurement.

Bigoted nonsense, but it probably kept a few spoiled honky transplants from getting themselves hurt. Where respect could not be taught, fear would have to do. But anyone who really looked could tell that the ghetto was not much of a threat to its white neighbors. Like every ghetto, Watts preferred to eat its own.

Rory turned off the westbound 10 on Crenshaw and beat the lights heading south ahead of a flock of cops on a zero-tolerance dragnet sortie. Three cars were pulled over within the first two blocks. Only one driver was white.

Amazing. Rich white kids still tried to come down here to score drugs.

Which still wasn't half as stupid as white folks coming down here trying to sell them.

"So, you got friends down here, too?" Faking an ease he didn't feel at all, Rory let his hands tap out their anxiety on the wheel. With the practice he was getting in tonight, he'd be able to keep up with Gene Krupa.

"We've got friends everywhere," Tommy said.

"So you know Richie Long pretty well?" Rory tried to catch Tommy's eyes in the rearview as he asked.

Tommy shook his big, knobby head and grimaced. It took a second to figure out he was laughing. "Richie's our main man. He's like a big brother to me."

Jesus, the balls on this kid. "Yeah, a lot of people say that. So, you've been in L.A. a long time?"

"A while. Long enough to know how it works, you know? It's not what you know, but *whom* you know, and who and what they know. A lot of people always harp on how fragmented it is, but they don't see all the amazing ways everything connects together."

"Is that what you're doing tonight? Connecting people?"

"Yeah. It's going to be beautiful."

"You're not worried about going down here on a night like this? I don't know if you follow the news, but—"

Vanessa's cool, dry hand pinned his to the wheel. He tried to show how strong he was by not flinching away. "We're not afraid, Rory. We have what everyone really wants. We make new friends everywhere we go. You should try it."

"We can take care of ourselves, if that's what you're worried about." Now Tommy leaned forward and touched Rory's arm.

Rory was rushing to catch a stale yellow light at Slauson, but he hit the brakes hard to bite down on the line. The Lincoln rocked on its badass shocks. Rory's weight surged up against his seat belt, but Tommy wasn't wearing his.

The lanky kid launched off his seat and crashed into Rory's padded headrest. He gave only a surprised grunt, but his fingers turned into fishhooks as he dug into the meat of Rory's left shoulder.

Rory's arm instinctively shot out to stop his passenger flying into the dashboard. Vanessa was belted in, but force of habit made him catch a handful of tit.

His hand shrank away fast, but he shamefully felt the memory of its taut shape in his palm, more muscle than mammary flab and most definitely 100 percent real.

"Sorry," he said, nodding at the black-and-white ghosting through the herd of Slauson cross-traffic.

She giggled a little. "That was fun."

If he bird-dogged the cop, he could get pulled over, and let them deal with what he was sure they'd find in the trunk. And they would be sure to take the word of a two-time felon into consideration when they decided who to bury. If all these idiots did tonight was get him arrested, maybe he'd be lucky.

Rory turned around. "Hey, I'm sorry, man, but you really should have your belt on . . ."

Tommy returned to his seat and tilted his head back, pinching the bridge of his nose with his long fingers. It was bleeding, but it wasn't bleeding blood.

The stuff was white, and looked like glue.

Beside him, the twins sat with their arms wrapped around each other. Shaky from the sudden stop, they stroked each other's arms and locked lips in a long, soft kiss.

Tommy had to snap his fingers in Rory's face. "I can see that you're not down with all this. You're coming at tonight's experiences from a purely selfish perspective."

"It's just a job, man. I'm just the driver. But—"

"Our risks are your risks tonight. Your brother offered you, what, two thousand, to squire us around town?"

Rory tensed up even more, which was no mean feat. "If it's all the same to you, I'd rather not discuss—"

"Would you feel better if you got five?"

Slauson's light turned yellow, and a bunch of desperate left-turning cars darted into the face of oncoming traffic so as not to be stranded in no-man's-land.

Half the major intersections in L.A. still didn't have left-turn lights. It had to be for a reason. Weed out the truly unroadworthy, those with no killer instinct.

Where the hell was his head?

"Sure," Rory answered, "and I'd like to be home eating

my wife's pumpkin pie right now, too. You don't have to make me any promises, sir."

Tommy tapped his shoulder again. Rory reached up to brush his hand away, but he grabbed a tight roll of bills instead.

He took it and looked, expecting a few twenties or a counterfeit hundred over a wad of Albertson's coupons. These crazy motherfuckers couldn't be for real. But it was hundreds all the way down. Thirty brand-new hundreds that his fingers told him were real, or better.

"Don't worry, Rory. We won't make you do anything illegal that you wouldn't do anyway, to save your own skin. Just drive like the professional that you are. And we'll have you home in time to get to your wife's pumpkin pie, before somebody else eats the last slice."

The light turned green. Rory punched it, grimly satisfied when he got a scream out of the Lincoln's tires.

TEN

The place overlooked the Inglewood Cemetery. Apartment projects at the dead end of Seventy-eighth Street: six sprawling three-story buildings on the block. Rory balked at rolling into the parking lot, which wound around the crappy landscaping and dead, dusty stretches of lawn studded with two-kilo piles of dog shit.

"Go on in. We're safe."

A couple bangers in baggy starter jackets hung out in the lot, but they faded when Rory cruised by. Most of the narrow windows glowed cathode blue.

The other cars in the lot were a study in contrasts—rusted-out old shitbox sedans and minivans, and tricked-out late-model Japanese street racers with more plastic accessories stuck on them than they had guts under the hood. But the complex knew the peculiar kind of peace that settles on a place where everything worth stealing, everyone worth hurting, is long since off the table.

"Park out here," Tommy said. Rory stopped in a vacant spot with space around it and popped the trunk. Tommy and the twins got out and took another suitcase up the path between the buildings, passing under a spastically flickering fluorescent light.

Vanessa sat back and slammed a bottled water.

"You sure you don't need to go in and, you know . . ."

"What?"

"You've been, uh, drinking a lot of water . . ."

"I'm fine. How are you?"

He looked away, fiddled with the radio again. Five minutes to one. He should call Trixie, let her know he was okay, but he didn't want to talk in front of Vanessa. And he didn't think it was a good idea to get out of the car.

He slipped his phone out and sneaked a quick text. ALL IS WELL. HOME LATE BUT WORTH THE WAIT. He didn't like lying to her, but was he lying, exactly?

He didn't want her to worry. He could take care of himself a lot better if she wasn't weighing on him. Guilt slows you down and jumbles up what should be a clear reactive mind. He'd gotten paid, and if these people got into trouble, he was just a dumb bystander.

So why did he already feel so guilty?

Maybe because guilt was easier to deal with than admitting how afraid he was.

He'd already decided that, present activities aside, these people were not drug dealers by nature or trade. They looked like clueless roadkill-to-be, but they acted like a cult. If they got through this insanity intact, he'd take their money and patiently wait for Richie to get out of jail, then patiently kick his ass.

Setting aside his quite natural fear of getting caught or worse out here, what gnawed on his head the worst was the question of how these freaks knew his brother.

All their lives, Richie had been a silver-tongued social chameleon. He knew someone at every track, behind every bar, and out front of every club, in every town they ever visited. Since he became respectable, he'd gracefully shed most of his low connections in favor of shiny new ones. He had a city councilman and a newscaster who was banging the mayor on his speed dial.

Amateur nut jobs like these would never have gotten Richie's number, let alone his help in some retarded gangster fantasy-island suicide mission—but the Richie he knew, the one he said yes to, would probably never have gotten busted driving with drugs on him.

The more he thought about them, the less sense it all made. All he knew about them was that they seemed to know their way around, and they paid in cash.

Vanessa chopped out another batch of lines. "You change your mind yet?"

Fuck. These people were doomed.

He shook his head. "How long have you known Richie?"

"What time is it now?" She checked the dashboard clock. "About three hours. Feels like longer . . ." Bending to snort the lines on the tray, she paused and looked around, as if she was lost. Her pupils were the same size now, at least, but both were big enough to show him his reflection when she looked at him and silently mouthed, *where am I? Who are you?*

He reached for the tray, gently, so as not to spook her. "Maybe you've had enough of that shit already."

She blocked him with the hand holding the bill, while her other slipped into her purse. He saw something else silver inside.

"I'm okay," she stammered. "Just . . . keep your hands to yourself, okay?"

"Fine, I didn't want to try anything . . . I mean . . ." He was still trying to figure out what he wanted to say, when he saw the big, smiling black guy outside Vanessa's window.

The guy waved politely, then raised a hand to knock on the glass.

"I told you that was a bad idea—"

He knocked the window out. A blast of safety glass pegs sprayed Vanessa and scattered all over the seat.

Vanessa shouted, "Damn it!" and lifted her purse, but a big arm in a Raiders parka snaked in the window and wrapped around her neck to jab a short but sturdy Buck knife into the hollow behind her jaw.

"Pass up that bag," the carjacker growled, savoring the role as he shook Vanessa.

An even bigger, blacker guy knocked softly on Rory's window with the chrome barrel of a snub-nosed .22. "Yo, please present your license, registration, and all your good shit." He didn't smash the other window, so they must want the car.

For her part, Vanessa was way cooler now than a minute ago. She rolled her eyes at Rory as if she'd been rehearsing this scene all night. "You gentlemen want something from us?"

"Purse, bitch."

"You're making a big mistake, fellas." Rory rolled his window halfway down and raised his hands into plain sight. He put on a sunny, unconcerned expression that he once saw on TV. "We're not lost. We're here to—"

"Shut up." The barrel of the gun rapped the bridge of Rory's nose. He jolted back in his seat and brought his hands up to his face. It took every ounce of will he had not to reach for the gun and take it from the fucker.

Vanessa took her hand out of the purse. The knife at her throat twitched and pricked her, but even the guy on Rory's side had a little heart attack when the big bag of white powder came into view.

"You boys can have this for free," she purred. "Take it and good night, God bless. Anything more is gonna cost you."

"Get out the car, white boy." The gun's barrel came up close enough to kiss Rory's left eye.

Rory didn't move. He could see no way not to get killed, but no fucking way was he yielding the car.

Any minute, Tommy and the twins would come out, and this shit would get sorted out. These assholes were either flunkies or cowboys, and either way, they probably weren't going to get away with this.

"Bitch, gimme the motherfuckin' purse." Vanessa's assailant was beside himself.

Vanessa turned to face him. The knife skated across her neck, laying open a shallow wound that spat blood down her little black dress, but she didn't seem to notice.

Before the knife could reassert itself, Vanessa came up with the shortest sawed-off shotgun Rory had ever seen, and pressed its yawning double-barrel mouth to his ample belly.

His coat slid apart, and Rory gave a disgusted groan.

"Is that what passes for body armor around here, man?" Rory asked.

The guy with the pistol cocked it in Rory's face, but his friend moaned, "Hold up, hold up, time-out—"

Under his Raiders parka, the carjacker wore a Snugli harness, in which rested a baby of indeterminate age and gender.

In its Raiders footy pajamas, with a wizened preemie face that reminded Rory of those miserable Cabbage Patch dolls, the baby looked like it was teething, so naturally it put its mouth on the stubby barrels of Vanessa's shotgun.

"Bitch, that's cold-blooded. My homey got white boy down cold. Gimme—"

"Let's make a deal," she said. "Come on, proud papa, do you want what's behind Door Number One—" She shook the bag of coke, which was easily two ounces . . . "—Or will it be Door Number Two?" And she tickled the baby with her shotgun.

The babysitter took the bag and dipped a pinkie into it, rubbed some on his gums and seemed to freeze over and thaw out in about ten long seconds.

"Yo, fuck this," Rory's jacker grumbled, and yanked on the door handle. "Get out the fuckin' car."

His partner took a step back from the Lincoln and . . . bowed? "Let's go, G. We got shit to do."

"What the fuck, cuz? Fuck you—"

"Let's go, G. Now." The guy with the baby pocketed

Vanessa's bag and strolled away. After an awkward moment, his partner jogged off after him.

Rory broke out in cold sweat. He itched all over. "That was the stupidest thing I've ever seen anyone do."

She giggled like a little girl and, flicking bits of safety glass off the tray, finished her lines.

"We should call it a night when your friends come back."

"Don't worry about those fools. They on the line now."

He was about to ask her what the hell that meant, what any of it meant, when he heard loud noises from the building that Tommy and the twins had disappeared into.

Now, even Vanessa sat up and looked worried.

Rory heard a big dog's frenzied barking—then two dogs, and men shouting.

And then he could hear nothing but guns.

Eleven

The doors to the van flew open; and as Trixie backed reflexively toward the garage, she counted the jolly freaks piling out into the driveway, none of whom looked like they worked in a day care center. Or anywhere else, for that matter.

They looked like street urchins, not a one over twenty-three: the kind of raggedy Hollywood panhandlers that slept in packs under low-hanging bridges. And as they hit the open breeze, it was also clear that something smelled really wrong.

There were seven in all: glassy-eyed and chattering over the howling of the dogs, as if they'd all just arrived at the world's greatest party.

God, Trixie thought. *They're coked out of their minds.*

"We're closed," she said. "Sorry. You have to go."

"Aw, man!" the driver hooted, and the others laughed. He looked like a dreadlocked Jesus. He wiped sweat-streaming hands on a faux-vintage T-shirt that said FRESNO NEVER SAYS NO, and struck a wounded, pouting pose. "Rory said it would be cool."

"Rory said *what?*" That kind of threw her for a loop.

"Well, you can hear how bad it's running," came the guy from the shotgun seat, a scrawny cracker in nothing but greasy cargo shorts. "He said we could drop it off, and wait for our ride."

"Wait a minute." Trixie scrolled her memory banks, came up blank. "Rory didn't say anything to me."

"So Richie didn't call?"

And that was the magic word.

"Hold on," she said, still backing away, as her heart began to pound. "What's this about Richie now?"

"He said it was cool to just hang out with you till Rory comes home. Or our ride shows up. Whichever comes first . . ."

"Oh, no no no. That's not gonna happen. I'm sorry. You can leave the van, I guess, but you'll have to wait on the corner . . ."

They all started laughing again, and moved like a wave toward her.

"That is so uncool," said Dreadlock Jesus, pulling out an ounce of blow and a pocketknife. "Maybe you ought to get on the same page with Richie."

"Renee!" Trixie yelled, loud enough to wake the neighbors. "Shut the door!" And to her relief, the grinding whirr of the big garage door started almost at once. Renee was way ahead of her.

That was when she turned to run back up the driveway, the door slowly lowering, Renee white-faced behind it. From the panic in her eyes, it was clear that Trixie wasn't the only one running.

In her mind, she wasn't picturing the deadbeat horde behind her. She was picturing the wall of tools in bay number one, to her left, and what she'd have to do with them if these people actually violated her space . . .

. . . and then Trixie went under, ducking her head, the door at five feet and closing. Her gaze locked on a tire iron. She ran to it, hefted it, whirled.

Dreadlock Jesus came in under the door, skimming his back as it hit the three-foot mark. A second later, the cracker rolled under, and then they were down to two.

A third tried to slither up on Trixie underfoot. She kicked him in the face, kicked him again, kicked him back out the shrinking gap. "I. SAID. GET. OUT!"

The others started to bang on the outside of the door as it dropped the final foot with a clang. Trixie brought up the tire iron like a baseball bat, advancing.

Dreadlock Jesus cut a slit in the bag of coke, brought a little white mound up on the tip of his blade. "You wouldn't believe . . ." he started to say, as if he didn't believe she was really going to hit him.

Trixie swung straight for his head. His arms came up, and one of them shattered, his yelp of surprise morphing into a shriek.

"You think I'm PLAYIN'?" Trixie growled, and kicked him square in the nutsack.

"JESUS!" yelled the cracker, as his buddy collapsed and the baggie and knife went flying. "Why do you got to be like that? All confrontational and violent and shit?"

"DIDN'T I TELL YOU TO GO?" Trixie bellowed.

Outside, the banging abruptly stopped. Dreadlock Jesus was down on his knees, making a noise somewhere between vomit and laughter. Trixie kicked him in the belly and bent him in half. He fell forward on his upchucking face, and a reeking white pool spread out before him, its consistency somewhere between marshmallow fluff and moldering coconut milk.

From outside, she heard the sound of retreating footsteps, took that as a sign that her message had been received. She turned her attention to the cracker, who was now sensibly backing away and helplessly casting his gaze for either an exit or a weapon. But that blissed-out shit-eating grin was still on his face, and that disturbed her to no end.

"Renee? Call nine-one-one."

"I don't have a phone—" came the terrified squeak behind her.

"It's in my back pocket. Come here. Stay close." All the while advancing on the cracker.

He wasn't backing toward the yard. He was crossing bay two, coming up on bay three, staying parallel to the garage doors, heading straight for Rory's drum kit.

And before she could think *oh, don't you mess with Rory's drums,* he was sprinting toward them, going "WOOOO!"

Trixie took off after him, but he had a good five yards head start, his hands snapping up Rory's high-hat stand and whipping it around like a shield and spear before she could close the distance.

She swung as he thrust, little cymbals clanging and cracking under the tire-iron onslaught. But he did not let go, swinging the stand back at her. It clipped her side, then jabbed hard enough to remind her she could lose.

Now the cracker was having fun, with a five-foot metal extension between them. He braced the tripod legs against his groin and lower belly, thrust forward with his body, like he was trying to bang her long-distance.

She couldn't reach him with her swing; and when she tried to grab the cymbals, they pinched her fingers, breaking skin. She screeched and pulled back for a second, then whipped the tire iron at his skull: a sidearm throw that whined through the air, then whacked him across the face.

As he started to tumble, she grabbed the cymbals with both hands and shoved with all her might. He tripped backward over the drum stool, brought the snare drum down onto his lap, losing his grip on the high-hat stand, which she promptly winged halfway across the garage.

Trixie tipped the bass drum down onto the cracker, leaned into it, crushing him underneath. He couldn't get leverage, couldn't get a grip, could only flail as a rib snapped.

Trixie hefted the bass drum, brought it back down hard

on his head. Something went crunch, and it wasn't just the drum's acrylic finish.

It occurred to her that she might have just killed him, but all she could feel was relief.

And then the screaming came from inside the house.

TWELVE

Renee was in shock. For her, the world now moved in painful slow motion; and the things happening before her could not possibly be real.

She felt herself coming up behind Trixie, heard the animal howls and the human screams. But she could barely feel her body. It was as if it were happening to somebody else.

Trixie turned to her sloooowly, with such rage and urgency in her eyes that Renee couldn't bear to look directly at them.

Looking away almost cost her her life.

Something grabbed her by the ankle. Before she knew it, she was falling, incredibly fast, arms flying out by reflex so that she landed on her elbows, the pain mercifully muted as her legs kicked out, the free one connecting with something hard.

She pulled her other leg free and started to scuttle, looking back at the dreadlocked, milk-bloodied face. He was starting to rise now, struggling back to his feet, which was something she couldn't quite manage to do . . .

. . . until somebody grabbed her by the arm, hoisted her up, up and up, while all she could do was scream . . .

. . . and then Trixie was slapping her face back and forth, one two three, dragging her forward once again . . .

. . . and she could see that the guy under Rory's drum kit was getting up, too, impossibly alert and moving, even with a skull like a crushed pumpkin . . .

. . . and Renee was being yanked backward at a run, a slow-motion run that felt like floating through harsh airline turbulence, her legs on abstract automatic . . .

. . . and she turned to see Trixie hauling her forward, aiming not for the door, but just beside it, for reasons she did not understand . . .

. . . looking over her shoulder, at the two men running toward her . . .

. . . and then Trixie was pushing her off to the side, Renee twirling out toward the night and then coming round again to see the men in the garage closing in on Trixie . . .

. . . who waited until they were almost on her . . .

. . . and then the heady Thanksgiving scent of turkey fat loomed large, pluming out with the gallons of boiling oil that sluiced from the overturned King Kooker, rolling toward the men in a violent tide.

As the oil hit their feet, the men slipped, screamed, and sizzled, rolling and crying and frying in the scalding flood. As they tried to rise, their flesh sloughed off in crispy stringers, stretched between the floor and their agonized bones.

The smell was overwhelming, the sight too much to bear. Renee teetered at the brink of consciousness, felt the oily smoke and sickly sweet stench of deep-fried flesh enfold her and make her an instant vegetarian.

And then Trixie started dragging her again.

There was no time to fuck around. Fran and Edie were still screaming, but the laughter from inside the house was even worse.

Trixie grabbed the flat-headed shovel from the tool rack with one hand, while trying to pull Renee with the other. She couldn't even express how furious she was with her friend, and there wasn't time to do so if she could.

"COME ON!" she screamed; and when that didn't work, she let go of Renee and started running toward the gate, past the damaged cars to the unmowed lawn, until the back porch with its unlocked screen door was the only target that mattered.

A familiar engine vroomed, and headlights streamed up the side of the house from the driveway. "NO!" she screamed, as her catering truck revved its engine, kicked into reverse.

But the screams were still coming from inside the house. And the dogs were almost as loud, almost as close.

The headlights disappeared from the driveway, and she heard the distant skid of her own tires squealing. The porch, on the other hand, was three steps before her.

She was in and through the kitchen before the next person died.

She couldn't even see whom she hit. The living room was dark, and somebody rushed her, and the shovel came down, and that was that. She maneuvered to the right, eyes adjusting or trying, felt the hands grope for her throat before she saw the silhouette.

There wasn't room to bring the shovel around, so she snapped back with the wooden handle and cleared some-body's mouth of teeth. The attacker fell back, and she pushed forward, trying to get to the front door, trying to clear the way for her friends . . .

. . . who, she suddenly realized, were no longer screaming . . .

. . . and then somebody turned on the lights.

The crib was painted red. That was the first thing Renee noticed. The bodies on the floor were just like semaphores and arrows, pointing her gaze in that direction.

The crib was red, as if a gallon of paint had exploded inside it.

Splayed out at the foot of it, Fran and Stan were red as well. Red and white, as if their faces had been dusted with flour. Both their necks were bent at unusual angles.

Fran's eyes wouldn't stop blinking.

Renee started to scream.

Trixie stood frozen in the center of the room. The horror didn't just paralyze her; it sucked out all of her will to live.

There were still three freaks in her living room: one curled up on the floor with her skull slightly flattened; one slumped against the stairs with a frothy toothless maw; the last one still wavering over the crib, clutching the butcher knife that—just hours before—Rory had used to carve the turkey.

All of them were blinking in the sudden light, as if *they* couldn't believe what they'd just done either.

Then something began to slam at the front door.

It was Trixie's turn to get slapped in the face, galvanized back to life by the thundering sound. She was closer to the door than the freak with the knife. Dogs were howling behind it. She could feel their mad clamor through the floor, running up her spine.

As he started to attack, she turned and raced to the door, throwing the bolt and turning the knob, waiting for the blade to tear into her back . . .

. . . and the door flew open, propelled by not one, not two, not three, but six German shepherds, knocking her out of the way as they snarled and leaped on the sonofabitch with the knife.

"RENEE!" she roared, turning to her screaming friend as a herd of smaller dogs streamed berserk through the doorway. The toothless freak in the staircase tried to stand, but the dogs were on him at once.

The dogs smelled the wrongness in these people, just as she had smelled it back in the driveway. That's why they'd been barking. They knew something was horribly wrong, and it drove them crazy.

"COME ON!" Trixie bellowed, and Renee finally responded, staggering unmolested through the canine swarm.

Trixie reached for her keys, on the rack by the door frame, then remembered those fuckers had stolen her truck. But the last she recalled, the day care van was still running. They hadn't even bothered to shut off the engine.

"COME ON!" she repeated, yanking Renee out through the door; and then they were racing up the sidewalk toward the rumble and clatter in Rory's front drive.

Not only was the engine still running, but the doors were all wide-open. Trixie jumped in the back, still clutching the shovel, making sure no lurking assholes were stowed away for surprise attack.

Satisfied, she dragged the sliding door shut behind her, crawled into the driver's seat, while Renee grabbed the shotgun seat and slammed her door shut.

The second she shifted into reverse, she knew they were in trouble. The transmission was holding on by a thread. They may have been home-invading freaks, but they weren't lying about the truck.

She slipped into neutral, coasted backward down the drive onto Fernwood, hit the world's shittiest brakes, and then shifted into second and hauled ass down Hyperion.

"Omigod omigod omigod," Renee muttered, a mantra of shock she probably didn't even know she was uttering out loud.

"Baby?" said Trixie. "Renee? I need you to do something."

"Omigod . . ."

"Renee. I need you to take my phone . . ."

"What?"

Trixie shifted straight into fourth, with the gas pedal pinned, watching the speedometer jitter up toward fifty. "I need you to call Rory."

"What—" Renee's voice was thick and slurry. "What— didn't you want nine-one-one?"

"I'm going to the children's hospital on Sunset. It's just a couple more blocks away. We'll get help there. We'll send doctors and cops."

"Doctors and cops," Renee repeated, and started sobbing.

The van screeched off Hyperion, careened onto Sunset, running the red light. Nobody was there. No longer going uphill, the van edged up toward sixty, the engine's squeal a clattering echo of her panic.

"But we need to tell Rory what happened," Trixie continued. "I need to know that he's okay."

"Okay . . ."

Trixie took one hand off the wheel, skootched her ass up to pull the cell phone from her pocket. "It's number one on the speed dial. Can you do that?"

"Yes."

"Thank you." Handing over the phone, and leaning both hands back into the wheel.

She ran the red light by the Vista Theater, gritted her teeth heading into the next intersection. It was one of the worst in L.A.—the place where Hollywood, Sunset, Virgil, and Hillhurst all painfully converged—and she started leaning on the brakes despite herself, praying to God Almighty that nobody was coming from any of those multiple directions.

All she had to do was swing a hard left, go maybe three or four blocks, and the children's hospital was right there on the left. Not a diddly-crap clinic, but L.A.'s finest. The cream of the crop.

She heard the faint ring-through, thought her lover's name out loud, began to skid into the turn . . .

. . . and the last thing she saw was her own catering truck, blowing in off Hillhurst, ramming into the passenger side.

Then everything was spinning and flipping and pain turned to blackness triumphant, and consciousness lost.

THIRTEEN

"I think your friends are in trouble," Rory said. He thought Vanessa would jump out of the car and run for the apartment, or worse, order him to go in after them. But she just sat there, returning his stare, as if he were putting her on, and she didn't quite get it.

"No, they're fine." And just like that, the gunfire ended.

How many shots had there been? No more than a dozen, and then just like that, the night was empty and quiet again. A baby cried, and the TVs in every apartment got turned up louder.

"But they might need your help. Maybe it's already too late, and we should just—"

"I'm good right here. You need my help more than they do."

"Me? I don't need any help. I . . ." He left off when he belatedly caught what she meant. The sawed-off shotgun miraculously slid back into her purse, but the purse rested on her lap.

The moment she was out of sight, he would leave. Of course he would. Those weren't his friends in there, and this was none of his business. And he'd already been paid more than enough for what he'd done.

He wasn't a greedy man. Offering him any more wouldn't make him a fanatic. What was wrong with these fucking people?

Vanessa looked at his chest and smirked, like she could hear his heart beating.

In his breast pocket, his phone rang.

"Go ahead, answer it. I won't eavesdrop."

He looked at her as hard as he could, but didn't move.

Her phone rang. She patted him on the shoulder and got out of the Lincoln, strolling away across the parking lot in her heels. Broken glass sparkled around her feet as she took her call. Her back was turned, but the purse hung from her shoulder.

Relieved, Rory took out his phone and answered it.

"Baby, I'm fine—?"

But no one was there.

Suddenly, he saw a hooded figure carrying a limp body across the lawn. Passing under the epileptic light, they crossed the lot at a fast clip, Tommy holding a girl in both arms and struggling with a duffel bag strapped to his back. The other twin followed close behind, sweeping the lot with a machine pistol.

The kid just moved past him, mumbling, "She just fainted. Needs some water." The girl's blood left a shiny black trail across the lawn.

Vanessa joined them to take Tommy's bag and dump it in the trunk. Rory came around to help her, but she didn't need him either. The bag rolled in next to the other one. The zipper yawned partway open. Inside, he saw packs of twenties.

"Your friend needs a doctor. She got shot—"

"She's fine. She just needs some water."

Under the tenement's flickering light, two, then four hulking shapes gathered and checked their weapons. Time to go.

"Is that what you're doing this for? Is that even real?"

"Some of it probably is," she answered, totally unconcerned. "Get behind the wheel. We're halfway done."

Rory got the car started and whipped it around to roll for the exit.

"What the hell happened back there?"

Tommy took the wounded twin's nine-millimeter automatic, while she gulped water poured into her by her mute, maddeningly calm sister. Half of it seemed to spill out her mouth, the rest out of the bullet hole in her throat.

"Look sharp, dude," Tommy said. "It's not over."

Rory saw nothing moving in the lot but the four big guys watching them leave.

Two more guys loitered by the driveway. The carjacker in the Raiders parka turned and waved.

Rory floored it, racing for the street, when he saw the slammed Toyota racing up Seventy-eighth, on a kamikaze course with the Lincoln.

With its headlights off, the other car was close enough for Rory to see the driver was wearing sunglasses. His passengers were cocking guns.

"Goddamn it, you fucked us—"

The Toyota spun almost ninety degrees on its wafer-thin sport wheels to block the driveway. Rory steered left to aim for their rear axle, which would be a hell of a lot easier to plow out of their way than the engine block.

Two Crip soldiers in blue bandannas jumped out of the Toyota.

Before they could raise their weapons, the carjackers popped up assault rifles and executed them.

It was not like gunfights on the news, or even in movies. Nobody jumped behind cover; nobody fought like they planned to live through it. Neat sprays of lead to the head of each moving target, like in a video game, as if the guys on the curb had played this level to death already.

The two Crips sprawled in the street. The Raiders parka jumped up on the hood of the Toyota and burned off his clip into the windshield.

The Toyota stalled and jumped once. Dogs barked and lights went on all up and down the street. The carjackers gave Rory a big thumbs-up.

"Drive on," Tommy and Vanessa said, at the same time.

Steering around the Toyota, Rory barreled over the shrubbery and hopped off the curb with a jolt that made a gun go off in the backseat.

Rory jumped, but the slug must've gone into the roof.

Tommy chuckled and slugged water, passed one to Vanessa, and offered Rory one. He passed.

"Here next," Vanessa told him, and stuck a note on the steering wheel. He turned south on Crenshaw again.

Even over the radio, even over his heart and grating teeth, he heard sirens, and saw the cold, bright God's eye of a helicopter searchlight probing the area east of the cemetery.

"There's a Kaiser ER right down the street. Your friend—"

"She's going to be doing better than you if we don't make it to the next stop in under thirty minutes."

Two cop cars flew past them, lights and sirens going full jackpot. The Lincoln swerved to the right shoulder with the other cars. They were invisible.

"We didn't want to hurt anybody," Tommy continued, "but some people react to change with fear and violence, and we don't want to die either, dude. Not yet." He took the wounded girl's hand. She smiled weakly and glubbed more water.

"Who's *we*, white man?" Rory snapped.

"What?"

"What planet are you fucking people from? You've been watching too many fucking movies. You can't just wave guns and drugs around and not expect to get shot."

"It's working pretty well so far."

They passed Hollywood Park. A cop car lurked at the turnoff for the training tracks. Rory hopefully gunned it, hoping to arouse his interest, but the car was a rent-a-cop, and probably asleep, as Rory blasted by, headed for the 105 on-ramp.

He thought about the shootings they talked about at dinner. The kind of "drug deal gone bad" incidents that peppered the news until they were just so much background noise to California life, like the earthquakes, and the fires that burned someone else's house. "Those drug heists all over town the last week. You guys know anything about those?"

"Demand goes up if you interrupt supply," Tommy said, licking his cracked lips and staring straight ahead with his brow furrowed, like he were watching a foreign movie with subtitles.

"I think I get it. You guys just came back from the war, right? You saw a bunch of shit over there, and you come back, and nobody understands, and you're just supposed to settle down to some bullshit job. I understand all that. But this isn't Baghdad. You just can't get away with this kind of shit here . . ."

Vanessa and Tommy and the other twin all laughed. The other one joined in as best she could, with a gagging rasp that somehow didn't convince Rory she wasn't dead.

"What do you need me for?"

They stopped laughing. "Dude, your guess is as good as mine. You were sent for. It'd be a lot easier without you, actually." Rory glowered at the smirking kid, who shrugged. "Jus' sayin' . . ."

They passed Imperial Plaza and jumped onto the eastbound 105, hugging the fast lane. Traffic was sparse and sleepy, and in no time, they crossed over the 110 and sliced right to get off at Central.

"In response to your earlier query," Tommy said, "we couldn't come to an agreement with the old captain of the Inglewood Crips franchise, so we picked a new one. Cut off the head of a gang, and the body grows a new one. Makes a lot more sense than having a single body, are you feeling me? Jesus, I'm thirsty."

He kept the rest of his questions to himself. Their answers only made it worse, and only made it harder to figure how he'd get out of this.

He was pretty sure, though, that what they were peddling wasn't garden-variety coke.

He'd heard a rant from a paranoid friend, about a victory in the war on drugs, or at least they called it one. The street price of coke had gone up a good chunk due to military interdictions, and every layer of the smuggling and selling parties had cut their losses by stepping on their product.

The top cop in the EU bragged that the average cokehead in the street was lucky if he could find product that was even 10 percent pure, and rattled off a list of awful shit they were inhaling along with their Colombian courage.

It was nothing less than chemical warfare, but the news that people were snorting carcinogens and poisons only seemed to mean that victory was even closer. To hear his friend tell it, the influx of cut drugs was just the next phase in the war the CIA had been waging on the black community since the crack wars of the 1980s. His friend would probably love to go bowling with these people.

The Central on-ramp came too soon. It seemed like less than half the streetlights worked on the avenue as he skipped the red light and turned south, heading into Compton.

The absolute ass-end of Los Angeles, Compton rose to legendary status because of the Blood-Crips war, as glamorized by gangsta rap. The rappers made a bundle off the image of the civil war going on down here before they all moved far away, but instead of making a difference, they just made it look cool.

The few cars on Central were predators and prey. Two helicopters hung over the neighborhood. Kids sprayed a big blue 187 on a black-and-white parked outside a liquor store.

They turned east on Compton. Rory kept to himself. *Trixie is okay,* he told himself. *Her phone crapped out, or she went to bed . . . but she has to be all right.*

It was easier than trying to figure out how he would save himself.

FOURTEEN

What a difference a day makes, Tommy thought, over and over, whenever there was nothing else to think, which was often.

Only twenty-four hours ago, Tommy Rubini had no purpose, no dreams, not even the cocoon of illusions that let others believe they're the center of their own universe. He only wanted to get away from it.

But L.A. was not just a place; even from halfway across the country, you could feel it like a living entity, calling you. The city had treated him like shit for so long, he'd lost his faith, but L.A. had only broken him to build him into something new. You could not hope to make your dreams come true, and find your destiny. You had to listen to the city's dreams for you, surrender yourself and let them come true.

Of course, he was not without fear. But it just didn't matter anymore. Only made it sweeter, in fact. This night, this life, was something he could never have imagined yesterday, let alone inhabited, but here he was.

Tommy had died and been reborn more times than he could count since he left that shitty loft party this time last night, and now he knew that he would live a thousand times more before he died.

And if and when he did die, he knew exactly where he was going.

Certainty like that paid dividends. Fear was a language

he no longer understood. It was only a lot of funny faces, meaningless, annoying noises others made. The ones who refused to grow.

Rory's fear stopped amusing Tommy when he turned into the AM/PM parking lot and tried to get out of the car. "I gotta piss," he kept saying.

Vanessa offered him one of her empty bottles. "We're on a tight timetable," she explained. Tommy and Lucy put their guns behind Rory's ears and cocked them.

Funny how Vanessa's patience with Rory exhausted Tommy. They were all here to learn, and to teach, and to take what they learned with them back to the source, but Rory's resistance was beginning to enter the realm of those things that defied logic, and could only be removed.

"Okay, goddamn it, I'll go later."

A few blocks down Compton, Vanessa caught him pocket-texting on his phone and took it away. BBAY CAL COPR. SEMDTO 13FU8 CAQROCB . . .

"You don't use this thing a whole lot, do you?"

Wendy was fading fast. Her breathing was too shallow to inhale any more powder, but the holes in her neck and belly had sealed up. She squeezed his hand as she smiled up at him. "It's gonna be so beautiful, isn't it, Tommy?"

"Sure, Wendy. You'll see it. We all will."

"Make sure I—please make sure that I get . . . if I die . . ."

"We will, Wendy. Don't worry. You still got too much work to put in to check out now."

Her grip on his hand tightened a little. One of her eyes bulged out of its socket, but she winked the other one and said, "I'll hold on a little longer."

Inspiring.

In stark contrast to their driver, who couldn't go a mile without bitching. "Just let me call my wife. I'll drive the fucking car. I'll help you. Just let me call her once. I need to know she's all right . . ."

"You just need to relax," Vanessa said. She turned the

knob on the radio to the sound they loved, and turned it up. Better than any man-made music, it contained multitudes of tunes in its almighty roar. He heard them all at the same time, like all the foreign thoughts, all the little bits of lives, flying through his terminally dazzled brain.

Tommy guzzled water, wondered where it all went. He wasn't sweating, and he still didn't need to piss. He hadn't slept or eaten since long before last night, and he'd thrown up before he went onstage. Funny thing, he used to be so afraid of something he felt driven to do. He knew, now, why he always used to get so sick. He'd been trying to live someone else's life.

This was *his* life now. God, but he loved it.

The last holdout in the strip mall on Carob had boarded up its windows only weeks ago, but the 8 Bowl Gaming Center went under over a year before. The big sign in the parking lot—showing an eight ball knocking down a frame of bowling pins—loomed over the black bones of a Pioneer Chicken burned for insurance.

No cars were parked out front, but the polarized glass facade of the 8 Bowl had been knocked out, and chrome glinted in the cavernous darkness within. He counted at least four cars.

Rory brought the Lincoln to a lurching stop around the side of the bowling alley. Screened from the street by a massive Dumpster and some concrete planter boxes, they all did another bump to put the moment in perspective.

Rory sat ramrod-stiff in the driver's seat, looking ahead. Tommy reached out and touched his shoulder, felt dancing muscles under the ill-fitting blazer.

"Listen," he offered. "I used to be just like you—"

"I doubt it."

"No, please, Rory, hear me out. I used to think I could change the world, if I could just make everybody listen to me. If they could just see themselves as I see them, I thought, everyone would stop fucking everything up, and the world would live as one."

"That wasn't my problem."

"Don't you see? You'd better try, Rory, because right now, my problems *are* your problems. It's about ego, man. It's about letting all that go, and getting right with the rest of the world. It's about this."

And he blew a white cloud in Rory's face.

Problem solved.

Rory wheezed and spat and wiped his eyes. "Mother-fucker—" he cursed, before it hit him. Tommy could almost hear his racing heartbeat.

"Keep the engine running," Tommy said as he climbed out and helped Wendy follow. "These dipshits are going to try to ambush us."

If Rory heard, he gave no indication. But that didn't matter. He'd know what to do.

Now that he was on their side.

The trunk popped, and Tommy got a suitcase. Lucy circled around back, while Wendy leaned on him all the way to the hole in the wall. The kid on the corner drew a ruby laser dot on them, but let them pass.

Inside the 8 Bowl, two huge thugs behind the shoe rental counter told them to check their weapons and meet their party on lane one.

Tommy let them pat him down, but Wendy balked. She threw up when they bent her over, which made them laugh, until she got some on them.

They got led back down the alley to lane one, picking over debris in the harsh glow of the headlights of parked cars.

The rest of the lanes had been gutted, the polished hardwood floor and all the ball-retrieval tracks underneath ripped out to make a series of huge, open pits and trenches for dog fighting and cruder, crueler entertainment.

Tonight was not a fight night, apparently, but the place was packed.

Tommy carried Wendy down the stairs to the scoring table, where a bald black mountain sat beside two kids whose eyes were swelled shut. Tommy smiled to see someone he recognized, at least by reputation. These two were the ones he'd come to do business with.

"You look lost," said the bald black mountain.

"I'm right where I should be," Tommy countered, "but you do have me at a disadvantage. Stymie, right?" Tommy knew damned well who this guy must be if he found out about their deal and crushed it this quick. "Are you friends or business partners with Yung Huck and Cheeseburger?"

This cracked up the peanut gallery.

Stymie the bald mountain rose from the scorekeeper's bench and strolled around behind Yung Huck and Cheeseburger like a master trial attorney advocating for his defendants. "We're the law around here. When outsiders come in and try to poison our neighbors, friends, and loved ones, we take an interest. You arranged a transaction with these two individuals. Why?"

Tommy eased Wendy into a seat and very gently set down the suitcase. "We have mutual acquaintances in county lockup."

"I doubt it," Stymie said. "Yung Huck here is still a juvenile. He's a comer, front-office material for damn sure, if he lives long enough. Huck's got his finger on the pulse. He watches the news, don't you, Huck? He still goes to school, can you beat that? He knows every damned thing about Africa. That's how he got the idea, I guess, to build himself a child army."

Yung Huck didn't look like much of a general right now. Just a skinny kid too young to drive a car, beat within an inch of his life. He struggled to keep his head up.

"Now, we like Yung Huck, and we got no beef with the Cheeseburger, heh. Most the shit they sell goes to those white kids in Palos Verdes. Call themselves wiggers, can you believe that? But Yung Huck is not the law around here, y'know what I'm saying?"

Tommy figured he'd played helpless long enough. "Okay, I admit it. We reached out to Yung Huck because we didn't get anywhere with you."

"There's a good reason for that, I don't think I have to tell you." Stymie picked up a bowling ball. Deep red like petrified blood, deeply scarred and cracked, the old house ball was a twenty-pounder, but the holes were too small by half for the mountain's fingers.

"We've all come a long way from the Wild West days, when brothers were cappin' brothers everyday like a goddamn snuff minstrel show on the TV news. We got a machine now. We got chains of command. We got loyalty. Cheeseburger, put your hand on the table."

A fat kid with a nose like roadkill, Cheeseburger obeyed without hesitation.

"When the FBI infiltrated the Black Panthers and started the feuds that became the Blood-Crip War, we were happy to play along. When the CIA flooded the ghetto with crack cocaine to fund the contras and reelect Reagan, we eagerly participated in our own genocide. But nobody's gonna buy us, nobody's gonna poison us anymore. We serious about this."

The mountain brought the bowling ball down on Cheeseburger's hand.

The fat kid yowled like a cat.

Crushing the bones into crumbs and breaking the Formica table in half, the ball crashed to the floor and rolled over to Tommy's feet.

"You're angry about something else, I guess," Tommy said. "You want somebody to blame for your problems."

Guns clicked and pointed. Red laser dots roved over Tommy's face like alien acne. Yung Huck sat stock-still, his empty face etched with the numb serenity of the condemned.

Cheeseburger held his ruined hand to his galloping boobs and silently sobbed. Only Tommy seemed to notice that he was laughing.

Stymie came over to stand nose to nose with Tommy. "Yeah, truth be told, we get a little pissed when some mother-fucker nobody knows tries to sell a load of shit the very next day after somebody else nobody knows jacked half the shit coming into L.A. It's some suspicious shit, right there."

"It's not poison. We're not trying to harm anyone, or take advantage of you. This is not the same stuff that was stolen. It's like nothing else you've ever tried . . ."

"Nobody on my crew uses that shit," Stymie growled.

Someone circled behind him, but Tommy pretended not to notice. "We didn't mean to upset protocol. Tell you what . . . keep the product. With our compliments."

"That's mighty big of you. But you think that's the end of it."

"If you're still upset, I'm open to how I can make it right."

Wendy hunched over her ruined belly, let out a fitful stream of foamy white puke onto the hardwood floor.

"Your girl is hurt real bad," Stymie said. "You smiling like you understand, but you don't know. This is business. Life or death."

The guy behind Tommy stepped up and wrapped a braided telephone cord around Tommy's neck, squeezing. He was too short to lift Tommy off his feet, so he kicked Tommy's knees out from under him.

Tommy dropped into the noose and his eyes bugged out. Everything went solarized, sizzling black spots obscuring the view of Stymie watching him die.

He couldn't see Wendy rolling off the chair with her hand pressed to her gut-shot belly, digging out and point-ing the .22 she'd stuffed into the wound.

Stymie stepped back, hands up, yelling, *Shoot the bitch!* too late.

And from the ball-return slot on lane one, a white hand with a machine pistol commenced to spray the room.

Stymie hit the deck and started scurrying on hands and knees. Tommy's strangler wasn't so quick; a garland of blood roses bloomed across his chest. Tommy's weight dragged him forward as Tommy dropped to the floorboards, gasping. The jumping, humping, bullet-riddled body fell as well, pinning him to the floor.

Stymie's crew opened up on Wendy. The wounded twin staggered back into the seats. Bullets slammed into her soft white flesh, blowing off the already half-dead outer shell to reveal the softer, whiter insides.

Tommy yanked the pistol from the waistband of the corpse on top of him, began to struggle free. But before he could squeeze a shot off, bullets pelted the dead strangler's body, made it dance some more. Tommy shrieked and started firing, took one fucker out at the knees.

Wendy kept firing till her gun was empty, impossibly still alive. Bullets slapped into her like insults on a playground, but she was all rubber, they were glue.

Blind, wild sprays of automatic fire from the ball return cut the strings on two more of Stymie's puppets, sent six or eight others scattering to their cars.

Someone fired a shotgun at the ball return, peeling back the hard plastic and fiberglass. Lucy emerged in all her furious gunslinging glory to drive the shotgun back behind cover.

She tossed the empty machine pistol and leveled a pump shotgun on a sling she must've taken from Stymie's backup guys.

Before she got to use it, a lucky shot punched out her left eye and flipped her into the dog pit.

In the midst of it all, Yung Huck and Cheeseburger sat like wax dummies at the scorekeeper's table. The fat kid was giggling, but his partner finally stood and plucked a gun off the deck, grabbed Cheeseburger by the neck, and levered him up.

Advancing on the parked cars, he took out the surviving gunmen one by one. The idiots tried to shoot him through Cheeseburger's XXXL torso, but the fat kid kept walking toward them, even after everything above his bulging eyes was a smoking memory.

Cheeseburger finally ground to a halt by the shoe rental counter, but Yung Huck was the only man left standing in the alley when the shooting finally stopped.

"Damn," Cheeseburger said, and collapsed.

Tommy got up and went after Wendy, who was dead, and Lucy, who was dying. The product was gone. So was Stymie.

One of the parked cars leaped forward and smashed Yung Huck into the shoe counter. His arms flew out and he let out a scream, just air escaping from his crumpled rib cage as the SUV plowed through the counter and hit the load-bearing columns behind it.

Backing out with Yung Huck's body on the hood, the SUV grazed another car, jumped the window frame and the curb, then whipped around and peeled off into the siren-crazed night.

The product was gone. There was never any money, but it was never about money.

Another successful transaction.

More satisfied customers.

Tommy only discovered that he'd been shot when he took out his phone: one in the back and another in his left side. His voice was a husky, bubbly mess when he told Vanessa, "Come help me with the twins. Bring the hacksaws."

Working together, they harvested Wendy, Lucy, and Yung Huck, but alas, there was not enough of Cheeseburger, so they left him behind.

They came back out five minutes later, and still no cops.

A police helicopter had swept the lot, but then darted off elsewhere. Left alone in the car, Rory had not moved a muscle. He popped the trunk for them to throw in the bowling bags; then they got in.

Tommy passed a new Post-It note to Rory. "Last stop," he said, "then home."

Rory didn't look at it, but he was smiling as he sped out of the lot and onto Wilmington, headed south.

"I know where to go," he said.

FIFTEEN

There was a long, dark tunnel, infinitely long, cold, and dark.

But Trixie saw a light at the end, and sensed someone waiting on the other side, watching her from within, and guiding her out of the darkness. She struggled up toward the light, and the face of the angel who smiled to see her arrive.

"Do you know where you are?" the angel asked.

Good question, fella. She couldn't see, couldn't move.

"What's the last thing you remember?"

Getting broadsided by her own truck; driving, crying, trying to get hold of Rory, because she ran away from their house when people came in and killed their friends.

She blinked and squinted at the blinding white light. She wasn't dead. "My name is Trixie Wright, and I was attacked . . ."

"No, ma'am, you were just in a traffic accident. You're in the ambulance now." The voice that stirred her ear was soothing. The breath, not so much, with that sour dung smell guys get when they don't drink enough water. "We're going to the hospital."

"That's great, but . . . I can't move . . ." *Oh God,* she thought, *I can't move* . . . Everything ached, but nothing moved when she tried to sit up. *But calm down, girl. A minute ago, you thought you were dead,* and the cold white light inside the ambulance poured in now, showing her the hovering shadow of a chunky Latino man, whose name, embroidered on his powder blue uniform, was Angel.

"You're in a restraint until we can be sure you didn't damage your spinal cord. Can you feel my hand?"

She could feel it indeed, touching her hand, giving it a little squeeze. Her arms were strapped down at her sides, and a big plastic collar stretched her neck. She tried not to squirm, but it was impossible not to. "I think I'm all right, really. Can't I get up—"

"You'd better not try . . ."

"Listen, I need to speak to the police. My home was invaded, people are dead—"

Angel pulled a rueful face, moved out of view. "We'll be at the hospital in two minutes, Trixie. There'll be a policeman waiting to take a statement about the accident from you there . . ."

"Which hospital? And where's Renee?" The last she remembered, they was three blocks from Children's Hospital of Los Angeles.

"I'm sorry?"

"My friend! She was with me when we crashed—"

"No. You were alone in the truck."

"That's not true!"

"Trixie, you're getting hysterical."

Trixie tried *not* to get hysterical, but she couldn't see Angel when he wasn't looking down into the contraption that held her paralyzed. "No, please, you don't understand! I had to leave my house because people came in and killed my friends, and my husband—"

"*Shhhh*," he said.

Then he pricked her with a needle.

And the last words she heard were "It's all good."

As the blackness returned.

SIXTEEN

There were times, in every life, so hurtful and confusing that drowning oneself in action was the only refuge. And if any other action were possible for Rory, he would have taken it without hesitation.

But beyond driving the car, he could not seem to move or talk.

Ever since Tommy blew that shit in his face.

He'd had only an instant to close his eyes, and that was not enough. His sight whited out and he cursed, spitting foam.

Then stopped himself, crazily, with the image of Bill Clinton. *I never inhaled.* That was the famous bullshit phrase.

Suddenly they were words to live by.

It wasn't easy. Behind the sting like onions in his tear ducts, the biting mildew stench fueled a swift and violent allergic revolt. Snot bubbled out of his sinuses, which swelled shut with painful urgency.

Tommy and the twins left, but he was still dimly aware of Vanessa beside him, watching with naked interest as he struggled not to breathe.

Drowning in the driver's seat.

Until he could take it no more.

Wiping his numb lips and pinching his nose shut, he flopped his mouth open and sucked in air. It burned going down, pinpricks of dry ice in his throat and lungs.

Oh, fuck, he thought, in both rage and terror.

He started coughing. Explosive gouts of snot flew from his nose. Tears burst from his flaming, sightless eyes.

"Let it happen," said Vanessa.

And just like that, it did.

The first thing that struck him was *this is not coke*. It struck him in the same moment that euphoria overtook him: not completely, but enough to let him know that something very special was inviting him to happen.

God*damn* it felt good. Like a great weight lifting. Like a full-body massage in one-tenth of a second.

Just like that—from that tiny amount—he was stunningly, almost unbelievably high.

"Whoa," he muttered.

"Uh-huh. Mmmmm. Yeah." Vanessa let out a low, throaty chuckle. "I told you it was nice."

"Holy shit—"

"It's all good, baby. Believe it."

"Whoa—"

"You're feelin' me now, aren't you?" she said, and leaned back in her seat like a *Penthouse* fantasy dream.

His raging mind took flight, lifted up on the rush of endorphins right out of the corner they'd backed him into. He was nobody's slave, nobody's servant. He was his own man, the author of his own destiny. He could do whatever he wanted.

And what he wanted to do most of all, tonight, was drive this fucking car.

It was really remarkable, wasn't it, how a tiny trace amount of a substance could turn your whole perspective around.

Rory reeled as the waves of exhilaration pinballed around inside his head, lighting up all the dead pleasure centers that only the most incredible peak situations could even brush against.

But mostly and most unbelievably, it turned the crushing paralysis of negativity into a dynamo of positive energy.

To his bleary sight in the rearview, it almost seemed like light poured out of his runny eyes. He wiped his face and grinned a fitful rictus at Vanessa.

"You want some more?" she asked.

"More," he managed.

Best idea he'd heard in all his life.

He wanted more, and he wanted to share it around. His new friends and their mission suddenly made perfect sense. It was natural, when something felt this good, not to try to hoard it, but to take it far and wide, to friend and enemy alike.

"Don't hide it, provide it . . ." He chuckled and rubbed his hands together as his bowels clenched all the blood out of themselves, sent it rushing to his heart and his brain. He could and would drive all night and when he went home with a fat roll of cash and a bag of magical powder, even Trixie would have to come around and everything would be—

No. That almost shut the buzz down, because he couldn't see Trixie being okay with anything like this. She never touched the stuff, and had helped him put it behind him for good.

If he brought something like this into their home, she wouldn't be okay with it at all. In fact, his hyperexcited mind could picture her looking very steadily at him and asking, just once, *Is this how you really want it?*

And then she'd leave him.

The thought of it left him breathless for a very long while, and he just sat there, unaware he was babbling every thought out loud in a stage-whisper.

Trixie would never come around, but maybe he could keep it from her . . . but sooner or later she'd find out, and if she just tried it once, she'd feel what he felt, and it would all work out, and if she had to be forced, that one time, then what of it?

The pleasant rush had petered out minutes ago, leaving

him with the prickling anxiety of leaving something wonderful behind, something greater than mere pleasure. He knew these selfish thoughts had no place in his mind, right now, when he was on a mission, and on the verge of discovering something so great, so much larger than himself—

Drug people talked all the time about shamanic and religious rituals for reaching altered states of consciousness, but mostly, they were just rationalizing their own bad habits as some kind of spiritual journey. Rory was always quick to call bullshit on such talk, but he couldn't deny that there was something there, in rare flickers and glimpses, where one did not feel alone in one's head and heart.

A connection to something larger could be felt when he raced flat-out and risked his life for nothing but the rush, as if his ancestors looked over his shoulder and lifted him up, saying, GO. In those rare drunken late-night conversations with the right bunch, bits of wisdom older and deeper than the sum of the group could come out of your mouth, when the brain was too pickled to fret over its selfish pet peeves. Stoned and jamming or drawing, his artist and musician friends always said they weren't making stuff, so much as finding it, and the bemused awe they showed as they looked at their own work from the outside was much more than just being too stoned to remember doing the work.

Sort of a silent article of faith it was, then, with Rory, that somewhere that might as well be heaven or hell or both, there was a collective mind, a dream of God that knew everything that the human race had ever known or wished or lied, and sent its dreams to those happy and damned few who could speak for it.

To hear it even for a moment demanded that you shut out the world and your own petty desires and open up your head with drugs or drink or some other ritual to exorcise the self, but to those who chased it, a split second of clear vision was worth a lifetime of sacrifice.

And Rory had almost seen it.

He could see it again.

If he wished, he could go to it like a moth to a candle and bask in its glow, know all that it knew, and take its message to the world.

All he had to do, was a little *more*—

Vanessa held out the silver tray and the rolled-up C-note. A while ago, somebody tested a bunch of retired twenties and said that three-quarters of the currency in L.A. had traces of coke on it.

"Do you understand now?" she asked.

He nodded. The anxiety had become a nagging on par with a public-radio pledge-drive announcer, promising the secrets of the universe and a meet and greet with the collective unconscious and the PBS tote bag, if he just snorted a little *more*—

From inside the bowling alley, the shooting started. Big and little guns, machine pistols like a prolonged sneeze, then the deep boom of shotguns. The bowling alley backed on some huge industrial complex with towers and conveyor belts and floodlights every fifty feet, but beyond the parking lot, not a creature was stirring.

Looking around the lot, he silently begged for a police chopper, a wailing pack of squad cars, a SWAT team with the tank and the bomb squad robots, but all he could see was a couple kids on skateboards, who rolled blithely by the Lincoln, peeping with open curiosity. They sped up and hugged a tree when an Escalade backed out through the broken window and spun around on the sidewalk, then peeled out for parts unknown.

The nagging in his brain became a howling televangelist with a sermon on the holy love of drugs, and the hellfire of self-denial, the heavenly glory of MORE.

But he did not move to take the bill.

He did not want it. Trixie would not want it. The part of him that wanted it might be smarter and smoother than the rest of Rory, but that part of him had wrecked his car in a street race and landed him in jail twice. This was just a drug talking, and something much more potent and dangerous than cocaine.

He'd barely ingested a few grains of the shit, through his throat and eyes. His sinuses still rebelled at the shit, but he wanted it, even now, even if it cost him more than he'd already lost. "Maybe later . . ." he mumbled.

Her phone rang.

"What was that?" she answered it. And a bit later, she said, "Okay," and hung up.

"Stay here. Call if you see cops." She got out and went to the trunk, then slammed it and jogged over to the gaping hole in the bowling alley.

Her phone lay on the seat, beside the silver tray.

She'd spelled out his name in cursive script, with the white powder.

Rory.

It called him.

Oh God, how it called him.

It could show him things he'd never dreamed of, connect him with something so vast, so fundamental, that he would never be the same again.

The howling in his head became a dental-drill chorus. His sinuses throbbed, but yawned wide-open, hungry for it, now. Ready for it.

He reached over and touched the phone. He couldn't even think of whom he wanted to call.

He reached for the silver tray and picked it up.

He couldn't think straight until this was over and done with, and there was only one thing to do.

He dumped the shit out the window and blew the silver tray clean, then put it back on the seat.

There. The second the die was cast, he felt the raking, agonizing need subside to a dull throb, no worse than the pin in his elbow when it rained.

Trixie.

He had to call Trixie.

He picked up her phone and punched her number. He got her message on the first ring, again. He hung up and the phone rang. He answered before he looked at the incoming number. "Hey, baby, where—"

"How are you feeling, Rory?" Vanessa asked.

"Better. Amazing."

"Great. Bring the car to the door."

He put the car in drive. He turned and looked out at the street. A few cars rolled by on Carob, but no sign of flashing lights, no wailing sirens. Nobody knew, nobody cared, what happened here.

He could get away—

Vanessa tapped on the glass. "What kept you?"

He popped the trunk. How long was he sitting here, spacing out?

Tommy came out with a brace of bowling bags and an assault rifle. He slung the bags in the trunk and climbed into the backseat, handed Rory the last address.

"I know the way," he'd said, trying to fit in, but he felt uneasy, because he did know where they were going, and the street names played through his mind uninvited as he drove, four blocks before he crossed them.

"You forget the twins?" Rory asked, trying to sound casual. Sounding wired was easy.

Tommy looked like he'd just served two terms as president. His eyes were sunken in, his skin pasty and sheened with something oilier than sweat, and reeking of mold. His hoodie was sloshy with blood from at least two bullet wounds in his torso, but he didn't seem to care. As they pulled away, Vanessa served him up a fat pile of the white shit.

"Our boy's got a healthy appetite," Vanessa said.

Tommy polished off a couple grams of powder and two bottles of water. Vanessa turned the radio to another dead space between AM frequencies and cranked it up until it sounded like they were driving inside a thunderstorm.

Heading east on the 91, he got them to the northbound 5 and followed the bouncing ball in his head to the city of Commerce.

People lived in Commerce, but damned if Rory could figure out why. Next to City of Industry, Commerce had the highest carcinogenic pollution levels in the state, and fine black particles clung to every surface in the daylight.

Outlet malls crowded the frontage roads, but behind Waterbed World and the Halloween Superstore, the big, anonymous buildings where Freon refrigeration coils or diamond-tipped cutting tools were manufactured by day became a ghost town at night, yet every few blocks, a few sorry clusters of condos and apartments turned up.

They crossed a tangle of train tracks and turned down a side street that dead-ended at a rail siding, with a couple dozen abandoned freight cars blocking the view of the freeway, and a row of enormous palm trees to keep up the pretense that this was still California.

Rory parked on the street behind a dust-caked Taurus and killed the engine. Tommy couldn't get out of the car, so Vanessa did the honors.

The kid sat back and smirked at Rory, stroking his new G3 assault rifle. "So, you wanna do another blast?"

"Thanks, I'm good."

Tommy's smile broadened. "Are you?"

He shivered at the thought of taking that shit into his body again. It seemed to work almost like PCP, keeping them going past the point of exhaustion and shock. And yet, he still wanted it. Without it, he was running uphill just to stay awake and alert in the moment.

He tried to smile at Tommy the way they smiled at one another, but the kid wasn't buying it. He turned and looked out the window.

The huge palm trees shivered as if in a high wind, but none was blowing tonight. His headlights startled the steady stream of rats darting up and down the nearest trunk, from the huge, unkempt leafy nest fifty feet up, to the roof of the crappy old Taurus.

The Taurus's taillights were barely glowing, like the battery was almost dead. A garden hose dangled out of the exhaust pipe and wrapped around the passenger's side to feed into the cracked-open window.

The engine wasn't running. Probably ran out of gas a while ago, maybe a week or more, and the rats had the run of it.

This was the last stop. After this, these ruthless assholes were done for tonight. They might just tell him where they lived, and tip him handsomely as they got out to go upstairs and shower off the night's depravity and murder. Or they might just cut him down and leave him behind, like they had their other friends.

Rory turned and checked the road ahead and behind. A street sweeper rolled down the cross street in the rearview, but he wasn't due to discover the dead guy in the Taurus until the first Thursday of next month, according to the parking sign.

"You're not with us," Tommy said. "I can tell." He leaned forward confidentially, as if they were being eavesdropped on. "I know how you feel. Richie knew you would try to sabotage this."

At the sound of the name, Rory tensed up. His voice strained to get out of his control. "What do you know about Richie?"

"Your brother always looked out for you like he thought your dad would have. Tried to keep you out of trouble, keep you from settling for a normal jack-off life. He was angry that he didn't have more, and he was afraid that somebody was going to take away what he had. But he got over all that, the same way I got over my selfish bullshit. He wants to help you get over yours."

Rory's hand snapped the plastic turn signal indicator lever clean off the steering column.

"I hope someday you can join us," Tommy sang in a cracking, achingly sincere voice. "And the world—"

Rory turned and buried the turn signal up to the hilt in Tommy's right eye. "Am I the only person in the world who can't stand the fucking Beatles?"

Rory started the car and gunned the engine.

" 'Imagine' was a John Lennon song, dummy."

Rory looked up at Vanessa, who leaned in the smashed-out passenger window and pointed her chunky purse at him.

Throwing the car into drive, he hunkered against the wheel and stomped the gas. Almost instantly, the Lincoln slammed into the back of the Taurus.

The airbags burst out of the wheel and dash, hiding him for a split second. Vanessa's shotgun went off, shredding the balloons and shattering the driver's-side window.

He shifted into park and started the car again. Vanessa had cracked the windshield with her head, but she looked a lot more clearheaded than he felt.

"Why are you trying to fuck up everything?" She sounded genuinely hurt.

Into reverse as she raised the shotgun, but the car dragged her and threw off her aim. Rory floored it and sat up to take the wheel. The Lincoln jumped the curb going backward and swerved toward the rows of rat-infested palm trees.

Vanessa unloaded the other barrel at his head. The headrest exploded behind him.

He chopped at Vanessa's extended arm. She dropped the empty shotgun and reached out to rake his face with her nails.

Screaming, "Traitor!" she gouged at his eye and left four

parallel welts down his cheek before she was suddenly and brutally ripped from the car.

The first palm tree slapped her legs back into the wheel well, and her feet must have got caught under the wheel. She threw out both arms and slipped out of sight, and the superb independent suspension rolled over her like any other speed bump.

Rory steered off the curb and into the street, whipped the huge luxury sedan around so it stood on the center line, then shifted into drive, and hit the gas.

He felt both better and worse when he looked in the rearview and saw Vanessa up and crawling in the street, dragging her mangled leg toward the dead guy's Taurus.

Never say die, lady, he thought with a hysterical burst of laughter.

His ears were ringing too badly to hear what was on the radio. He found Vanessa's phone on her seat and hit History, redialed Trixie's number. Got her message line again.

"Damn it, baby, where the fuck are you? Something bad's happening, and they've got Richie . . . he's part of it . . . Baby, we got to get the fuck out of town . . ."

The phone rang in his hand again. He didn't recognize the number or the area code. He answered it.

"Are you finished?" The voice on the other end was flat and businesslike, but Rory recognized it at once.

"Happy Thanksgiving, Richie," he said.

SEVENTEEN

In her short, lucky life, Trixie had spent very little time at the hospital. Her parents nursed an almost dogmatic aversion to going to the doctor that Trixie later figured was equal parts healthy frugality and immigrant superstition, with a healthy pinch of plain old fear of racism. When Trixie thought of her mother warning her of summer pneumonia and treating every scratch like a triple-bypass, she used to laugh with her friends, but she'd never had to spend the night in a hospital as a patient or a visitor, and she had never once had to ride in an ambulance.

Even if nothing else was wrong tonight, Trixie probably would have been scared out of her wits, and so Angel was probably right to sedate her.

When she woke up again, she was still strapped to a gurney, but she was parked in a corridor. Her mouth tasted like cotton balls and she was missing two teeth on the right side of her mouth, but she didn't feel all that bad, otherwise. She could see just a few squares of stained acoustic ceiling tile with a speaker mounted in it. The fluorescent light overhead was shut off, and the nearest lit one blinked like it was only half screwed in. An IV bag on a metal stand dripped cloudy fluid into a rubber tube that she supposed must be going into her arm, which explained why her arm hurt.

She could hear voices agitated and upset and a TV blasting entertainment news in the nearby waiting room, and mushy Muzak from the speaker. Perhaps it was relaxing to have screaming loved ones drowned out by "Do You Know the Way to San Jose" and a breathless special bulletin about Kim Kardashian's feud with the media about how they described her butt, yet it just pushed her further out of reality.

This couldn't be happening to her. Any minute, she'd wake up in the beat-up recliner in the living room to the sound of her friends' snoring, and Rory, bleary and exhausted and home safe, bundling her off to bed.

In bad dreams, sometimes, she had to wait forever in long lines or traffic—you couldn't live in L.A. and not have those dreams—but even her most fevered nightmares didn't have Muzak. When "San Jose" segued into "Winchester Cathedral," she started shouting.

"Hey, how long am I gonna have to wait to talk to somebody!" People came and went down the corridor, but no one took any notice of her. Some sort of crisis at the far end of the wing had alarms going every few minutes, but she could hear a bustling traffic in injured and ill bodies moving all around her.

She'd heard plenty of horror stories about the ERs in L.A., but always took them with a grain of salt. People saw such things through the filter of their politics, but she'd known staunch advocates for the homeless and illegal immigrants who underwent instant conversions to conservatism after waiting to see a doctor.

"Hi, how are we doing tonight?"

Thank God, she thought, and strained to turn her head.

"Don't try to move." A man's voice, older, polished, in love with the sound of itself. "Your chart says you were knocked out cold. Can't be too careful."

"I'm sorry, I can't see you . . . oh, there you are. Are you a cop or a doctor?"

The man smiling down at her, she somehow instantly knew, was neither. Maybe it was his glasses, which looked

like they cost more than her car. Or the artful way someone had seeded his bottle-tanned skull with silver hair
grafts from his back, or his teeth, which looked like sugar
cubes. Yet underneath all the expensive TLC, he was a
pretty ugly older guy whose ear hair grew like kudzu. If this
guy was a doctor, he was a Beverly Hills plastic surgeon
with a third-tier reality show. But if she had to guess, she'd
say he was a tax lawyer.

"Lady knows what she needs. I wish I could help." Again
with the ostentatiously fake smile. All that money for
teeth, you'd think he could've put in some lips. "But I'm
just here with my wife. She's the looker in trauma three."

She didn't trust herself to reply right away. Being hog-
tied in an ER could work wonders for your patience with
assholes. "You must be very worried about her, Mr. . . . ?"

"Wenzel, Leonard Wenzel, Esquire. You're banged up
pretty good."

"Right . . . I'd shake your hand, but . . . is there any
chance I could talk you into getting a nurse for me? I don't
know how long I've been parked out here, but it's really
kind of important that I talk to somebody."

Leonard Wenzel took off his expensive glasses and
cleaned them off on a no-doubt expensive silk tie that
Trixie couldn't see. "I'll try for you, Trixie, but I tell you . . .
everybody's pretty busy tonight. It's my wife who's causing
all the commotion over there . . . Bitch never knows when
to quit. They're pretty shorthanded tonight, actually, but
they're literally packed three deep out there." He winked.
"Literally."

"What hospital is this?"

His phony smile finally faltered. "Wow, you really are
out of it. I tell you what, I'll go find the nurse for you. Stay
right there, ha ha."

"Hey, Leonard Wenzel!"

"What, Trixie?"

"You didn't answer my question."

"Um, you're at the old Rampart Citadel, sweetheart. Don't worry, they'll take good care of you."

He turned to go, but just before he left, he did something to her IV bag. Trixie couldn't quite see, but she thought he squeezed it really hard, just once, before he left.

Her arm felt cold and heavy. She started to say something snarky as he left, but her tongue felt sluggish, her mind dull, and neither would cooperate.

Trixie twisted in her bonds. Her arms were strapped securely to the steel frame, but her legs were just tied down. Her collar was connected to the wooden cradle under her spine.

Trixie was still wearing her old jeans and one of Rory's T-shirts. Her Vans slip-on shoes were gone, and she found she could twist her leg out of its bonds and lift it up to touch the Velcro restraints on her right wrist. *So much for spinal trauma*, she thought.

She managed to get her toes around the wrist strap when a cold, rubber-gloved hand pried her foot away. "Quite the acrobat, aren't we?" A starched white cap and an arched eyebrow loomed into Trixie's limited theater of vision, and her gurney began to roll.

Finally, thank God. "Are you the nurse? I've been trying to get somebody to listen to me—"

"That's wonderful, dear, you can speak. We'll get to the rest of you in a few minutes. Put her in four, Jinder. That's great."

They rolled her across the trauma center and parked her under some differently stained tiles, and drew a curtain around her gurney. In the next stall, the unfortunate Mrs. Wenzel, and on her right, someone quietly sobbing.

Somebody whopped the curtains back, then sealed them up again and scooted up on a stool. "Hi, don't mind me, I'm just here to take some blood."

"Nurse, can you please help me? I'm sure the police are looking for me . . ."

"Now, you're going to feel a little poke, like a bee sting." Why did nurses always say that? If there was anything less comforting to people than a needle, it was a needle with an angry bug on the end of it.

She felt kind of queasy and weak, were they really supposed to draw all that blood? "Please, I need to talk to a cop . . ."

"We'll be with you in a jiff, okay, darlin'? Kind of crazy tonight." The blood-taker scooted away on her stool. Over the erratic beeping and rustling in the next stall, Trixie heard the blood-taker talking to another nurse. "Not responding to treatment," they said, over and over.

What the hell? All things considered, she felt fine. If they were so overloaded tonight, why couldn't they just check her out and let her go?

In the next stall, a doctor was talking to the lady who never knew when to quit. "You're in the Rampart Citadel hospital, and you've had an overdose. Your heart stopped for several minutes. Do you understand what I'm saying?"

No answer, but the beeping got louder. The doctor called for help to "stabilize the patient." His voice sounded oddly familiar, and suddenly, Trixie realized what it was about this place that had made her so uneasy from the first.

The nearest hospital to her house was USC Medical Center. Rampart Citadel was one of the hospitals she had always heard stories about. Horror stories. Ghost stories. But all the stories were old. Rampart Citadel was closed down at least five years ago.

So they reopened it. *Good for them.* There was a crying need for more ERs everywhere in L.A., especially in the poor neighborhoods, but that didn't begin to explain the chaos all around her, or the sense that this hospital was not open yesterday. The stagnant air stank of disinfectant, but underneath it, the dust and mildew of a long-abandoned building, and the stink of piss and shit that said people with nowhere else to go had lived here.

Strapped down as she was, parked in that curtained-off stall, yet Trixie began to feel like she were falling. This was wrong, so wrong, but it was all of a piece with the invasion of her house and the attack on the road. They kept coming and coming, and she didn't know what they wanted.

"I know why they tied you down," someone said. A dry husk of a woman's voice, reeking fruity alcohol and menthol smoke breath. Hands clutched at her arm as if to tug her off the gurney.

Trixie was startled out of her wits. "Hey, don't sneak up like that! I'm fresh out of blood, if that's what you're looking for."

"I'm not one of them."

"Who?"

"The hospital people. The stopping stoppers." The paranoid lilt with which she whispered this last into Trixie's ear told her what she was dealing with. The smell under the booze and smoke was the deep, ground-in body odor of a street dweller, like the Dog Lady, but so much worse. Like all those people who wore THE END IS NEAR and YOU DESERVE TO GO TO HELL sandwich boards on Hollywood Boulevard, she had finally found something worthy of her most insane fantasies. And she, alone, seemed to notice Trixie.

"I could sure use some hospital people . . . or maybe a cop. Can you maybe try to find a cop for me, please?"

"There's a cop out in the waiting room, but he won't help . . . he's one of them."

"Who?"

"You get hit in the head, too?"

Trixie was losing patience with this Alice in Traumaland routine. "Listen, whatever you want, I'd be happy to help you, but I'm tied down . . ."

"It's because of the medicine." As the bag lady went on, her voice grew higher and louder to compete with the ongoing crisis in the next stall, and the no-doubt deafening voices in her head. "They tried to make me take it, but I won't take it. They gave it to you while you were sleeping, but they're afraid to come in here with you, because it's not in you. They came in here and made this place look like a hospital again, but they're not really helping people. They're—"

"Hey . . . hey . . . hey, slow down. I want to help you"— Trixie coaxed her voice down to a whisper—"*but I'm tied down.* What's your name?"

She heard lips smacking and thought she felt a tear drip on her arm. "I'm—Lois, my name's Lois." Saying her name out loud seemed to calm her down, to make her human again. But then she hastily added, "You don't know my last name, so you have no power over me."

"Well, Lois, my name's Trixie. I'm not one of them. Can you help me?"

"I can't see it in you," Lois babbled, "but maybe you're already dead. I can't let a dead person go free, you'd eat my naked soul. Jesus, it's hard to know what's right . . . I used to have medicine that worked . . . but the bats took it away, those dirty ear-fuckers . . ."

Trixie almost let out a frustrated scream, but she heard the purr of Velcro and her left hand swelled up like a balloon filled with needles. "Thank you, Lois," she practically wept.

Instantly, before she could even control her hand, she was clawing at the plastic neck brace, trying to find a seam or a latch, but there was nothing. The bag lady's ranting hitched up in a wordless screech, and then she leaped away, ducking through a gap in the curtains to retreat to her own stall.

"Attagirl, Lois. They've got your discharge papers up at the front."

Finally, she thought, with nauseous dread. This new voice, she instantly knew, was the doctor. Male, younger than she, but deep in a reassuring way that airline pilots have, so in control they're barely awake.

It was too late to hide her untied hand, so she reached over and unstrapped the other before he could stop her.

"Here, let me help you with that." He bent over her and smiled down into the tunnel of her neck brace. For just a second, she almost thought this guy used to be her doctor, or a guy she briefly had a crush on in school, but she was sure she knew him from somewhere—

His sandy blond hair tumbled into his eyes when he looked down at her. "I think we can safely rule out a spinal injury, then." His arms snaked around her brace and fumbled with the latches for a while before it finally, with an anticlimactic series of clicks, released her neck.

Trixie broke out of the brace and sat up, then almost toppled out of the gurney. She reached out for the instrument tray to steady herself, but it rolled away on squeaky wheels.

"You're probably a little light-headed," he said, checking her pulse and her pupil response. "I probably shouldn't tell you this, but we're all pretty worried about you. That's why they had me come to consult on your case, because I'm a doctor who thinks out of the box . . ."

This corny line snapped home a trigger in Trixie's mind. "Hey, I know you—you're that guy from that one show . . ."

"Yeah, I'm not a doctor, but I play one on TV, ha ha." He tipped her a wink and turned to an instrument tray. "They're really shorthanded tonight, and I volunteered . . ."

Now she remembered, and her mind went into overdrive. She tried to avoid following the tabloids, but it was like trying to ignore the pot smoke at a Phish show in this town. By osmosis, she'd absorbed the stories of so many marginally talented, maximally entitled celebrities who flamed out brighter and faster every year.

And this one she remembered, because he was the young, hot doctor on that show about a decade ago, the one who so effectively portrayed the horrors of drug abuse that he won an Emmy and got canned for drug abuse in the same season.

"I know what you're thinking . . . has this guy lost his mind? But I was a doctor, before I became an actor, did you know that? Almost literally. In my last year of medical school, anyway, before I came out here. So nothing to worry about, you can trust me."

In and out of rehab so many times his career became a role, the endless scenes of misbehavior and begging for redemption. And when he wrecked his Maserati on PCH in Malibu, someone up there must've liked him plenty, because he walked away, while his passenger was still a vegetable, using machines to breathe. The jogger he hit was killed instantly.

And she still couldn't remember his fucking name—

"Stop him, Trixie!" Lois shrieked from the other side of the curtain. "Stop the stopping fucking stoppers!"

The actor turned around and held up the biggest syringe she'd ever seen. Inside was more of the cloudy fluid, but almost opaque with swirling white particles. "Trust me, Trixie. I've done this hundreds of times, just tonight."

"No, thank you," she said.

He stopped, frozen, only a squirt of fluid from the wide-gauge needle in her direction. "What do you mean? Do you want to be discharged or not?"

"Oh, I'm going, don't worry . . . but I think I'm well enough, without another shot in the arm."

Trixie reached for her foot restraints and undid the last of them. She was almost done when he grabbed her arm. "I'm afraid this one doesn't go in your arm, darling."

Before she could react, he wrapped her neck in a sleeper hold and brought the needle up before her eye. "Hold steady, sweetheart. You'll be hella fuckin' sorry if I get it up the wrong nostril."

Trixie brought her head back hard into the TV doctor's

handsome face. His nose crunched like a plastic airplane model. She drove her elbow into his gut and tried to push the needle away from her face.

His grip on her only tightened. His nose was bleeding down her shoulder. "If I miss with this," he panted in her ear, "you're liable to lose your whole frontal lobe, is that what you want? Like the lady in the next stall?"

Trixie brandished the scalpel she'd snagged off the tray when she overplayed her fainting spell, and slashed his sleeve open down to the elbow. "I'm not a doctor and I've never been on TV, but you should see me with a good knife, honey."

In the next stall, something moved. The alarms went off again, and a hand reached out to stroke the curtain.

The shadow left a slimy trail on the rubberized fabric.

Through a fluttering crack in the curtains, Trixie could see only tubes and wires, and a rubber-sheathed form spilling off the gurney and trying to rise, despite the nurses' best efforts to push it back down.

He seemed to think about this for a while. Any reasonable person, Trixie believed, would have just let it go. When she saw the big needle coming for her, she couldn't believe it. She tried to argue with him. "Wait, hold on, now, let's talk about this—" She argued more because she really couldn't bring herself to stab a human being with a knife.

But her hands could do it all by themselves.

She jabbed him in the wrist with the scalpel and saw a bracelet of bright blood erupt around it. For a nasty split second, she thought it would just fall off, but hands are made of sturdier stuff. The blade snagged, trapped between the radius and ulna bones of the forearm.

He dropped the syringe and his fingers curled up like dead spider's legs, but he still hugged her close.

In the next stall, the dying woman threw off her covers and lunged through the curtains. Trixie kicked out in hysterical disbelief.

This wasn't a woman, this wasn't human, but it was real, and it was coming for her.

The woman was probably quite beautiful, before. But her head had split open, and something had been stuffed in between her skin and muscle in great bubbling clumps all over her body, like some runaway boob-job disaster.

The cleft in her head yawned and spat up bubbles of fibrous white tissue and questing roots that stuck to the curtain and tore it away when she lumbered into Trixie's stall.

A wall of rancid foulness wafted ahead of her. She had no eyes, and her teeth only chattered mindlessly, but her body undulated in a sick travesty of what her hot, surgically perfected body once did best.

Trixie kicked again, but only shot the gurney out from under her and at the woman, who raked it aside and kept coming.

The TV doctor couldn't hold her one-armed, and when Lois pounced on him from behind, he dropped them both and staggered, falling on his paralyzed hand. "They're still sick! Don't let them leave!"

Trixie got up and yanked the IV out of her arm, ran for the nearest door with an unlit exit sign over it.

But when she shoved the door open, the passage was clogged floor to ceiling with trash bags mixed with fresh (and not-so-fresh) corpses. The walls were stained and covered in layers of graffiti. The door wouldn't open wide enough for her to squeeze through sideways, let alone for Lois—

"I'm not going anywhere," Lois cackled, "you stopping eye-fuckers! *Get out of my house!*" And then the sick woman fell on her.

Lois swung at the thing with Trixie's IV stand, snapped it in half over its "head."

The bloated white sacs blooming from the cleft in her skull split open and showered Lois with a torrent of creamy white discharge like curdled milk. The bag lady fell on her knees, growling and thrashing and beating her head against the linoleum tile.

With no eyes or ears that Trixie could see, the shambling thing climbed up off Lois and came after her again.

A heavyset nurse tackled her, but Trixie plunged the scalpel into her back and kicked her in the face until she let go. The other staff and most of the patients were torn between coming after her and restraining the other patients and loved ones trying to escape the ER.

The eyeless woman—Wenzel, it must be the intemperate Mrs. Wenzel—hissed at her, and hundreds of tendrils emerged like worms from her slack, slobbering mouth.

Worst of all to Trixie, somehow, was the utter absence of blood. This monstrous deformity—parasite, whatever it was—had eaten up all the blood in the poor woman's body, and turned it to something else.

Jumping back from her fumbling hands, Trixie darted into Mrs. Wenzel's trauma stall and grabbed the big, gaudy gold Coach purse off the chair with the woman's clothes piled on it, turned and ran down the corridor, with the eyeless monstrosity in hot pursuit.

Down the corridor toward another set of double doors, until two orderlies blew through them and came rushing with their arms out and their heads down like linebackers.

Trixie juked left and faked out one of them, then bolted through the nurses' station, shoving carts and overturning trash cans in her wake.

As she ran through the ER, she was overwhelmed by the thin and seedy quality of the sham they'd put together. The staffers were bag ladies and bums and gangbangers, their street clothes under their antique mint green scrubs and yellowed smocks.

The hospital had been a flophouse and a dump for years; and in hours, these people had tried to turn it into a semblance of a working hospital again, but not to heal.

She vaulted over the counter and slipped through the grasp of the TV doctor squealing, "Wrecking it, you're wrecking my scene—" In his working hand, the long, heavy syringe dripped. Trixie darted away from it and through the heavy swinging doors into the waiting room.

A TV mounted in a corner was turned up full blast. The newscaster sagely predicted that tomorrow would be the biggest shopping day of the year. At least thirty people sat on folding chairs or lay propped against the wall. Half of them were asleep. Many of them were doubled over with pain or injuries, and looked up hopefully as she barged into the room.

Every face in the room was brown or black. Every blood-shot eye that rolled up to take her in registered only the slightest pulse of interest as she tore through their midst, screaming, "Get out of here! *Apurate!* These crazy gringo motherfuckers are poisoning *la gente!*"

They just stared at her. The doors flew open behind her and the nurse she stabbed shouted, "Stop her! She's a thief!"

Nobody moved. Whatever they were doing to the people in the ER, they hadn't got around to these people, yet.

Or so she thought.

Someone's leg shot out and tripped her. She tumbled into a grandmother who threw out her arms and caught Trixie by her ponytail.

Her hacking cough blasted spit and phlegm in Trixie's face, but she couldn't bring herself to hit the old woman, who was at least eighty.

"*Be still, young lady,*" the grandmother cooed in her wheezing Spanish. "*Whatever ails you, they will cure it.*"

Her grandkids piled on Trixie's back, kicking her in the kidneys and grabbing for her arms. She swatted them with the purse, but couldn't get purchase to lift herself out of the grandmother's lap, let alone fight off the fat kids.

Trixie cried out, but no words came. The sound she

made would have given any normal person pause, but they kept piling on her back.

A fat old Mexican guy in red boots and a cheap black cowboy hat caught one foot in his arms and another in his jaw. Pale and shaky as if he'd just had a heart attack, he got three more people to catch her kicking legs, and they dragged her, feetfirst, back toward the ER.

"Goddamn it, let me go!" Trixie shrieked herself hoarse and clawed at passing legs that slipped out of her grasp. Laughing children stepped on her hands. The old woman made a gesture like a papal benediction at her and smiled.

Her nails broke on the cracked linoleum tiles she raked up and threw at them, but nothing could stop them.

"LAPD! Freeze and drop, all of you!"

A police officer stood in the open doorway she'd been running for.

Thank God, she thought. "Help me! Officer, please get these people off of me!"

Young, white, and frightened, the cop stood with his legs braced wide and his gun out, but his voice cracked as he tried to get a grip on the situation.

"*Drop the lady!* Get down on the floor! *What the fuck* is going on in here? *Drop her!* Goddamn it, don't any of you people speak *English?*"

They stopped dragging her, but the hands on her limbs tightened their grip, straining apart as if they meant to make a wish and rip her in quarters.

Sweeping the crowd with his gun, he stepped into the waiting room. He reached for the radio handset on his shoulder and keyed it on. "Dispatch, Two-Four-Two here . . . I need backup at the old Citadel hospital ER . . ."

"Two-Four-Two, take a number . . . we have nineteen incidents in progress and two officers down . . ."

They ignored him for a precious few seconds. Then the sick and wounded men, women, and children sprang from their chairs and rushed the cop.

His gun went off twice before they crushed him. Without speaking, without making a sound, the mob attacked. The rest of the shots went off under a pile of bodies, smothered like coughing in a theater.

Trixie kicked the fat cowboy in the gut. He grabbed his chest as he folded. Before they could grab her foot, she twisted into a ball and wrenched the grabbing hands off her other leg.

They fell on her, but the healthiest, heaviest men and women were still wrestling with the cop. She kicked and punched children and old people at death's door, but she was past seeing or caring what she hit. If it held onto her, she hurt it.

Breaking free of the dog pile with a ragged scream, she grabbed a folding chair and swung it around her, cracking a crawling bald man over the head and knocking down the fat grandkids who tried to bite her ankles. Tossing the chair into the tangle of bodies, she turned and ran for the door.

The bodies on top of the cop had broken up into a weird tableaux that trapped her eye even as she ran past it, flailing her arms and running for her life.

The cop struggled under the bodies of wounded and dead civilians, still screaming for backup. A teenage girl in a cheerleader's outfit shot him with his own Taser gun. The electrodes speared his screaming face and jolted him into a crazy break dance, but the current made the living and dead bodies dance, as well.

A dirty *campesino* in a sheepskin jacket doused the cop with his own pepper spray, and another who might've been his twin brother hammered the cop with his baton. The nurse knelt over him, trying to slide a syringe up his nose. "Hold still, damn it!"

Trixie knew she should turn around and try to do something for the cop, but they came staggering out into the parking lot after her. If she stopped, they would tackle her and drag her back into the hospital.

Dodging past the locked police cruiser, Trixie raced among the scatter of parked cars, desperately digging around in Mrs. Wenzel's ridiculous purse for her keys.

Most of them were wrecks and junkers abandoned in the lot months or years ago. Still stumbling forward, whooping for breath, she tossed out a sunglass case and two CVS bags filled with prescription meds before her hands caught something like a key ring.

Rich folks couldn't be bothered with keys anymore, it seemed. The jumble of artifacts on the ring had nothing so plebian as a simple mechanical key, but there were remotes, magic wands, and Fastpasses aplenty. Mashing the buttons all at once, she heard a faint chirp from the far end of the lot and went running after it.

A lady in a housecoat and a drunk with a broken arm hobbled after her, but they couldn't keep up.

She reached the end of the row and jumped into the Lexus SUV. At the push of a button on the dashboard, the instrument panel and headlights fired up, and the whole cabin thrummed with a hushed but absurdly powerful engine.

Blank-eyed, they followed her and threw themselves in front of the big luxury truck.

She swerved to avoid them, but the SUV handled a lot more fluidly than her catering truck. She clipped the guy with the busted wing and smashed into a beater pickup truck held together only by CRISTO ES LA VIDA! bumper stickers.

The impact threw her against her seat belt, but it wasn't even enough to trigger the air bags. She sailed through the wreckage with no other harm done, except for the piercing wail that suddenly filled the cabin.

At first, she wondered what kind of fancy car alarm she'd triggered, but then she turned and looked into the backseat, and saw the crying baby looking back at her.

Eighteen

When the whole world seemed out to get him, Rory always knew that he could talk to his big brother. Richie alone would hear him and know what he really meant.

But tonight, he was at a loss for words.

Richie tried to help. "If I had asked you flat out, you would have refused, wouldn't you?"

"Goddamn right I would have refused! What's going on out there? I can't get hold of Trixie—"

"I don't know the answers, man. I wish I did, but I don't even know where you are."

He didn't answer right away. Turning onto a main drag over the snarl of abandoned train tracks, he passed a fuel truck and a couple cars, keeping a nice, even speed, just another luxury taxi driving around with its windows open in November. It was easier to drive like he wasn't running away from anything if he yelled at his brother.

"Someone's making you do this, right? Someone in jail's got a gun to your head, and they made you reach out to me. That's how it was, right, Richie?"

"I know you think you're having a bad night, but this is gonna be a hard time for everybody, buddy. I tried to give you a chance as a way to say, hey, you know, I'm sorry . . ."

"A chance? Sorry? What the hell—hold on, damn it . . ."

Rory slowed to a crawl behind a pickup truck with flashing orange lights on the roof. It was a spotter for a huge flatbed truck with an entire Krispy Kreme franchise on it.

"I always held you back, little brother, and I wanted to make it right. Now, don't say anything, I know what I'm talking about. You always put your trust in me, and I tried to look out for you, but just as often I used your temper to keep you in trouble, so I'd always be the responsible one, and you'd always be . . . Rory."

Rory didn't know what to say. He checked the oncoming, then punched the gas and passed the convoy. The surreal sight of the repossessed Krispy Kreme passed from view, and he cruised up to a four-way intersection with stop signs. The car on the right was just sitting there, and Rory almost blew through the intersection when he realized the other car was a police cruiser.

He stopped hard, making the brakes squeal, but the Lincoln's big, sleek nose heeled just shy of the warped white line. The cop car didn't move.

"This is a golden opportunity, little man, are you feeling me? You get in with me on the ground floor of this, and there's no telling where we'll end up come Monday morning."

"Shut up, Richie." Rory hit the Speaker button and dropped the phone into his lap. Up until now, the hands-free law they just passed in California made perfect sense, but he found himself thinking, *oh shit, what if the cop saw me talking—*

They might stop this. They might get him out of here and find Trixie and deliver them safely from these fucking freaks. They might even help him out with the guy he'd murdered with his own hands in the backseat of this car, and who was still just slouching there with a turn signal jammed into his eye socket, with Rory's fingerprints all over it. And maybe they wouldn't just put him in jail for the rest of his life, just to be safe.

"Rory?" Richie's voice, tinny and suddenly sapped of its power, burbled out of the phone. "Don't you have a headset yet? Jesus—"

"I hate those fucking things."

"Well, how the hell d'you expect to take a call when you're driving—"

"When I'm driving, I don't want to talk. What the fuck, man?"

The cop just sat on the line, the swords of his headlight beams crossed with Rory's. He'd been stopped when Rory pulled up, and Rory had been waiting for at least ten seconds.

What the fuck was he waiting for? Rory pictured starting to move, only to have the cop pounce on him.

Whatever happens, I'll make it happen. He reached up to signal his intent to turn left onto the frontage road and the freeway on-ramp.

Oh, shit.

He could go straight and try to backtrack, or he could just bull through with a hand signal. He was still weighing his options a few seconds later, when he got rear-ended.

Rory sat back hard in his seat. His head whipped back and bounced off the shredded headrest. Tommy hurtled halfway over the seat and lay facedown in Vanessa's seat.

The Lincoln's tail end rose up a bit off the road and the car launched into the intersection. Rory reacted instinctively, stomping on the brake pedal to arrest his slide, but he fucked up. Or maybe he meant to hit the gas all along.

Roaring in overdrive, the Lincoln powered out of its skid and swerved left as it peeled out for the frontage road.

Out of the corner of his eye, Rory saw the flashing lights perk up, and heard the siren. One cop jumped out and ran for the car that hit him. The other car—the fucking Taurus with the suicide's garden hose still dangling from the tailpipe—stalled in the intersection with its plastic grill smashed into its radiator.

Gushing green coolant like a dying Martian, and yet it lit up and took off after him. The windshield was caked with dirt and dust, but through the slots scraped clear by the windshield wipers, Rory could see Vanessa clearly enough. And she, laughing and waving, saw him.

The cop waited a few seconds for his partner to jump back in, but by then, they were gone.

Rory hit the turn and floored it onto the frontage road before he remembered he was driving a boat. The Lincoln handled better than it had any right to, but he still drifted to the outside of the bend in the road. Vanessa's impromptu vehicle selection left her with even lousier pickup than the Lincoln, and the gutted radiator would kill the Taurus within minutes, but she somehow caught up to him and rammed his right-rear door. Her hysterical laughter cut through the symphonic crunch of their colliding cars.

The wheel whipped out of Rory's hands. The out-of-control Lincoln slewed into the chain-link fence and concrete K-barricades between the frontage road and the freeway. Sheets of white sparks sucked in Rory's window.

Rory accelerated out of the skid and battled back across the yellow center line, pulling away from the Taurus. He had the pedal to the floor, but the fucking red needle was still climbing at its stately pace up past sixty.

Steam shrouded her car as she gained on him again, but he twisted the wheel right and sailed across her path into the parking lot of the outlet mall.

The big livery sedan caught air and skewed right when he swerved to avoid the gigantic Santa Claus balloon the Halloween store was setting up in the parking lot. Jesus, it came earlier every year.

The Taurus stayed on the frontage road, and sped up to head him off at the next driveway. Rory had lost a lot of speed with his maneuver, but he picked it up on the open tarmac and paced the Taurus, with only a bank of juniper hedges separating them.

The on-ramp was only a hundred yards past the drive-way. Rory pumped the brakes and turned hard left through a gap the hedges, jumped the curb, and shoved the Taurus aside.

Vanessa swung across the frontage road and banged off the barricade to ride his left flank. Banging against his heavier frame in frenzied frustration, but her face was a blank, as if she were waiting for a parking space at the mall.

But she kept coming. The 5 North on-ramp was a sharp left turn around and under the Garfield overpass. It was only one lane wide, and he couldn't shake her off.

The turn came too fast for both of them, but Rory braked and turned into her rear as she passed. He meant to shove her onto the overpass, but the Taurus was overheating, and slowing down. His grill kissed the Taurus's trunk hard enough to knock it sideways, blocking the on-ramp.

For just a moment, as she lost control of the car and it skidded across his path, Vanessa looked dead into his eyes and something like true rage finally cracked that blithe, blank face. Funny, when she got angry, she somehow looked just like Richie.

Then she was gone.

Neat as a nine-ball bank shot, the Taurus rammed into the concrete abutment backward, and he passed her onto the freeway.

"Yeah, baby! Fifty million Elvis fans can't be—!"

He choked on his victory whoop when he heard the siren and saw the flashing lights coming up fast behind him.

Oh yeah, the cops.

Even louder, he heard the crash as the police cruiser T-boned the Taurus and clogged the mouth of the on-ramp.

Rory was feeling pretty good about himself, right then. This time, it almost lasted thirty seconds.

Somewhere around Washington, he became aware of a cramp in his thigh that, when he reached down to probe it, turned out to be Tommy's hand.

His long, knotty fingers dug into Rory like corkscrews.

Without looking, Rory screamed, "Fuck you!" and elbowed Tommy in the back of the head, over and over.

He didn't let go, and he didn't seem to get hurt, but his head seemed to give way like a rotten cantaloupe. Thick, clotted white fluid spurted from his skull and sprayed the floor and seats, creamy like custard and somehow, despite the eye-watering mildew stench of rot that exploded in the car even with no windows, it smelled so fucking good he wanted to lick it off his arm and the steering wheel, and even off Tommy's head—

But even as Rory beat on him, Tommy only seemed to gain in vigor. Lashing out now with both arms, he tried to gouge Rory's eyes and wrestle him for the wheel.

They slewed across three lanes in front of a semi towing two trailers of Vons ice cream that sounded a horn like a huge cow god's moo at him.

He didn't dare break anything else off the car to hurt Tommy with, but his hand found the empty shotgun. There might even be shells in here, somewhere—

It worked pretty good as a hammer, too. Most things do, if that's all you need. He smashed Tommy's nose in with it, then split his eyebrow, then used the butt to stove in his snarling, blood-rimmed mouth.

His eyes were gone, and not just the one Rory pushed in. Ropy white tendrils, exactly like the "eyes" that grow out of old potatoes, burst out of his sockets, as well as his nose and ears and the bullet holes in his chest.

Even as Rory beat him, big, pulpy ulcers were blooming on his head, and bursting. The shit was making him sicker, even as it tried to make him eat it.

As if he could read Rory's mind, Tommy grumbled, "No . . . little man, it'll make you *better*. He wants you to—"

"Fuck you, motherfucker! You don't know my brother, and *you don't know me!*"

Rory jammed the heel of his hand against the turn signal. "Are you feeling me, fucker?" The chrome rod slid in with sickening ease, until the butt was flush with Tommy's cheekbone, and he felt the jagged end scrape against the inside of Tommy's skull. Those white tendrils twitched and tried to curl around his hand as he brushed them away.

And still the fucker kept talking.

"Rory, please, don't destroy me . . . he wants you to understand . . . this . . . is a wonderful thing . . ."

Finally, he relaxed and slid off Rory's shoulder, collapsing onto the backseat.

Rory tried to pull his undershirt up and breathe through it. His hand burned where he'd touched the shit growing out of Tommy's head, like the acid burns he got once, taking a corroded battery out of an old Firebird.

His head hurt so fucking bad, his brain felt like a jack-in-the-box, about to pop out of his skull. Everything else was out to lunch.

He'd been a hothead and a violent guy all his life, but he'd never actually killed anybody. If you had to do it over and over again, did it still count as just one guy?

They flew through the Atlantic underpass when he saw Tommy get up again.

In his rearview mirror, the lanky dead kid's silhouette was almost unrecognizable, distorted by bulging sacs of white shit and fumbling tentacles where his face should be. At least without eyes, he should have a hard time hitting Rory with the assault rifle he was aiming at him.

"*We weep for you*," Tommy's corpse said, and opened fire.

Rory slid into a ball under the steering column, straining as hard as he could to kiss his own ass.

The runaway automatic fire filled the car with thunder and lightning. Lead rain punched out the windshield, the roof, the dashboard, and the seats. Incredibly, he wasn't hit once.

The Lincoln veered left and collided with a car in the next lane. Rory crawled sideways on the floor and found something that was either a lipstick tube or a shotgun shell.

Pretty impressive stunt, buddy, but who's driving?

He popped up and reached out to steady the wheel.

The Lincoln was riding against a late-model Honda with the kind of cheap tinted-window job that blisters and turns to a hideous alligator pattern after a couple years. The driver was a young Asian guy who must have his cruise control on. He'd caught a couple of Tommy's bullets in the head and neck. His hangdog face leaned out the hole in the badly tinted window and stared sightlessly ahead as his car sped on down the road.

Rory disengaged the Lincoln from the dead car and pulled away, into the open car-pool lane.

He heard Tommy fucking with the rifle in the back. It was jammed, and he was making it worse trying to clear it with his pulpy, oozing hands.

With one hand still on the wheel, Rory broke open the shotgun and loaded the shell.

The last human remnants of Tommy's head had fallen away from the pulsing, clutching mess that grinned at him and pointed the rifle again. The voice that came from it had no teeth or tongue, but it still cut him to the quick.

It was Richie, imitating their mom. "Why, Rory, why d'you always gotta ruin everything for me?"

Rory always had a smart-ass answer for his mom when she berated him, but he had nothing to say to this faceless thing that knew how her voice went up an octave and three decibels halfway through every question.

He pointed the shotgun at its temple and pulled the trigger.

It wasn't lipstick.

Ears ringing to beat the band, but he heard a harpy shriek from the right lane, pumping her horn and screaming, "Pull over! *Pull over, you cocksucker!*"

Dear God, not another one . . .

The car racing alongside him was a white Lexus, the driver a beautiful platinum blonde ice queen of the blue-blooded variety that common slobs like Rory could only hope to encounter on the road.

She pointed to a dent and a black streak on her door panel. She seemed to think he had something to do with it, and she was shouting into a phone. *"Pull over, goddamn you! Look what you did!"*

"Wow, sorry to ruin your night, lady." He supposed he must have grazed her when he ducked under the wheel to avoid getting shot. Amazing how he hadn't noticed hitting her, but then she somehow must not have noticed all the automatic-weapons fire coming out of the Lincoln a minute before. Incredible, the things people don't notice.

"Look, lady," he shouted across the gap between cars, but this would never work. Instead, he pointed the slime-caked shotgun at her.

She slammed on her brakes, hot pink lipstick in a big O leaving a vapor trail as she dropped out of sight like a falling elevator.

He turned to look after her just in time to see her get rear-ended by the dead Asian kid. God bless the guy who invented cruise control.

At his feet, the phone rang again.

Nineteen

The baby couldn't be more than a year old, tops.

It wore little black sweatpants and a black muscle shirt with the words *Adore Me . . . Or Else* embossed across the chest in silver cursive letters. Trixie guessed it was a boy, but she couldn't be sure. Despite the fact that it was red-faced and screaming, it had beautiful little blond-tufted blue-eyed chubby cherub features that—at this point in its development—could totally go either way.

There wasn't a speck of pink or blue to be seen, except on the toy that it fervently clutched in its stubby little fingers: a toy cell phone, with big bright-colored buttons that beeped as the baby stabbed at them again and again, adding a catchy backbeat to its tantrum.

Trixie screeched to a halt on the hospital ramp, thirty feet from the West Temple Street exit. She remembered Wenzel saying something about leaving *Rocco* in the car, and had figured it must've been a dog. This had to be Baby Rocco Wenzel. Which meant that they'd left it in the god-damn car the whole time they'd been in the ER.

Not that it would have been better off with them . . .

"Oh, *baby*!" Trixie moaned as—for the first time since the accident—she allowed the red crib in her living room to well back up inside her. And the horror of the memory was so huge that it slaughtered her, right there in her seat.

She looked at Baby Rocco, transposed little Edie's face on it, and helplessly did the emotional math.

Babies equaled babies, whether their parents were sweet-hearts, strangers, or abominations.

And suddenly she couldn't stop sobbing.

Right up until the first headlights lit up in the parking lot distance behind her.

Fisting the tears out of her eyes, she screamed, "FUCK!" and stomped on the gas, wheeling onto Temple with her soul torn in half.

The road was clear, so she sheared left onto Hoover, looking up at the 101 freeway as she passed underneath it at something like seventy miles per hour. From below, it looked gridlocked and angry, bathed in crimson brake lights; and somehow, that just made horrible sense.

She made it back to the foot of Hyperion—with the baby screaming every inch of the way—before the first headlights showed up seven blocks behind her, continued down Temple, and were gone.

"I'm sorry," Trixie said, veering off Hoover and onto the home stretch. She was talking to the baby. She was talking to herself. She was talking to her dead friends.

The baby was talking to its phone. Hiccuping and sniffling, Rocco seemed to have rediscovered his toy phone, burbling at it as he made the buttons light up. The toy beeped and burped and chirped in a robotic Speak & Spell voice, *"Let's call . . . Mommy!"*

Which reminded her of whom she should be talking to—whom she needed to be talking to—right this second.

Feeling like an idiot, Trixie reached back into Mrs. Wenzel's purse with her right hand, her left on the wheel. It was amazing how much shit was still in there, after the meds and sunglasses were gone; but the cell phone was easy to distinguish by touch.

She pulled it out, flicked it open, punched in Rory's number with her thumb without even looking.

"Please answer," she muttered, as the phone began to ring . . .

. . . and suddenly he was there, shouting into her ear.

"You wanna know where I am? I wanna know where YOU are, you mother—"

"Rory, it's *me*!"

He seemed to hesitate for a moment, as if he couldn't believe it. *"Trixie? Oh, baby, thank God! Are you okay?"*

"No." Without hesitation. "Are you okay?"

"No, I'm not." His laugh was a bark of fury. *"I'm most definitely not fucking okay."*

"Oh, sweetie . . ." Trixie started crying again. But not nearly as loud as the baby in the back. Rocco was babbling gibberish and waving his chubby arms in the air like a toothless Mussolini.

"What's that noise? Is that Edie? You need to get out of the house and—"

"SHUT UP!" Trixie screamed at the baby as she roared past Sunset. She saw a stretch of sidewalk parking space immediately before her, slammed on the brakes, and made the SUV fishtail, screeching to a halt at the curb.

"TRIXIE!" His voice, so tiny from the phone, as she unbuckled her seat belt and whipped around, the light on Sunset turning red behind her.

The blue-faced baby glared defiantly at her, arching its back in its seat as it ratcheted the volume up even higher. Its anger was shocking, but she was so furious right now that she didn't blame it a bit.

"Hang on a second," she said, as much to Rory as the baby, as she swept her gaze along the backseat for something to offer as comfort for the child. A blanket. A bottle. A ring pacifier.

She leaned over the seat, and there was the bottle: on the floor, nipple dribbling milky whiteness on the shag. Trixie oofed and bent all the way over, snagged it up, and handed it to the raging baby, who almost seemed to know he was the last of the Wenzel clan.

"Here you go," she said. The baby wedged the phone

between its thighs and took the bottle with both hands, greedily sucking the nipple into its mouth. "That's right. What a smart baby! Good . . ."

"*TRIXIE!*"

The baby's eyes rolled back, as if nothing else existed. Slurping down what was probably the last bottle of his mother's milk on earth.

"I'm here," she said into the phone, settling back into her seat. The screaming had stopped at last, and that was a blessing.

If only she could stop shaking . . .

A car slowed down as it passed her, the driver peeking in, then continued down Hyperion. She felt every pore on her body constrict. Then it rounded the corner, and was gone.

"Rory." Gathering herself. "What the fuck is going on?"

"*I don't even know where to start—*"

"Well, I do," she said. "You get a phone call from Richie. And away you go. And a couple hours later, people come in our house—"

"*Omigod—*"

"And they say they know you, but I know they don't. But they sure seem to know Richie—"

"*Motherfuck!*"

"And I fought as hard as I could, but—" Now she was choking on the words. "They killed our friends, Rory. They killed them in our house—"

Her hysteria was catching. The hitch in her voice when she said his name, the pleading that he'd never heard from her before, the helplessness and terror, all combined to make him even crazier.

But she needed to talk, and he needed to know. So he listened to her story, from the attack through the escape, barely speaking except to curse under his breath.

And when she had gotten all the way through, he took the deepest breath he could, fought his way toward icy calm.

"I think I was with the same people, or whatever the fuck they are. And whatever they are, they're spreading."

"Rory . . ."

"Listen to me. You need to get out of town right now. Don't go to the cops. Don't call anybody, not even our friends . . ."

"I'm not going anywhere without you."

"These fuckers have a place where I was supposed to drop them off, and I wouldn't be surprised if Richie was there, right now—"

"Don't you go up there. Call the cops."

"I can't, baby. I'm sorry. I didn't do anything bad . . . but I can't go to the cops about this."

"Fuck Richie! You can't cover for him—"

"This isn't about Richie. I hurt people, Trix."

"Jesus Christ, Rory! You said it yourself: we don't even know WHAT they are anymore! But they're not just people— they're squirting white shit out of their heads—and either you're coming with me, or I'm going wherever you're going."

"Okay, okay. You're right. Shit! Where are you right now?" He realized, as he asked, that he wasn't even sure where he was right now. He'd been driving on automatic since the call began. Trawling like a wayward shark through black water.

"I was—Jesus." Her voice sounded calmer now that she'd gotten her way. *"I'm only about a half mile from the house. How stupid is that? What was I thinking?"*

"Oh, baby." Fighting the panic in his own voice. "Get out of there now. Go south. I'll meet you."

"Where?"

"I dunno. Just—"

And then it came to him.

Trixie had shifted from park into drive, was waiting for the word from Rory's end. She checked the baby in the rearview mirror—still swigging. The bottle was a little more than halfway gone.

"Rory?"

"Trix?" And she could have sworn that he was on the brink of tears.

"Yes, baby?"

"Remember our first date?"

She laughed. "Oh, yes, I do. Of course I do!"

"You remember how to get there?"

"I think! Down the—"

"Shhhh!" His hiss was urgent. *"Don't say it out loud. If you don't remember, we'll pick somewhere else. I just—"*

"Don't know who's listening. I understand." Looking at the baby in the backseat, who could not appear less interested.

She thought about it, reconstructing the picture in her head. Off Carson, down the 405 toward Anaheim. Less than twenty-five miles.

"I think I got it."

"Then that's where we gotta go."

"You promise?"

"I promise. I fucking swear, I'll meet you there."

"I love you, Rory."

"I love you, Trix."

"Don't hang up."

"I won't."

"Stay with me."

"I will."

"Okay," she said, pulling away from the curb and wheeling right back onto Sunset, blazing the yellow light and taking the hard left east. There was very little traffic, none of it urgent. So normal it almost lulled her back to normalcy.

"You still there?" he said.

"I am." Driving through the comforting punky funkiness

of her favorite neighborhood, as Los Feliz turned to Silver Lake. Downtown was ahead, but she needed to cut west. At this hour, Olympic Boulevard seemed like her best shot.

"Tell me a story."

"No, you tell me a story. I already told you a story."

"You don't want to hear it."

"Yes, I actually do."

And so he did, in painstaking detail, seeming grateful for the chance to do so. Unburdening himself of the long, hellish ride, as she crossed town unnoticed and uninterrupted.

It was amazing, listening to him as she cut west across the bottom of Beverly Hills, how *not insane* Los Angeles seemed to her right now. There were none of the car wrecks he described, no riots in the streets, no monstrous eruptions of chaos. Just stopping at red lights, rolling on greens, the occasional beeping of the baby's toy phone.

She knew it was true, but it all just seemed so surreal. Like a TV series they'd each caught different episodes of, shot in familiar locations, but almost entirely unrelated to their actual lives.

It wasn't until she nearly reached the 405 that she realized she was being followed.

A number of thoughts came together in Trixie's head, at that moment.

1) This phone belonged to Mrs. Wenzel, who was currently one of the damned.

2) Mr. Wenzel was one of them, too. And the last time she checked, he was still alive and kicking.

3) The swank SUV she was tooling around in, as if she hadn't a care in the world, had a fucking GPS monitor built right into its goddamn dashboard . . .

"AAAAUGH!" Trixie screamed, taking a sudden hard left across oncoming Olympic traffic that screeched and honked and swerved, down a side street she didn't even know the name of, rapidly calibrating her options as she zipped past the storefronts into humble residential territory, little one-story houses mostly darkened in slumber, curbs lined with parked vehicles. There were plenty of open driveways there where she could ditch the Lexus, but they were all in plain sight, and too close to where she'd turned.

Nobody was on her ass now. But they could be, at any second.

"*TRIXIE!*" Rory bellowed through the phone.

And the baby began to scream.

At the first opportunity, she took another hard left, running the stop sign and nearly clipping a van parked at the corner. She saw a parking spot ahead, wasn't sure if she should take it. Where the fuck would she go from there? And what about the baby?

In the rearview mirror, Rocco intently met her gaze, as if trying to understand why she was driving so crazy.

"*TRIXIE!*"

Or maybe it was more than that.

Trixie suppressed a shudder of deepest dread, pressed her lips tight against the mouthpiece, hoped that Rory could hear her clearly, and took a hard right at the corner.

"I can't talk to you anymore," she said. "They're onto me. I gotta ditch this phone."

"*No! FUCK!*"

"I gotta ditch everything. I gotta—"

"*Trixie! Ditch the car, but hang on to the phone!*"

"But—"

"*I need to know you're safe, baby! Please!*"

There was a metallic click from the backseat, promptly followed by a thud. For a moment, she thought she hit something.

Then she looked in the rearview mirror.

The baby seat was empty.

And all the noises had stopped.

Trixie panicked and slammed the brakes on, skidding. The phone flew from her hand as she brought it to the wheel, steering out of the skid just in time to keep from clipping the vintage Chevy Malibu to her right. The screech of burning rubber masked the fading outrage of the Chevy's horn, and then nothing but the smooth thrum of the engine.

Then she was sitting there, hyperventilating wildly, afraid to turn and look. But according to the rearview mirror, there was still no one in the baby seat.

Reluctantly, she turned on the cab light overhead. Steeled herself.

And turned to look behind her.

There was nothing in the back but the baby seat, its baby seat belt undone. Not broken. Undone.

She heard a stirring on the floor, as something unseen moved under her seat.

It would have been so easy to get out of the car, lock the door, and run like hell. This was, in fact, her plan.

But she had to know.

She leaned forward over the seat . . .

. . . *and the baby was crouched down there, smiling at her . . .*

. . . *with its mouth open wide, to show the glistening white polyps growing out of its pink gums, not baby teeth at all . . .*

. . . *and she suddenly realized what was in that bottle . . .*

Rocco grabbed her by her hair, tiny hands viciously yanking her with a baby's uncanny strength. Pulling itself up into her face.

And vomiting white foam.

Trixie pulled back, feeling hair yank from her scalp in ragged, bloody clumps. She bit back an agonized scream, clamping her eyes and mouth shut just in time. But Rocco came up with her, seventeen pounds of shrieking, homicidal meat. She grabbed the baby by its shoulders before it could grab her hair again.

Rocco clawed for her eyes, and she swung it against the windshield in a full body slam. The glass didn't give, but the baby went sickeningly limp as it flopped back into her arms. Torn between throwing the body and cradling it, her reflexes short-circuited. Her horror at the thought of killing a baby was almost but not nearly as huge as her horror of being killed by one.

She dropped the body in the passenger seat, watched it roll and shudder. Instinctively turned and cut the engine, pulling the keys and stuffing them into her right hip pocket.

From the backseat came a grating musical ringtone.

Rory, she thought, scrambling over the front seat and leaning down to grab it, as it rang again.

But it wasn't Mrs. Wenzel's phone at all.

It was the baby's.

And suddenly, all that beeping from the backseat made terrifying sense.

Trixie stared at the brightly colored but clearly-not-a-toy phone in stunned disgust. Who the fuck gives a working cell phone to a one-year-old? Who would *manufacture* such a thing, much less invent it? She helplessly blamed the Japanese. But more precisely, she blamed the Wenzels.

The baby grabbed her by the tit and bit down hard through her shirt and bra, bringing the issue sharply back into focus.

"YAUGH!" she roared, grabbing the baby by the ears and yanking back hard and hurling it against the passenger door. Rocco hit the padded leather and laughed, leaped at her again.

She punched it in the face.

She couldn't help herself. She was so fucking mad that she punched it again, until the laughter stopped, bringing back her fist to look at the white slime on her knuckles, then smearing it off on the upholstery.

Beating up a baby was not getting her any closer to Rory. What she needed was to get out of here, just as fast as she could.

Trixie threw the door open, slid outside, slammed it, and locked it. Across the street and three doors down, somebody's living room lights flicked on. She knew how bad this was going to look. She had to work fast.

She popped the trunk, went straight for the spare. One thing she could say for the wealthy: they often had excellent tools, whether they knew how to use them or not. The tire iron and tool kit had never been touched.

But all that was about to change.

In the distance, she could hear a car coming. Her tail, catching up at last. She ducked into the nearest front yard and crossed it to the back, climbing the fence with jungle gym ease, coming out at the next street and doing the same for the next three blocks.

Dogs howled, but they were not for her.

On the floor of the Lexus, sandwiched between the passenger seat and the door, the discarded cell phone rang and rang and rang.

It was hard for the baby to get to the phone. But the tiny, clumsy body had become possessed by the patience and persistence of a fungus as, stretching and straining until its arm almost popped from its socket, the baby reached the phone.

Tiny fingers popped the top, pried the mouthpiece from the ear so the screen lit up. The baby liked buttons, and this one was silver.

"Trixie?" cried the tiny voice. But the baby's was tinier still.

"Rory?" it said, with an infant's lazy tongue, and a mouth

unaccustomed to forming words. But getting the hang of it real quick.

"*Who IS this?*"

"Everybody." Grinning. "Everybody but you."

And then hung up the phone.

As the others closed in.

TWENTY

Rory stared at the phone, felt icy cold flood him: half rage, half despair and 100 percent terror.

They had her now. There wasn't a doubt in his mind. They had her, and they would turn her if they could. Pump her full of their poisonous shit until her eyes popped out of her head.

And if that didn't work . . .

"Shut up. *Shut up!*" he hissed at himself, at the sadistic little fucker in his head who kept spooling those horrible brain-movies. This was no time for panic. This was time to rev up and roll. If he wanted to save her, he would have to act fast.

And God as his witness, the *only* thing he cared about in this whole mad, swirling world of shit was saving Trixie. Making sure she survived. And not as one of them, but as her own amazing self.

If they were trying to bait him, he had a pretty good idea of where to head next. And if they wanted a war, then they would fucking well have one.

But he would need reinforcements.

With that in mind, Rory punched in a number, and stomped on the gas.

PART FOUR

The Thin White Line

Twenty-one

On nights like this, Sergeant Ruben Placido genuinely wondered what the hell he was doing, still trying to be a cop in this fucking city.

As if he could read Tony's mind but couldn't quite *read*, his partner loudly declared, "Shit, Sarge, is this whole town on the rag, or what?"

"You know that kind of talk doesn't just piss off women, right?" Placido pulled them up sharply at Highland and Sunset, head-checked the intersection for motorists running the red light, for odd looks from the motorists flanking the cruiser.

An old black lady hobbled past, shoving a wire cart with a broken wheel in a panic, as if she was sure they were going to run her down.

"Sorry, Sarge . . . But seriously, it's not a full moon, so what's up with all these bogus calls?"

Placido wished he knew, but he couldn't admit it to the rookie. "People lie to the cops, Glen. Everybody does. Sometimes, you get called in by a guy whose pot plants got stolen, and he wants you to get them back. That's honesty for you."

"Shit, whatever, dude, but . . ." With his usual grace, Officer Glen Dolfuss gathered his thoughts halfway through his sentence. "Some shit's going down tonight, I know it, but every call we bounce on, there's like, a cover-up, or something. How are we supposed to help them if they fucking lie to us?"

The kid was built like a tank and could've had a future as a pro linebacker, if he'd had the brains. Born in Wyoming, broken in over a hitch riding convoys in Iraq, the kid came back looking for a safer brand of the same kind of action. He was addicted to moving faster than he could think, but as Placido's project, Glen was making huge strides. He would probably always be a little too slow to work the streets on his own, but he'd never be quick to draw down without proper cause either.

And what scared Placido was that he had a point.

"Lemme tell you something you better get down." Placido lazily drove off the line. Other cops made it a point of pride to lay a patch at every intersection, or just ignore the lights altogether. Those guys made his job harder than most of the crooks. "There's no 'us' and 'them.' There's all of us, or there's just you and everybody else. You go around like those old hard-ass guys"—he didn't say *white guys*— "who live up in Simi Valley, you treat them all like hostiles, that's what you'll get, every time. You think of this as our house, and that we suffer them to live in it, and you'll come to grief. You can't forget that *we* work for *them*, all of them. We're all one big family, or it's every man for himself, *mijo*."

"Okay, okay, shit, I get it. One big happy family." Glen scanned the parked cars on Highland, the shifting shadows of lurkers just outside the blazing pink lights of a strip club. "Hey, Sarge, is that your sister over there, giving my cousin a blow job?"

"Watch your fucking mouth, kid." Placido flipped the lights and goosed the siren as he chopped into the strip club driveway.

The lucky couple were going at it right in the parking lot of the liquor store next to the club in front of God and everybody. A few wasted club patrons took off running, but the guy just shaded his eyes and waved, while his special lady friend went on doing her job.

"Lemme take this one, Sarge. Don't sweat it, I'll be totally color-blind."

Placido called in the stop, soaked up the chatter. Bad ground signs racked up. False alarms and 911 calls, shots fired and no perps, cops on the radio saying, "Everything's cool, stay cool . . . it's all good."

The dispatcher sounded half-asleep as she read a general call. "All units, look for a black '02 Lincoln Con, livery license T511C4 . . ."

Glen ambled over to the happy couple. His broad, black-uniformed back hid them from the headlights' glare, but he rolled up on them with one hand on his stick, instead of his gun. Good boy.

The dispatcher tried to make it sound boring, but some maniac was drag racing in Commerce and totaled an LAPD unit, then shot and killed two people on the northbound 5. Present whereabouts unknown.

Christ. As long as he'd lived here, and the Placidos had lived in L.A. for four generations, he couldn't sort out the cutoff point in the cycle of bullshit that fed on and fueled itself. Hollywood glowed like a big bug zapper, attracting all the creeps in the world, who came here to fuck the magic, and their bad behavior only fed the mystique that dragged the gutters of the earth for the Hollywood screw-ups of tomorrow.

The people who really lived here were like the people everywhere else. They just wanted to live and work and stay out of trouble.

Ruben's father got his skull cracked open by white sailors in the Zoot Suit Riots. His parents' house burned down in the '68 riots. And his cousin got shot in the back by a Korean storeowner in the Rodney King riots, so if anyone had a reason to nurture a chip on his shoulder, it was Ruben Placido. But, like his mother used to say, *To err is human, to forgive is Mexican.*

When Placido joined the LAPD in '82, he thought he

was taking a step to reclaim the police force. He believed the law could never protect people south of the 10 if it always wore a white face. He never wanted to get off the street. He was a stabilizer and a teacher, a counselor and a confessor. People understood that he didn't want to bust them; he didn't measure success that way.

If shit like this happened every night, he'd just give up, unsure if he'd finally won, or if it was all too far gone to even recognize.

The night had started out like any third-watch family holiday: slow and sloppy, with tired, drunken relatives and neighbors calling the cops on one another, but nothing special. They had responded to three domestic calls in Hollywood and two noise disturbances in Silver Lake, and in every instance, they found nobody to swear out a complaint, let alone arrest. All lights out, everybody gone.

One Adam Twelve, see the crazy naked lady running down the street screaming that her husband wasn't her husband. By the time they found her, a crowd had formed, and the naked but now quite reasonable lady just wanted to be driven home.

A weird night. And then the kicker . . .

The accident at Sunset and Hyperion was a big one, by the initial report; but when they got there six minutes later, the victims were gone. The vehicles were there, a crappy old van T-boned by a catering truck that turned out to belong to one of the noise disturbance complaints. But the paramedics from Kaiser were totally flummoxed. An eyewitness told them an ambulance had already rolled up and collected the driver of the van, but a passenger had run away, and now nobody could find either one of them.

It was enough to make you start believing there was a Them, and They were playing a game way above your head.

Glen finally turned around and followed the couple back to a skeevy Camaro, checked the guy's papers.

"Wrap them up," Placido shouted. "Let's go."

Glen ambled back to the squad car and jumped in. "I took a page from your book, Sarge. I asked first, I listened actively, and guess what? They're married."

The couple sat in their car. They didn't move or turn on their lights. "It's still a three-one-one, Jethro. And if they weren't pushing, they're probably looking out for someone who is—"

Like nothing else, the nickname usually threw Glen into a fit, but he just snorted and sneezed. "I issued a citation. The guy just got out of jail today. I thought I'd cut him some slack."

Just as well. The freeway shooter was northbound, and could blow past them any minute.

Glen was uncharacteristically blasé about the possibility. "It's probably bullshit, like everything else tonight. But you wanna know about something really amazing—"

Placido cut him off with an angry glare, peeling out of the parking lot to ram home his point. "Don't assume you know everything this job can throw at you, *mijo*. I've seen guys go to domestic violence stops and take a beater away, only to get stabbed by the wife. I've seen—"

"I get it, I get it. You're showing me that nothing is what it seems. Race and class are useful levers of social control. You're an excellent teacher, Ruben."

Placido looked sidelong at his partner long enough that he ran a red light at Fountain. Horns honked after him, but he hardly noticed.

Glen returned his look and smiled. Sweat broke out on his forehead and neck. His nose was bleeding. His eyes looked glazed and dry as onions, but he didn't blink. Placido found he was driving down the road looking into his partner's eyes, waiting for him to blink and suddenly wondering, *who the fuck is this guy?*

And that was when it clicked, for Placido, when he realized what had felt wrong all night. Everybody lies to the cops, but all night, Placido had been listening to cops on the radio, and he knew in his gut that *they* were lying.

"Something you trying to say to me, Glen?"

"If you're talking, you're not learning, right? Go ahead, I'm all ears."

The radio cut in before he could start another lecture. "All units respond . . . Unit Eight-Three-Eight requests immediate assistance . . . shots fired at nineteen-hundred block Laurelmont and Olympus. Officer down . . . nine-one-one calls report that the shooters are in a West Hollywood Sheriff's car . . ."

"Goddamn it!" Placido hit the siren and floored it.

He didn't recognize the unit number, but it didn't sound like one from their precinct.

"Unit Three-One-Three, en route," Placido replied. "You know who's in that car?"

"No idea, One-Three."

The cruiser hit seventy-five ripping through scattered sleepy Hollywood traffic like drifts of steel snow. Placido turned west on Sunset, which was somehow still crowded with pedestrians strolling arm in arm down the street, like a rave just got out. People barely hopped out of the way, waving and laughing. Glen laughed and waved back.

Something was wrong with the night. With the city.

With his partner.

They blew through the next five lights and whipped around the corner onto Laurel Canyon Boulevard. A flock of paparazzi followed a drunken starlet up the street from some nightclub to her Maserati. A Hummer stretch limousine was stranded sideways on Hollywood Boulevard and traffic backed up all the way to Vine.

Above the boulevard, the featureless flatness of L.A. gave way to the loopy foothills, and the shacks and shitbox apartments that warehoused L.A.'s teeming millions fell away to let the palatial estates of the happy, famous few look down on them. At the top, the massive gated community of Mount Olympus squatted like a huge crown, the unattainable realm of the self-proclaimed gods of Los Angeles. The abrupt surge in property value was enough to give Placido the bends.

Past Sunset, they were in what used to be Hollywood Sheriff's backyard. Placido was old enough to remember the vendettas between LAPD and the old Hollywood Sheriff's deputies, who used to run cover for Mickey Cohen's syndicate. West Hollywood Sheriff's turf ended at Fountain, but included the dots of unincorporated territory on this side of the hills.

Glen fiddled with the radio to find West Hollywood's calls as they blew through the last light. The road squeezed down to two squirrelly lanes winding through a narrow canyon jammed with houses and compounds. Traffic was way too heavy for this time of night on a holiday, and every car seemed to stubbornly hold the lane for precious seconds before drowsily yielding to their wailing siren.

The radio blared "*—ly shit, they shot us, they fucking shot us! Danny's down, and I can't raise Sam and Vince . . . Where's the fucking ambulance, Didi?*"

"We're trying to get through to them, but the call centers are jammed. There's rioting on Hollywood . . . store windows are getting smashed—"

The deputy's reply was interrupted by sprays of gunfire. Glen rolled down the window and hooted, "Fuck me! I can hear it!"

"Tell them *we're getting fucking killed!* Get us some goddamned tactical and run that plate through the system—"

"LAPD units are en route, Stu. Stand down and tell Danny to hold on, we're getting Cedars to send—"

"NO! *Don't let LAPD in!* Didi, didn't you hear what I fucking said? Run that plate to make sure it's not stolen—"

"I did, but—"

Honking and making the siren squawk, Placido finally reached Laurelmont and turned up the crazy-steep hill.

Just over the next ridge, the road turned into a private driveway for Mount Olympus. When these people had crime problems, they didn't call 911. They had their own cops.

"Goddamn it, Danny knew the big guy, Burt something! They're fucking cops, Didi! Get on the phone with nine-one-one dispatch and find out why *LAPD is shooting at us!*"

"Jesus Christ! Glen, leave it . . ."

Glen unlocked the shotgun. "You never know, Sarge. Nothing is what it seems, right?"

Placido heard shots just as he saw the black bulks of three cars in the street. The streetlights were out overhead, but their headlights picked out the deputy who must be Stu. His phone in one hand and his shotgun in the other, he turned and screamed, *"Get the fuck back!"*

"Whooeee!" Glen jumped out and rushed the sheriff's car.

Placido went nowhere.

His stomach, simmering all night, began to boil over. Hot bile shot up the back of his throat, and a most unwelcome tingling in his right arm warned him that he might not need to get shot to die tonight.

Suddenly too old and heavy to lever himself out of the squad car, he could only watch.

Glen ducked behind the engine block. The deputy dropped the phone and brought up the shotgun. The windshield dissolved into a starry snowfield of shattered glass, ejecting Placido from the car on reflex. He kicked his door open and dove out onto the pavement, fumbling for his old service revolver—none of that molded plastic automatic Glock bullshit for him—but finding his gun and bringing it out of the holster was like trying to pull a chandelier out of his pocket.

This situation was totally out of control, he knew. His mind was trying to do what his body could not, trying to put on the brakes before somebody got killed. But muscle memory and a million half-forgotten nightmares ripped the reins of his body out of control. His partner was in danger. He was in danger, and no matter what it looked like, he had trained his body to defend itself.

"Stop shooting! *Hold your fucking fire!*" Placido shouted, but nobody did. From behind the deputy's car, muzzle flashes sparked up and barked, and the few intact lights and windows on the deputy's car burst and scattered.

"Get some!" Glen popped up and fired twice on the deputy.

The deputy dove into his car, wriggled across the bench seat and slid out on the passenger side. A big splash of blood marked the flank of the car. Glen got him in the leg or the back, Placido figured. Good, maybe this was over.

"Glen, stand down, damn it! You up there, stop shooting! *LAPD, motherfuckers!*" Placido came around the car with his gun up.

Glen came out from cover and threw his hand up as if to give Placido a big high five. The deputy laid the shotgun over the trunk of his car and shot Glen in the face.

Placido reacted instantly, aiming and squeezing three times, sure at least one hit the deputy in his neck.

The silence that fell over the scene was heavier than lead. Placido cautiously stepped from cover and looked around.

Glen was down and never getting up. The left side of his head was rudely scraped off by shotgun pellets down to the bone, and big flaps of flesh lay splayed out on the tarmac, pointed in the same direction as the shotgun carelessly thrown out alongside his big, dumb dead body. *They went thataways . . .*

The dull ache in Placido's right arm cranked up the voltage until he felt like he had a car battery wired to his heart. His face felt four feet thick and tingled like it was going to sleep.

While he still could, he grabbed the radio and bleated,

"Dispatch, we got a man down . . . men down . . . West Hollywood sheriff's deputies, and uh, it's . . . *oh my God, what did we do . . . ?*"

The voice that responded did not share his panic. It was not the dispatcher at all. "*And they shall plant vineyards, and drink the wine of them . . .*" The voice was sleepy and somber, like an old LP record on a player that was winding down.

"Get off this channel!" These newfangled cellular things weren't supposed to do that, were they? "Dispatch, any and all units—"

The low, leaden voice ground on over Placido's protests. "*And they shall also make gardens, and eat the fruit of them . . .*"

It was a record player. He heard a rubbery, stumbling dub reggae tune throbbing way back in the mix, and the warm fireside crackle that he'd mistaken for static. Somebody with a pirate radio station was jamming their fucking emergency channels, and playing old church records.

"*And I will plant them upon their land, which I have given them, your God.*"

Placido staggered back to Glen, who was still dead. Cars breezed by on Laurel Canyon, oblivious. The bubble would burst any second. Backup from both police forces and the private security from up the hill would surround them and sort it out, helicopters and news vans would pour into the vacuum left by all this pointless violence.

Cops killing one another . . . for what?

"*And the mountains shall drop sweet wine . . .*"

"Who the fuck is this? You're in a heap of trouble . . ."

A young male voice cut in, drowsy and ebullient, stone in love with itself. "*This is the voice of the New City, mon. Who the fuck're you?*"

Spooked, Placido dropped the radio and dug out his cell phone.

No service. What the fuck? He was on a hill in the most

connected, overdeveloped city in America, and he couldn't get a signal. He turned around and looked at the endless glittering bed of Los Angeles. He suddenly started to wonder if anyone was coming.

"Help . . . help me . . . please . . ."

Placido drew his gun and bent over to use his car as cover.

The deputy tried to sit up against the door of his cruiser. He was wearing a flak jacket under his tan uniform, but Glen had hit him low. His ear dangled from a sliver of gristle where Placido had hit him high. His lap was a red punch bowl that spilled ropes of gut on the road as he tried to grab his shotgun, get up and away from Officer Placido.

"Hey, man, calm down. I don't know what the fuck is going down . . ."

"Those fuckers were cops, too . . . you guys fucking declared war on us . . ."

Placido put away his gun. The other two cars, another deputy's car and the missing LAPD squad car, lay parked about twenty yards apart. A body lay in the road beside the deputy's car. He couldn't see anyone in or around LAPD Unit 838, from First Precinct, downtown. No sign of whoever opened up on the deputy from behind. Nobody coming.

Placido grabbed a first-aid kit from the trunk and went back to the deputy—Stu . . . Morgenthal his name tag said. Clumsily, he taped the ear back to his head. "What the hell happened here, man?"

"Your people are fucking dirty . . ."

"Hey, watch your mouth, *pendejo* . . . I'm trying to help you." Placido tried to compress the artery slowly spurting the deputy's life out of his pelvis, but the idiot kept fighting him. His swatting hands were so pale they looked like plastic mannequin hands, his movements weaker by the minute.

"Those cops . . . spotted them on Santa Monica, cruising. They picked up some kid on Robertson and shook him down. We came over to find out what they were doing on our boulevard. They were dropping weight all over the fucking place. Ounces of coke . . ."

"Man, I'm not saying you're lying, but you know how that sounds?"

"Fuck you, it's true . . . Hung back, followed them up here, and they opened up on us. Look in their trunk, you don't believe me . . ."

Placido got up and took the camera out of his trunk. He'd lived long enough to see every kind of scandal come and go. The last few had changed things quite a bit, but a blue-on-blue fatal shooting would screw up everything. Cops selling drugs was like the ultimate ghetto conspiracy theory. Everybody south of the 10 always knew the CIA was behind the crack explosion, but Placido never saw anything like this.

Placido looked inside Unit 838. Shot to shit. Tires flat, door panels shattered and blood and fuzzy white dust covered the seats. Empty water bottles and empty baggies piled up on the floorboards. He popped the trunk.

Ten-gallon trash bags filled with Ziploc sandwich bags, each stuffed with easily an ounce of cocaine. His eyes burned and the fine membranes of his sinuses tingled with the dust floating off the stash. Figure something like fifty pounds of the shit, and all the bags were less than half-full.

Placido stayed as far as he could from narco ops, but this kind of weight was how they moved cocaine into the fucking country, not around on the streets. But something was wrong.

The deputy said they were peddling it on the open street. But something was missing.

Oh yeah, money. And two dirty cops.

Placido climbed out of the car, reached for the unit's radio. He thumbed the Send button. "Dispatch and any and all units in Fourth Precinct, we have a goddamned blue-on-blue incident. Two are dead, one dying, and the shooters are still at large, so please send us a goddamned ambulance and some coverage—"

Hands grabbed his ankles. Screaming, he jumped back, but the grip on his legs yanked him off his feet. White hands, coated with slimy white fur. He fell hard on his ass and found himself staring as something inhuman crawled out from under the car and climbed up his legs.

Something in a cop's uniform.

"Lemme tell you something, all you old people out there," said the stoned voice on his radio.

Oozing chunky white slime out of its empty eye sockets, it crawled on him. Placido frantically crabbed backward on his elbows, kicking the melting white mess in what he took to be its face.

"All you blind people think you run this blood-clot city, you living in bubbles that about to burst. The people around you are real and alive, and you can't shut them out any longer. You're not the star of your own movie anymore."

Its jaw came off like hinges out of rotten wood. Bloated bladders swelling out of its misshapen skull popped and splattered white foam everywhere. Its features slid off to reveal the grinning skull underneath, but still it kept coming.

"You have nothing to lose but the walls between you. We come to show you the way to the New City, the way to oneness."

Placido rolled out from under the grinning thing, sliding hideously in a pool of white scum. The thing sat back and reached out plaintively to him, trying to say something through chattering teeth. Everything above its eyebrows had been blown off by a shotgun. His name tag was coated with slime, but somehow, Placido recognized him. Burt Subotsky. Called every Mexican civilian he dealt with, *Chico.* A storm trooper of the old Parker-Gates school, he still called in ghetto incidents as "NHI," or *no humans involved.*

Right now, that should be funny, somehow . . .

Burt reached out for help and gushed jets of white slime at Placido, who danced back cursing and shot the thing in the face. He shot it until he clicked on empty shells before it gave up.

"We come to tear down your walls and show you how good it can feel to come together." Placido swiped the radio off his chest and threw it away, but the voice wasn't coming from the radio.

"We come to save you from yourselves, Sarge."

It was coming from behind him.

He turned around too slow. The shotgun blast kicked his right leg out from under him, spun him around, and dropped him back on his ass.

"You change your mind yet?" Glen Dolfuss smirked and strolled up to stand over Placido. A little dizzy maybe, from having one side of his head pared down to the bone, but fine, otherwise.

Placido tried to speak, but only sobs came out. Where the fuck was their backup?

"Let me tell you something you better get down, amigo," he said, spraying bloody spit out the hole in his left cheek so he sounded a little too much like Daffy Duck. "This city you think you're saving, you just enable it. That's your bubble. You think you help people, but you don't really believe they're really alive, like you. Saving them proves to you that you're better than them, that you, alone, are *real*."

Placido tried to crawl away. Stupid, sure, but what else could he do? He flipped onto his belly. He thought he heard someone coming.

"This city is doomed. It's addicted to its own destruction. It wants to burn itself to the ground, but you know what?"

Lights cut through the dense eucalyptus grove shading the road to Olympus. Someone might come after all, someone might stop this insanity . . .

"We're going to save it."

Security guards in tactical gear jumped out of Hummers and golf carts, fanning out around Glen and Placido, waving assault rifles and flashlights.

Glen didn't drop his shotgun, but he lowered it and pointed silently at his partner.

Placido barely had the strength to fight as they flipped him over. "Why are you with them, Glen? What did they do to you?"

Glen just half smiled as they pressed a baggie over Placido's face.

He held his breath. He was bleeding out, going into shock. He would pass out and inhale the shit, or he would die. That would show them.

Down the road, the guards shot Deputy Morgenthal. Someone got into Burt's squad car and put it in neutral so someone else could hitch it to a Hummer and tow it up the hill to Mount Olympus.

Placido held his breath for a long time. The security guard leaning over him punched him in the ribs. He inhaled.

And in less time than it takes to tell, he changed his mind.

About everything.

PART FIVE

The Big Payback

TWENTY-TWO

Rory tried to keep a straight face as he looked over the giant scorpion that filled Jonah Stumbo's garage workshop.

The smoke-blackened steel armor was layered in segments that hid all of its intricate gas-powered servos. Its pincers were belt-fed automatic shotguns, while the stinger, curled against the cracked concrete ceiling, had a flamethrower.

"Don't you have anything a little . . . subtler?"

"Pussy," Stumbo grumbled. "Why don't you just go over in a G-string and dance for them, maybe give them a massage." Stumbo cut the power to the robot and slid off the remote-viewing goggles that let him see through its night-vision camera eyes. "You came to *my* house. I only do final solutions. Don't ask me to censor myself."

"This thing will kill a lot of innocent people."

"Heh. Not in L.A., it won't." Stumbo lipped a cigarette, flipped open the tip of the thumb on his prosthetic left arm. A blue jet of flame crisped the butt. He giggled out a gust of smoke. "I thought you wanted these motherfuckers dead, man."

Rory took a deep breath and ran his hands through his hair. His hands came away smudged with traces of Tommy's blood. "I have no idea what's inside. I was supposed to take them back there after they got done tonight. It's where the rest of the drivers and maybe the assholes behind this might be. Maybe working on the next step in the plan."

"You're fucking serious about this shit? You sure you don't want a beer?"

Rory shook his head. "I thought they were just amateur drug dealers, but there's something *alive* in the shit they're pushing. And it's trying to take over the city."

"And they came into your house. Took Trixie."

"I don't know . . . I mean, I don't know for sure, but—"

"So you haven't picked up a phone in almost two years, but when this shit happened and you couldn't get in there by yourself, you decided to come see me to help you fuck them up."

Rory smiled brokenly and just nodded.

"Thank God," Stumbo crowed. "I was starting to think we weren't friends anymore."

Rory called Trixie again, told her message center to get out of town. Go to her sister's in Chula Vista, if she had to, but get out of L.A. He would catch up to her as soon as he was done.

He knew exactly what she'd say, if she knew what he was planning. *"God, no, Rory, I don't want to lose you, too. Please don't do anything stupid, honey."*

"I'm not doing anything stupid."

"If you go up there by yourself, you're not coming back."

"I'm not going by myself. I'm on my way to Stumbo's."

"I take it back," she'd say. *"Go by yourself, please?"*

Jonah Stumbo was homeschooled, but got into Cal Tech, where his experimental SWAT robot blew his arm off. He drifted up to the Bay Area and found a home with an industrial performance group called Survival Research Laboratories, but quit after one of his installations set the audience on fire.

With a personality and skill set like Stumbo's, only Hollywood would have him. For every cheap-ass midnight movie you've ever seen that ended with an explosion or practical special effect that eclipsed the rest of the film and left no doubt that somebody got killed, you probably saw the un-credited work of Jonah Stumbo.

Lately, he was working on some secret project, and had been out in the desert for months at a time. Rory was lucky to find him at his windowless place in a basement under a strip mall off Sunset. Once an underground garage, the cavernous concrete bunker would make a perfect fallout shelter, if not for the grease that dripped from the ceiling into pans from the leaky deep fryers in the doughnut shop upstairs.

Stumbo finished loading his van, filled a thermos with coffee, and they hit the road.

He was cheerful at seeing Rory again, and at having a mission, but he had no other evidence but Rory's word. It was almost unnerving how easy it was to get him into this, but it wasn't just a matter of friendship. Stumbo thrived on trouble. He was a weapon you only broke the glass and took out when you planned on leaving nothing but scorched earth behind.

Rory could tell Stumbo hadn't hung out with anyone in weeks. He was quite the chatterbox. "Take over this fuck-ing city? That's rich. You know, that's when *The Turner Diaries* jumped the shark. Hang every fucking race-traitor in L.A. from a lamppost? Not fucking likely. You'd need a lot more lampposts."

Rory wiped his eyes and let the air clear. People of color thought Stumbo was a bigot; women thought he was a misogynist; hippies thought he was a fascist, and fascists just couldn't get away fast enough. The truth was, Jonah Stumbo just didn't know how to get along with anybody.

"But seriously, taking over L.A. is impossible. There's no strategic borders, no centralized systems of control. Doro-thy Parker was right, it's not even a city. It's seventy-two suburbs in search of a city."

"Wow, Stumbo. Dorothy Parker and *Turner Diaries*. You are one erudite motherfucker."

"Yeah, well, you get a lot of reading done when you never get invited to your friends' holiday parties."

Stumbo stuck to side streets through Hollywood. They heard sirens tearing up and down Sunset, but saw nothing and no one on the street. Turning up Laurel Canyon, they passed a line of parked luxury cars spilling down from Mount Olympus, the most ostentatious gated community in the hills.

Their target was not as fancy or as fortified, but Rory had scoped it out on Google Earth at Stumbo's, and found twelve-foot fences and walls encircled a dozen properties, and two exits with manned guardhouses. Parked down the street from the Lookout Mountain entrance, they saw husky, bright-eyed guys who were probably moonlighting cops sitting bolt upright at their posts, and cameras every fifty feet on the perimeter and at the entrance to each house.

"Fuck me sideways," Stumbo grumbled, "this won't even be a challenge."

Rory's rage for revenge began to die on the vine from the moment he looked over the defenses, but now it flared up at Stumbo. "They're going to see right through us if we try to bluff our way in—"

"I never bluff." Stumbo held up his secret weapon, opened his door to set it out on the road.

"Are you fucking kidding me?"

Waving away Rory's outburst with a gloved hand, he slipped on a pair of goggles and took out a wireless joystick from the racks of gear behind his seat. Pulling up the antenna and cussing under his breath at the little unit, Stumbo gunned the engine and sent the little remote control monster truck cruising up Lookout Mountain.

"You know what kills me," Stumbo chattered. "These rich jack-offs who move up here pay for their own cops, their own power and water lines, even their own fucking *fire department*, no shit, and then they have to rent out their fancy fucking estates to porn shoots and reality shows."

Rory watched the miniature headlights jitter and bob over the potholed tarmac, and somehow, the absurdity of all this turned his anger to fatigue. Trixie wasn't in here, and he began to suspect he wanted to believe she was, so he'd have an ironclad excuse to hit them. This was the Sav-On slingshot massacre all over again. He should call the cops and haul ass for the meeting place, and get the hell out of L.A. until all this blew over. Maybe for good.

But it was too late now.

"Bend over, bitches," Stumbo said. His mouth hung open as he fiddled with the joystick. Up the hill, the toy truck had rolled up to the edge of the harsh floodlights pounding out of the guardhouse. Rory fretted that Stumbo was going to try to distract the goons with the toy truck, but instead, he turned it into the shrubbery that buffered the barbed wire–topped fence by the wall.

"These retards even have their own fucking power grid, but they have a transformer outside the fence." He pushed a button and set the joystick down for a second, flipped up his goggles, and stared searchingly at Rory.

"Are you absolutely *sure* this is the right place?"

"Yeah. They're in there."

"Okay." Stumbo picked up the joystick and hit another button. "Let's have a war."

The transformer box exploded. The floodlights went out. Darkness fell, except for the spray of sparks from the bushes around the fence. Inside the Lookout Mountain enclave, all the lights went out except for two houses. One of them was the one they were going to break into.

"Grab your bag," Stumbo barked as he jumped out of the van. They met at the back and shouldered nylon day packs and snugged black ski masks over their heads. Stumbo carried a pair of bolt cutters, while Rory held a twelve-gauge shotgun.

A moment ago, he felt tired, like he could drift off to sleep, but now the old anger came back. His house was full of dead people. His friends were out in the streets, out of their minds, because of these people.

For all the trouble he'd ever gotten into, Rory had never actually killed anyone, before tonight. He didn't look forward to it, but he could barely think while these fuckers were out there. It had to feel better, if he could know they were gone for good.

Stumbo led him down the road to where the fence veered away into a steep, narrow canyon that cut into the hillside. The canyon was completely choked with chaparral, pepper trees, and a stand of straggly oaks, but the stray moonlight breaking through the clouds showed him a trail of sorts that paralleled the fence.

The Hollywood Hills were too steep and crumbly to build any lasting structures on, but the never-say-die residents burned millions on imported bedrock and telescoping stilts for their castles in the sky, and they had armies of immigrant laborers come in regularly to chop out the coastal scrub brush and funky imported weeds that made the hills a perennial firetrap. All this meant that no matter how inaccessible the terrain, somebody had to trek in on foot to cut brush, and Lookout Mountain was no exception.

The fire trail rambled up the canyon until they could see no signs of civilization at all. A misplaced grove of pine trees hid the neighboring hills. The house was right above them.

Through the screens of pine needles, Rory saw someone standing on the lowest of three balconies that wrapped the back of the house. He smelled cigarette smoke, and heard a woman's brassy voice.

"Yeah, I'll keep an eye out for him. We figured he might try something like that."

The woman was naked, except for an assault rifle hanging on a sling between her huge silicon tits. "Uh-huh. If we see him, you'll be the first to know."

Rory froze and closed his eyes, willing himself invisible. Somehow, he knew they were talking about him.

He heard a sliding glass door open and shut overhead, and turned to find Stumbo hacking a hole in the fence with the bolt cutters.

"We'd better get in there soon, buddy," Stumbo grunted. He pushed his backpack in and stepped through the hole. "Your wife is being held by porn stars."

The brush was head-high inside the fence, and Stumbo vanished into it. Rory stepped through after him, holding the shotgun up to block thorny branches. He almost tripped over Stumbo, who grabbed his arm and flattened him against the rough stucco wall of the house.

Stumbo hissed, "She's in there. I can feel it."

"How the hell would you know something like that?"

"You know how much she hates me?"

No point in arguing. "Yeah."

Stumbo rubbed his temples. "She's *definitely* in there."

"How are we supposed to get inside without getting her killed?"

"Well, if you knew what you were doing, we could split up and pincer-sweep the house. But you're more likely to shoot me than them."

"Thanks, man—"

"There's no reset button here, right? So just stay behind me and aim that thing away from my head."

Stumbo crabbed sideways along the wall to where the foundation climbed up the hillside. Passing under a huge deck on stilts, they crawled around the fiberglass under-body and pipe network of a hot tub. The jets were running full blast, and the thumping beat of a huge sound system made the crawl space throb with monotonous gangster rap beats. The air was sour with a potent moldy reek that made his eyes water and his memory go berserk.

Stumbo slapped something against the exterior wall of the hot tub and belly-crawled through the rows of Italian cypresses enclosing the side yard.

Rory heard the laughter and catcalls of an ordinary party. Maybe richer, dumber, and a bit more douchey than the crowd at his party, but how was this different from what happened at his house? He almost called Stumbo back. Any minute, Trixie was going to call him, and he would go to her, and put all this behind him.

He reached out for Stumbo, who grabbed him and pushed him out of the bushes and into the face of some guy who looked like he might've been a male model, before his nose rotted off.

Rory stepped back and cracked a winning smile. "Hey, pal, hell of a party, right?"

White-threaded snot gushed out of the handsome fellow's nose hole. "It's all good, bro, but who invited y—"

Stumbo smashed the guy in the side of the head with the bolt cutters, kicked him in the gut and ribs as he flopped over, vomiting teeth.

Stumbo got a machine pistol out from under him and tucked it into his belt. Rory helped him lift the body over the fence and tossed it down the canyon.

The garage loomed ahead of them, the side door sitting open.

"Rory, is your old lady in the hot tub?"

What kind of question was that? "I didn't look. Why would she—"

"Make sure."

Rory snuck back down the hill to peek between the waxy boughs of the cypresses. A pair of bleach-blondes sat up to their chins in foamy suds, listlessly making out, while two guys gave another girl a massage as she lay facedown on the deck. A mountain of cocaine and a big pile of guns lay on the table.

All in all, a typical Thanksgiving celebration in the Hollywood Hills.

The girl on the deck lifted herself up and looked around. The shape of the body was all wrong, but he could almost swear that it was Vanessa.

It couldn't be. Last he saw her, she got T-boned by a cop. He was shocked to find her alive, but if she was here, then his missing friends might also be here, and Trixie—

Rory turned and whispered, "No, she's not—"

The hot tub exploded. Foam shot twenty feet into the air. Vanessa flew out of the tub, howling. The other two vanished as the water swirled and dumped out the hole in the tub. The rest of the pool party leaped to their feet and grabbed guns, but they were shooting down into the canyon.

"Come on," Stumbo shouted and ducked into the garage. Immediately, Rory heard shooting.

"Rory! Get in here!"

Before he could think about it, Rory followed his friend.

Stumbo hunkered down behind a black Lamborghini with its windshield shot out. Stumbo emptied the machine pistol over his shoulder at the open door to the kitchen.

The noise and stench of gunpowder in the enclosed space was overpowering. Rory dropped to his knees and crawled up to the car.

A muscular guy in a Stars and Stripes Speedo thong jumped out from cover and fired a chunky pistol at them. "Hey, Rory," he screamed, "say hi to your old lady for me!"

Rory jerked back and fired the shotgun.

The stock hit his shoulder wrong, almost pulling it out of its socket, threw him against a metal utility shelf piled with trash bags, batteries, flats of bottled water. A big halo of destruction punched out the wall behind the buff guy and took a bite out of his waxed, rippling chest. With a wild war whoop that came more out of the hole in his torso than his mouth, the guy leaped onto the Lamborghini and took aim at Stumbo.

Rory brought up the shotgun and blew the guy in half.

"Clear?" Stumbo yelled.

Rory just looked at him. He had blood and chips of atomized bone stuck to his face. "They know me."

"Y'know what I never could get my head around?" Stumbo kicked the severed pelvis and muscular, shaved, and tanned legs. "How is burning a flag desecration, but wearing one as a fucking banana hammock is okay?"

"They're going to kill her," Rory said. Panic sent him running for the door.

"Wait!" Stumbo shouted. He threw something over Rory's head through the doorway and turned away to shield his eyes. Rory jumped back as he saw four guys and two girls in the kitchen, all armed for bear and waiting for them.

Bullets and angry swarms of shotgun pellets disintegrated the doorway. Rory hit the floor and rolled over debris, dropping the shotgun to cover his head.

Stumbo shouted, "Don't look at it!"

"Don't look at *what?*"

Stumbo's grenade went off in the dining room. The sharp sound of a huge slamming door followed a flash so bright it burned through Rory's eyelids as he pressed his face to the travertine marble floor.

The gunfire went crazy, blindly stitching up walls and smashing windows. Stumbo came bounding in from the garage and jumped over Rory with a nine-millimeter automatic in his right hand and a pipe bomb clutched in the steel robot grip of his left.

The big gun barked twice in his hand as he shot down two guys who looked like they could still see. The others rubbed their eyes and mewled incoherently as they fired at anything that made noise.

Stumbo walked around the room executing them, while Rory grabbed his shotgun and ran for the stairs.

Every room was on its own floor, disco strobes and intelli-beams burning his retinas, walk-through fireplaces and hot tubs in every room, and naked or near-naked bodies piled up everywhere like kindling.

They didn't look so much dead or asleep as simply empty: factory-fresh, surgically perfected porno extras, but some of them were missing arms or legs, neatly severed as if canni-balized for parts. Their faces were caked with white crust, and here and there bullet and knife wounds were packed with powder. Maybe the coke killed them before the other thing could take root and grow out of them.

Feebly, they reached for Rory, but he kicked them away as he ran from room to room, shouting, "Trixie!"

"I'm right here, baby," said a woman's voice.

He stepped into a hall and ran face-first into a huge fist. Rocked back off his feet, he tripped over a naked dead woman and sprawled across a futon.

Vanessa rolled into the room, naked and dripping. Rory's vision was still blurred, but something was wrong with her walk. Her left leg was corded with thick muscle and four inches longer—and three shades darker—than her right. The seam joining the leg to her hip was a clumsy hack job stitched together by dense white threads and cables. Same with her right arm, which swung like a wrecking ball to pulverize drywall as she stormed in and threw herself on top of him.

"Remember me, baby?" she crowed, and punched him in the balls with her oversize bodybuilder arm. Ripping the shotgun out of his hands, she turned it on him and shoved the barrel into his mouth.

Shaking with high, girlish giggles, Vanessa planted a massive man's foot on his neck and squeezed. She spoke in a voice three octaves lower than her own. "Why are you making this so hard, little man? Why do you sabotage every-thing I ever do to try to help you?"

Rory was fading fast. He could barely see Vanessa's

unhinged grin through the black stars and white snow-drifts filling his vision. He was dying. Maybe that's why he thought he heard his brother's voice coming out of her mouth. *"Richie—"*

"Would you really rather be dead, than be happy for the rest of your life? Really, truly alive?"

Rory tried to answer, but he couldn't move or breathe.

Thunder crashed and his head filled with pain. He curled up into a ball. Vanessa bounced off him and spastically beat her lopsided limbs on the floor. Thunder crashed again and again until she lay still.

Stumbo kicked him in the side. "Get up, dude, you're freaking me out."

Rory sat up. His ski mask was coated in white dust, so he pulled it off and shook it out.

Stumbo stood over Vanessa, reloading his automatic one-handed. "Whoa," he moaned, "head rush." He leaned against the wall. When he slid off it to head for the hall, he left a bloody smear.

"Stumbo, you're hit—"

"Fuck it. Are you still cool?"

Rory looked up to find the huge Cyclops eye of Stumbo's gun pointed at his face. "Don't fuck with me. Where's the rest of them?"

"They're holing up in the master bedroom. Come on."

Stumbling into the hall, Stumbo shot at the closed door at the end, then dodged to the side when an answering salvo destroyed the door and popped the bare bulb hallway light.

Rory almost followed Stumbo, but then grabbed his shotgun and went out the sliding glass door onto the deck. The huge picture window on the master bedroom was masked with black garbage bags, but he heard a familiar woman's voice screaming inside, and kicked in the glass.

He dove through the window and rolled up against a massive water bed just as Stumbo came in through the door.

Garbage bags covered the walls and the room was lit only with huge black lights, which made everything white glow as if radioactive. A crew of human scarecrows in surgical gowns and gas masks grabbed guns and turned to aim at his friend.

His view was blocked by a luminous white tree growing out of the water bed, reaching up to the ceiling.

Rory shot a masked naked guy who came at him with a scalpel. His arm flew off and sprayed bloody white curds at the ceiling.

Stumbo got tackled by three of them, but shot his way out, screaming, "Die, motherfucker, die!" until only the thumping bass beat from out back filled the silence.

Huge tanks filled with chemicals and drying racks laden with mounds of powder lined the walls. Digital scales and shelves with bags of glowing white powder were stacked to the ceiling.

Rory looked at the tangled orgy of bodies at the foot of the tree on the water bed, little more than withered limbs slathered in white slime, twitching and reaching for him. He hoped to God none of them was Trixie, but he couldn't tell.

"Dude," Stumbo growled, "I don't think your princess is in this castle." He approached the mound of bodies on the bed. "Fuck me, you weren't kidding, were you?"

It was not really a pile at all, for the bodies had grown together, fused by tubes and tendrils of white fiber and bulbous knobs of pulpy flesh brimming with white dust. The gnarled, pale tree stretched up to cling to the ceiling, and high above their heads, it bore a bumper crop of peculiar fruit.

Dozens of human heads dangled over them, drooling white slime and mouthing mute murmurs of ecstasy. Many of them were burst open and sprouting furry white horns that sprinkled powder like pollen onto the bed and the floor.

"What the fuck are we looking at here, Rory?"

"Trixie's not here," Rory said, in a flat, dead voice that was as close as he'd ever gotten to a prayer.

"She's not here, dude. Snap out of it."

"It's some kind of fucked-up life cycle," Rory said. "This shit comes out of them, and they harvest it, cut it with coke, and push it on the street. The people who inhale it get taken over, and start to produce more of it . . ."

"*Roooorrrryy*," the heads said. He made himself study their faces. None of them was Trixie, thank God. He stopped looking after he recognized Stan and Fran among them.

"I knew it," Stumbo snarled. "I always fucking *knew* it was something like this."

"We gotta get out of here," Rory said. "I need to find my wife."

Stumbo kicked over a tub of something highly flammable and rummaged in his bag for another pipe bomb. "Fine, let's frag 'em and go."

Stumbo lit a cigarette, then touched his thumb-tip lighter to the pipe bomb's ten-second fuse. "Back out through the garage, dude. Go now."

The mass of broken bodies on the bed stirred and tried to reach out for him. Rory jumped back and took aim with the shotgun, but four hands came up out of the tangle holding pistols. He shouted, "Stumbo! Get down!"

Stumbo took two shots to the body. One ricocheted off his prosthetic arm, struck a spray of sparks that set the floor alight. He cocked his prosthetic arm to lob the pipe bomb, but his grip wouldn't release. "Shit! Not again . . . You got a flathead screwdriver?"

Rory looked at his friend standing waist-deep in fire, and without a second thought, he waded into the blaze with his arms out.

"Throw it!"

"I can't!"

Rory reached for the bomb.

"Pull the fuse!"

"It'll kill us both! Just get out!"

Stumbo shoved him away. The fuse disappeared into the pipe.

Rory dove through the smashed window and hit the deck just as the pipe bomb went off in Stumbo's hand.

The concussion hurled Rory over the balcony railing. Spinning head over heels through the sky, he hit the triple canopy of pine branches and landed on his ass sliding backward down the canyon.

Pain jarred him back to awareness, but he still couldn't cover his head, let alone arrest his fall. Above him, the monstrous flaming tree of fungi and stolen flesh shrieked as it tumbled out of the burning house and came tumbling after him.

Rory rolled and fell until a sizable pepper tree stopped him cold. Scraps of burning debris rained down into the canyon all around him. The rustling black brush came alive with dancing orange phantoms, and somewhere behind him, the frying, dying collage of broken bodies thrashed in the canyon, wailing his name.

The first breath he could whoop into his lungs seared his throat with burning ash. Coughing, choking, he found his feet and crawled, then ran back down the canyon to the road. The fire raced at his heels, devouring the dry brush under his feet as quickly as he could put it behind him. When he finally spilled out onto Lookout Mountain Road, the fire had rallied into a raging wall that stopped begrudgingly at the edge of the pavement, then turned back up the canyon like a wild beast.

He got into Stumbo's van and dug the emergency key out of its magnetic holder in the torn headliner over the driver's seat. The engine caught right away and Rory took off down the hill.

His friend Jonah Stumbo was dead. His brother was part

of a monster, and might have taken Trixie down with him. And in his haste to slay the new monster, he had turned the oldest and worst monster of them all loose in the Hollywood Hills.

All things considered, Rory had never had less to be thankful for.

Twenty-three

Stumbo's van was not built for speed or invisibility, but Rory drove as fast as he dared back down Laurel Canyon. A fat Hispanic guy jumped out into the road and tried to flag him down, but Rory swerved around him, sending piles of heavy, expensive equipment sliding across the back of the van, before he realized the guy was a cop.

He kept driving, headed south with his phone in his hand, trying to think of whom he should call now, trying not to cry.

Maybe it was time to call the cops. There was nothing he could do, but make it worse. Maybe he'd call the cops from Ensenada. His thumb twitched on his contacts list. Manuel left early and had a good head on his shoulders. He wouldn't mess with the white shit. He had friends on both sides of the law. Euclid had friends at USC and the museums. He could figure out what the hell was going on, and make somebody in charge of the city take notice.

But everybody he called tonight seemed to get killed, or worse.

Where was he going right now? He had to get back to his own car, ditch Stumbo's van loaded with explosives and spy shit, and then find Trixie. He drummed the steering wheel with his fist, then lost it and hammered the dashboard. The cracked vinyl gave way and the stereo fell out into his lap.

She was out there, in trouble. Maybe she was already

one of them. Whatever they were. If she was taken over, would he be able to save her? Maybe, if she was one, then he already had no choice . . .

He turned onto Sunset as his phone rang. It was an unfamiliar number with a Westside area code. A cold, needling sensation ran up his arm from the phone.

He knew exactly what it would say.

Stop running.

We have your wife.

We have your brother.

Everything you thought you had is ours.

Pull over and wait for the next available mushroom head to come and fix you.

He almost didn't answer. He almost threw the phone out the window. If they had everything and everyone that mattered to him, then they had nothing to say that he wanted to hear.

But they might let him speak to her, for just a minute. She might not be one of them. She couldn't be, not Trixie. Never.

"Where is she, Richie?"

"*Oh, Rory, thank God!*"

"Trixie?"

"*YES! Where are you?*"

"Fuck that! Where are YOU?"

" *'Fuck that' my ass! I'm down here waiting for you, Goofy, right where I'm supposed to be! I've been here almost twenty minutes! Where the fuck are you?*"

"I—" He started to laugh, but it turned straight to tears. He could barely contain his relief, much less control his voice. "I—"

"*Oh, baby, are you crying?*" And the sheer compassion in her voice utterly slew him. No way you could fake that.

"I thought that they had you—"

"*Oh, no, no, no. I'm sorry. Didn't I tell you I had to ditch out?*"

He told her what the baby said, and her instant response was, *"That little son of a whore. I nearly put it through the windshield, and now I totally wish I had.*

"Rory, no. *I hot-wired this bitchin' '64 Ford Falcon, about six blocks away, and made it straight down with barely a hitch."*

"Why the hell didn't you call me?"

"I was dying to, sweetie, believe me. But the car didn't come with a phone. And I thought about stopping to steal one, but the road was pretty clear, and it just seemed like asking for trouble."

"Okay. I understand—"

"I spent the last fifteen minutes trying to find a pay phone that actually still works in this fucking dump."

"But you did."

"Yeah, I did. Soooo . . . are you coming, or what?"

"Just let me switch out my wheels, and there's not a thing in heaven or earth can stop me."

The phone clicked. *"You hear that?"* she said.

"Yeah."

"Unless they're tapping all the pay phones now, that means my $1.75 is almost up. Thank God the ashtray was full of change, or I'd still be wondering where you were. Not that you ever actually told me or anything."

"Beautiful, I am on my way," he said. "And I love you. You said the road was clear?"

"Last time I ch—"

"PLEASE DEPOSIT SEVENTY-FIVE CENTS FOR THE NEXT FIVE MINUTES," said the robot from Pacific Bell, or whoever was running the phone lines now.

"Save your change," he said, kissing the receiver.

And the last thing he heard was her kissing it back.

Twenty-four

Rory parked Stumbo's van in his garage, packed a bag with two pistols, the shotgun and some extra ammunition, and sealed it up. Jonah had no family and no other friends that Rory knew of. The place might go unopened until the day the building was condemned. *I owed you a hell of a lot more than this*, he thought as he ran to his car and peeled out heading south on Highland.

He had a bad feeling about the 10. When he passed it about two hours ago, it was a parking lot, and he flashed on that guy who jumped off the bridge as he passed under it. It was half past four in the morning, but the empty streets seemed charged with potential; the houses he passed, too many of them, had their lights on and doors standing open, as if they'd all evacuated to go to a hell of a block party.

He turned on Olympic and floored it headed west. He passed a police car parked on the curb at the corner of Mansfield, lights turning, but no one in sight. At San Vicente, where all the streets twisted south or north to bend around Beverly Hills and Century City, he passed a roadblock, with five BHPD squad cars straddling the six-lane avenue. A gang of cops with Tasers and clubs stood around a twitching kid like judges at a dance contest.

As Rory passed, he chanced a sidelong glance, just enough to feel like shit for driving by. The kid couldn't be older than ten. The woman who looked to be cheering them on might've been his mother.

He needed to hear Trixie's voice again, but he didn't dare run down the phone, which showed only a sliver of battery power left. He popped in a Johnny Cash disk, then ejected it. Whatever he listened to now would be tainted forever with the memory of this night. The radio stations all ran preprogrammed music and canned talk shows, like broadcasts from a parallel universe.

He ran every red light going through Century City, only feeling safe once he'd passed into West L.A. Which was stupid, because the street only got worse.

He turned south on Overland and sped around a couple of fender benders that clotted up the Pico intersection. People came running out of the bushes as he slowed to go around the lip-locked Lexus and Honda, like they wanted to wash his windows, but one was a Denny's waitress, and the other wore a spotless white tracksuit and gold chains. They waved shopping bags at him and left contrails of white dust in their wake. Rory blew by them and floored it to the freeway on-ramp.

The 10-405 junction was flowing smoothly, but traffic was surprisingly heavy for the hour. Maybe the deliveries to the Westside met some kind of resistance. Maybe Santa Monica just said no.

That was almost funny enough to laugh at. He decided to call Trixie, make sure she was all right.

The phone rang in his hand. He didn't recognize the number, but he took the call.

"Hey, Rory," a girl giggled. "*Where's the fire, big boy?*"

"Who the hell is this?"

"*Maybe you should hang up and watch the road, partner.*"

He looked around and saw a cute but skinny teen girl in the passenger seat of a lifted monster truck. Her head was cocked to hold her phone, and she waved at him just as the truck smashed into his car.

Rory whipped sideways in his bucket seat, choking on his seat belt. The Challenger swung wildly across two lanes, caroming off the side of a Miller Lite delivery truck. He fought the wheel to straighten out before the truck swung out of the car-pool lane to hit him again.

It was a lifted Toyota with gigantic dump-truck tires and Bionic-Tonic energy drink stickers all over it. The skinny girl hung out her window in a red tube top, waving at Rory like she thought he was a celebrity.

The driver was too short to see over the wheel, but he knew what he was doing. The monster truck closed in and swerved into Rory's front driver's-side wheel, then dropped back, skating against the Challenger's door panels. The maneuver would have spun Rory side-on into the Range Rover's chrome ram bars, and shoved him off the road in a bloody, burning wreck.

Rory slammed on the brakes and dropped behind the Range Rover just as it lunged into his lane. The Range Rover ground off the Dodge's front panel and went into an uncontrolled power slide. The girl ripped her tube top off and flashed her tits as they passed in front of him to collide with the Miller Lite truck.

Rory veered left and cleared the Range Rover, but he hit the concrete barrier a glancing blow at sixty miles an hour. His rearview mirror and door handle were wrenched off, but he was finally able to get control of the car and pushed it up to ninety in the car-pool lane.

Culver City flew by, and the LAX off-ramps passed without incident, but as Rory climbed through the traffic, bobbing and weaving across three lanes to claim any opening, he thought he saw someone smiling at him in every car, as they chattered into their headsets.

His phone rang again. He tried to ignore it, but it might be Trixie.

"Baby—"

"*Don't 'baby' me, asshole, I know what you did!*"

It must've been the car coming around the bend ahead,

headed the wrong way in his lane, flashing its brights on and off.

At his present speed, plus that of the car growing in his windshield view, he'd be disintegrated. Slamming on the brakes would throw the heavy front end of his car into the wall, and the fast lane was taken up by a pickup towing a speedboat.

Rory hit the brakes hard, then let off and ducked right. His fender clipped the boat trailer hard enough to throw the sleek fiberglass sled with its twin outboard motors skidding into the car-pool lane. The driver of the pickup, no doubt puzzled by the oncoming car, hit his brakes, too, but the wrong-way car swerved into his lane, doggedly tracking Rory as he hurtled almost sideways across the freeway, and smashed head-on into the pickup's grill.

The Challenger swerved and bucked under Rory's shaking hands, but straightened out again. No more white lights shone on his side of the freeway, but the northbound traffic was bunching up as sleepy drivers slowed down to look at the speedboat in the road.

He only had one headlight and his radiator was cracked. The car was good for maybe another mile. It should be enough to reach Trixie.

Less than a half mile ahead, four cars driving in a lock-step flying wing across all four lanes suddenly turned sideways and skidded to a halt, blocking the whole southbound 405.

About ten cars and trucks traveled ahead of Rory's Dodge but behind the barricade. One was a car carrier with two tiers of Cadillacs, less than two car lengths from the kamikaze cars when they crashed. The cab punched through the station wagon and chemical supply truck in the slow lanes, but the trailer overturned, luxury sedans tumbling off the racks and dragging the semi onto two wheels before it came unhitched.

Rory braked to a stop less than a hundred yards from the wreck. Another fifty or so cars filled in behind him. The southbound 405 was totally blocked up in at least three places from the wrecks they had caused, with his help.

Was this really about him? Or were they just closing off the city to make it easier to take over?

Two cars on the northbound side kissed off each other and blocked up the inside lanes of the oncoming traffic. The whole 405 was a parking lot, and they probably were doing it all the way to Orange County.

He was a quarter mile from the Carson exit—from Trixie—with God-only-knew how many people between them who wanted them both dead.

Honking and screaming, he cut off the white Mercedes (whose vanity license plate said—swear to God—CNTFACE) next to him. There was nowhere to go, and the mean old lady in the Mercedes told him this, but he rammed her aside and forced the Challenger through the gridlock and onto the right shoulder.

Two people jumped into the gap between the wreck and the concrete wall on the right shoulder. Rory leaned on his horn, and when they didn't get out of his way, he hit them. They didn't panic, they didn't jump out of the way. They looked right at him, with their cell phones to their ears. On the floorboards, his phone rang as he flattened them.

They weren't there to stop him. They just wanted him to run them down so he wouldn't see the semi cab lying on its side, blocking the shoulder just beyond the wreck.

Rory hit the brakes, but there was no room to stop, and nowhere to go. He smashed into the roof of the semi cab at a stiff forty. His knee jammed into the dash hard enough to break the ashtray, and the seat belt gave him whiplash. But he was still lucid when the car stopped sliding on two wheels against the concrete retaining wall.

He heard people screaming. Screaming his name.

He grabbed the knapsack and one of Stumbo's guns and climbed out the window.

People were running toward him. He fired a couple rounds over their heads, saw that it was hopeless for him down there, and jumped instead at the top of the wall. The edge hit him hard in the gut, crushing the wind out of him, but the gnashing teeth and pounding feet of the crowd below him pushed aside fear and even the need to breathe. Hanging on its summit, he threw a leg over, then rolled after it.

It was a hard fall, down the steep embankment; and by the time he stopped rolling, he wasn't sure if he could stand.

But he still had the bag, and he still had the gun.

He got to his feet, amazing himself as he painfully began to run.

TWENTY-FIVE

The crashes had been audible for what seemed like miles, as distant, troubling echoes; but the closer they got, and the more they escalated, the deeper her terror grew.

The last massive salvo of wreckage had been almost fifteen minutes ago, according to the clock in the locked front office of Speed Demons Go-Kart World. A blinking digital sign in the window blinked GET YOUR WHITE LINE FEVER PASS NOW!!! with no sense of irony. She'd been passing it every couple minutes ever since she got off the phone with Rory, as she had no watch or phone of her own, and pay phones didn't tell time.

There was no such thing as silence this close to the 405; but where she'd almost been lulled by the steady flow of traffic before, now there was only the dull thrum of a thousand idling engines, the contagious choruses of honking horns, the occasional scream.

And woven throughout it all, that terrible, jubilant laughter.

It had never occurred to Trixie that laughter so wholehearted and pure could make her flesh crawl like this. It wasn't mean laughter. It wasn't a bully's conquering crow. And it wasn't the harsh, nervous cackle born of fear.

This was a luxuriant, full-bodied expression of *ecstasy*: a giddy, drug-fueled merriment completely at home with its intimate marriage to mayhem and violence and death.

It was the kind of laughter she imagined at a Manson

family picnic, circa Tate and LaBianca. Utterly mad, and entirely sincere.

Echoing down on her, over and over.

Trixie was alone inside two acres of black-and-white race-car-flag-looking fence, surrounded by empty figure-eight racetracks built to the scale of the dozens of zippy go-carts parked along their lengths.

If Rory hadn't shown her how to sneak in after closing, all those many years ago, she'd have been left waiting on the street, hiding behind a skinny tree.

But this was the site of their very first date, and therefore imprinted on her memory banks forever.

They had fallen in love by fender-bending miniature hot rods into each other, at a whopping fifteen to twenty miles per hour. They hadn't even kissed yet, but after that, fucking came about as natural as air.

She'd thought it was just another one of her breakaway-from-the-past adventures, a Los Angeles rite of passage. She'd thought she was just sowing her oats, proving to herself that she could actually be the total badass she'd always hoped she was, and not just another shy pretty girl who bobbed her head and did as she was told.

Maybe it was the colliding metal, and the fact that neither of them could stop laughing. Maybe it was the fact that he took as well as he gave, careening away when she rocked him solid, and then veering in to chase her tail until the next inevitable collision.

And did she slow down to let him hit it if he fell too far behind? Of course she did. She didn't want to get away. She just wanted to play with him all night long.

One half an hour of vehicular foreplay later, they reconvened in his '68 Camaro, and backseat sex had never been so good.

Halfway through his second orgasm, he had murmured, "God, I love this."

She had taken *this* to mean *you*.

And she had been correct in that assumption.

There was, of course, some adjusting to be done. Getting him off the fucking blow, for starters. But mostly weaning him off his rage, of which the speed was less a cause than a symptom.

But was he worth it? Yes, he was. Because of a thousand things that she could itemize at will. His heart ran deep, moving much more than just blood. It was kind and tough and seasoned. He was smart enough to nail her flaws, and wise enough to wonder what he'd missed, all the while never losing track of her strengths and assets, and what a catch she was.

Many men had tried to sweep her up before. And more than a couple had succeeded. At least for a while. College students. College professors. Cute guys within casual cruising distance of her college dorms.

So why did she pick this guy?

Because he loved her.

And because she loved him back.

And because she felt, down to her marrow, that he was the guy that *got her*, just as she got him. A cellular understanding. Profound and mutual.

So where in the name of God was he?

"Don't leave me standing here," she said, as much to herself as to him.

And suddenly, there he was, stumbling out of the shadows toward her from the far end of the lot.

He wasn't walking like himself. That was the first thing she noticed, and it filled her with dread. He was still trying to manage his usual, cocky walk, but there was a wobbliness to it that was not at all like Rory drunk (a thing she had seen hundreds of times in the older, rougher days).

There was a bit of a zomboid shamble to it that she *did* recognize, from goofier times; and were she not so utterly traumatized, she might have thought it was funny.

But it wasn't; and as she moved toward him, she found

herself preparing for the worst, feeling the short hairs on her arms waft up like cilia designed to sense danger.

But the moment he saw her, a relief blew through him that almost sent him to his knees; and when she saw it, she started to run, that same relief blowing through her as well.

By the time he fell, she was almost on him.

"I made it," he said, and started laughing.

Coming from him—not them—it was the sweetest sound in the world.

After she did him—and there was *no way* she wasn't going to do him, on top, and to hell with their injuries—it was time to talk, snuggled in close on the big backseat of the Falcon. Rapt in momentary calm. Staring up at the starless predawn sky.

They filled each other in on what they'd missed, pausing periodically to stare into space and cry, trying to grasp the enormity of it, and laughing as much as they could. If there was one obvious bonding element in their love and perseverance, it was gallows humor. But it all sputtered to a halt, and a long, exhausted silence stretched out before them.

"So," she said, finally breaking the ice. "What do you think we should do now?"

"I don't know. We could run."

"Where?"

"Almost anywhere."

"And then what?"

"I don't know."

"That's what I'm gettin' at," she said. "Everything we have, and everything we do, and everyone we care about is back there."

He sighed. "I know."

"We already know that we can fight them."

"Baby? I don't know how much fight I've got left. I am beat to barely living shit."

"Can you drive?"

"If I have to."

"And I can fight."

"I know you can." Kissing her. "And I do have a couple of guns."

"God bless you. And God bless poor Stumbo . . ."

"He was amazing." Rory choked up for a second. "I mean, I know you, uh, weren't his biggest fan, but you should have seen him . . ."

"I know, baby. I know." She took his chin and steered his eyes back down to hers. "He did what he did for his own stupid, crazy Stumbo reasons, but he saved you. I don't know if he's off God's shit list, but I'm just grateful you came back."

He nodded gravely, not entirely convinced.

She disentangled her legs from his and sat up. The parking lot was empty, but she could still hear the horns and howling laughter on the wind. "I guess the question is: Do we land somewhere as homeless refugees, and start at the bottom, like all the poor bastards displaced by Katrina, without a hope in hell? Or do we fight for what is ours, and help the people who are still there hang on to what *they've* got, and maybe turn this thing around?"

"Sounds like you've already made up your mind."

"Not without you." Rubbing her nose against his. "If it's a choice between running with you or going home alone—"

A frown creased his weary face, but she knew what it meant. "You're not going anywhere without me."

"Okay." She smiled. "So where are we going?"

"Home," he said.

"But the traffic—"

He stopped her objection with a kiss.

And told her his plan.

Twenty-six

Up until they actually left the parking lot, it still seemed like a hell of a good idea.

Rory checked Trixie's gas one more time, then jumped in his cart and hit the gas. The Euro racer's 150cc engine whirred like a kid's toy, but by the time he passed the RV lot, he was pegged at fifty. And Trixie passed him.

A line of cars waited at the northbound 405 on-ramp. The traffic light cycled green, then red, but there was nowhere to go, so the cars were all turned off, flashers blinking.

"*Slow down!*" he screamed.

Trixie waved and disappeared into the slot between the line of cars and the concrete wall that shrank to a curb where the on-ramp bled into the gridlocked freeway. Rory followed her up the ramp. He knew the width of the flying cart was just shy of the wall and the parked cars, but his guts still dropped into the seat of his pants as he made himself speed up to catch Trixie, who flew up the narrow chute and dropped out of sight with a hearty, "Holy shit!"

A livid red river of angry brake lights flowed on over the smoggy northern horizon. For a split second, he marveled at the size and wasted power of it, all these vehicles going nowhere, like a clogged artery flooded with steel and plastic, and then Rory dropped into the pocket between the merging on-ramp lane and the slow lane, and all he could see were the towering cars rushing by on either side, and the narrow track ahead marked by a dotted white line.

At first, it was just like driving the carts on the track, just with less wiggle room. The stationary rows of cars were just a road hazard, but the big sport tires on the Euro racer squealed against the passing cars when he erred to any degree in his steering. Horns honked in their wake, though whether angrily or in support of their ingenuity, he couldn't tell. They had only one note with which to express everything that they experienced.

It reminded him of the brittle, insane laughter of dustheads, a moment before one crashed into his back end.

The whine of his engine was drowned out in a throaty roar that became a high-treble howl as the motorcycle popped a wheelie and crashed down on the cheap fiberglass spoiler that was the only protection for his rear engine.

He'd been doing a sensible thirty, but he floored it now. The cars looming all around him became blurred walls of factory colors. He screamed for Trixie, but she raced on ahead. The windows of cars on her right flank burst as she passed. Someone was shooting at her.

He looked in his rearview. The bike on his tail was too close to see, but more cycle headlights were growing larger as he watched.

Reaching into his waistband for the gun, he thought of the people in their cars all around him. But none of them was his wife.

Chancing a quick head-check over his shoulder, he caught a glimpse of the motorcyclist trying to wreck him. The asshole wore one of those spiky plastic Mohawks on his helmet. The visor was a copper-tinted mirror. His leathers matched the orange and black custom paint job on the teardrop-shaped torpedo he and his friends called "organ-donor cycles."

A passenger rode pillion on the asshole's back. Matching leathers and a pink plastic Mohawk on her helmet marked her as more than just a casual passenger. She stood on the pegs of the bike, then leaped up to crouch on the seat with her gloved hands braced on her boyfriend's shoulders, poised to do something totally awesome she saw on TV once.

Rory took out the gun and fired twice over his shoulder. He aimed for where he remembered the bike being. He didn't look back, but he hit something. The bike squealed and turned to bounce off the billboard walls of an RTD bus.

Something hit Rory's cart hard enough to send him lurching into a gap between two cars, pumping his brakes and swerving to avoid clipping the back of a stalled Smart car almost as tiny as his go-cart.

Two more motorcycles jumped their buddy's wreckage and came after him, shooting wildly.

Rory stood on the gas, but he was dragging something.

The girlfriend clung to his roll cage. She crawled up to look down on Rory. Quite a looker she was, too, if not for the white strings growing out of her nostrils and tear ducts.

Smiling, she flipped up her visor, cleared her throat, and hawked a lunger in Rory's face.

He wiped it away and looked for Trixie, who was suddenly gone. Just like his path between the lanes was gone, in about ten car lengths. *Nine—eight—*

Rory hit the brakes and screamed, "Trixie!"

Bullets zinged off the cars on either side of him. Horns honked, drivers screamed, but the lane to his right merged into the lane to his left, and he saw no sign of Trixie.

A big flatbed semi blocked the trench ahead, and two minivans honked and swore at each other as they jockeyed to cut in ahead of it. Something exploded at his back. His engine was hit and spraying smoke.

His hitchhiker spit on him again. Almost got it in his mouth.

He stepped on the gas, fully intent on crashing into the minivan just to spite the fuckers, when he realized where Trixie went, and followed her.

Jerking the wheel hard left as he came alongside the semi, he ducked under the flatbed trailer just ahead of the rear axle. The hanging toolboxes on the flatbed smashed the cycle chick in the head and wiped her off the cart.

The roll cage scraped the drive shaft, dumping sparks on Rory's head. He shot out from under the trailer and juked right just as a motorcycle tried to follow him. Laying the bike down like a pro, the cyclist barely clipped his head on the trailer, lost control, and slid into the wheels just ahead of his bike.

Trixie was almost a quarter mile ahead, but her taillights lit up. No doubt she saw the smoke.

He floored it, but the cart was losing speed. Before it could sputter to a stop, he jumped out and ran after Trixie.

A salvo of gunfire passed over him like a wave. He dove in a blizzard of shattered glass, crawling between the cars, screaming Trixie's name. Someone reached out of a car and grabbed a handful of his hair, yanked him against the door. He smashed the hand with his gun, then shot the owner of the hand without looking at them, and ran away.

The Euro carts had brakes, but no reverse. Rory ran until his sides were splitting. Even seeing her getting closer, he might have fallen down just then if not for the last motorcycle.

Rory heard him coming and dropped to his knees. The 400cc engine climbed in pitch as the rider closed in, hellbent on running Rory down. Rory shot the rider twice in the chest, punching him off the bike. He threw himself across the hood of a pickup truck as the bike tumbled past.

"*Get the fuck off my truck!* You motherfucking hoodlum—"

Rory slid back to the pavement and caught his breath. Through the horns and the shouting and the angry sounds of traffic-jammed motorists climbing out of their cars, Rory heard Trixie screaming.

Rory pointed the gun at the trucker and growled, "Get back in your fucking truck."

"Y—you're not the boss of me," the guy peevishly mumbled, but he obeyed.

Rory turned and went after the crashed motorcycle, righted it, and started it up.

Trixie was running toward him up the dotted white line, pursued by a howling mob.

"RORY!" She ducked something they threw at her. "FUCK!" A car door opened and someone started to climb out to get her, but Trixie kicked the door shut on the guy's ankle and kept running.

Rory gunned the throttle and raced at her like he meant to run her down, but as he drew up to her, he stood on the pegs and peeled out to bring the seat against her hip.

"I crashed," she gasped. "I don't think they're infected, but . . ." Pausing for breath, she finished, "They're definitely dicks."

She hopped on and wrapped herself around Rory as he pulled back on the throttle and rushed at the angry mob. Like high grass before a Weed Eater, they parted and flattened against the walls of cars to let Rory ride past.

"We gotta get off the freeway!" he shouted at her.

"Avalon's a half mile up—" she offered, but he cut between two cars and raced up the shoulder until he came to the bridge overlooking the Dominguez Channel.

Like every river in Los Angeles County, it was only a storm drain with a narrow stream of not-water flowing down it, but the rocky banks of the channel had been built to withstand a mighty flood. A dirt jogging trail ran alongside the channel.

"Hang on, baby," Rory shouted. He charged the guardrail and hauled back on the bars until the bike reared up under them. Trixie yelped and squeezed Rory with her thighs. Catching lift off the shallow curb, the bike leaped off the pavement and barely cleared the low guardrail to land on the jogging trail. Someone shot at them, but nobody followed them off the freeway.

Trixie clung to Rory even harder, now they were out of immediate danger. She pressed her face into his neck and breathed in the scent of him, rushing into her face on the stinking exhaust-breath of the city.

The Dominguez Channel turned away from the freeway to meander through mazes of warehouse stores and car lots. The red-gray sky seemed to sizzle with moisture that could never quite turn to rain, and then they were filled with a familiar shape that suddenly seemed strange and threatening in their adrenaline-drugged state.

Hanging low in the sky, an elliptical silver balloon two hundred feet long floated over a field of trimmed grass and an airstrip at which a line of trucks were parked.

"You want to change into something more comfortable?" he asked her.

She tried laughing. It came out high and frantic, but felt good. "No way are we stealing the Goodyear blimp."

The silver dirigible hovered almost directly overhead. Rory looked at it for a long moment, slowing to consider the idea she'd put in his head.

When they were kids, Rory dreamed of riding in the Goodyear blimp. His dad told him everybody got to, eventually; just a couple folks at a time, so it could take a while, but someday, everybody gets to ride over a baseball game in the blimp and look down on the event as God must see it, assuming he enjoyed watching the Dodgers get their asses handed to them every play-off season.

Richie must've remembered it, too, because he had this idea about using blimps as limos. Rich people who would pay through the nose got to fly over the city in a big, showy balloon that everybody stuck in traffic would slow down to marvel at.

"I meant a truck."

She hugged him even tighter. "This is fine. Just get us out of here."

He slowed to a stop and planted his boot on the edge of the road outside the Goodyear blimp airfield. The road forked to a frontage road heading south, and an on-ramp for the northbound 405.

"North?"

She sat back and let her arms relax. Her hands were shaking so bad, she could fall off the bike.

"Hell, yes. North."

And away they went.

Twenty-seven

They rolled north up Main as fast as they dared. Rory didn't like the idea of driving back through Watts any more than he liked the freeways, but no one seemed to take notice of them. In a city of some ten million people, not everyone could be infected already. The ones who were all seemed to know his name, though.

Whatever was going on, Richie was at the heart of it. The streets they rode felt like the jaws of a trap, and by going back, they were taking the bait. Begging the trap to snap shut on their necks.

Main turned to Woodlawn and banked east to feed into the vast cobweb of avenues surrounding downtown. Rory pulled off at an Arco station and parked behind the tanks to fuel up. With one hand in his jacket, he cased the place. The clerk, a Sikh with a long black beard and burgundy turban, sat in a booth behind bulletproof glass. The glass was smeared with gobs of green and white slime, drying to a flaky crust as it dripped on the candy bars.

The mouth of a sawed-off shotgun jabbed out the speaking slot. It wagged at Rory as he crossed the store to stand, hands up, before the cashier.

"I don't want any trouble," Rory said. "Just some gas, and stuff."

"Is not my fault," said the clerk. "He was disrespectful."

A body lay on the floor in front of the counter. Raw

meat loaf from the neck up. The body, in grubby jeans and an ancient Members Only jacket, lay in a halo of red and gray soup, but crazy, drunken spiderwebs of white fiber stretched out of the shattered skull, and little white toadstools bloomed in the cracks of the linoleum, where the biggest clumps of brain matter had settled.

"He's lying to you, man," said the body on the floor.

The clerk barely looked at Rory as he took cash for gas, corn nuts, and sodas, but as he passed Rory's change through the steel drawer, he asked, "Do you know, where are all the police tonight?"

"They're busy," Rory said. "Or they're not police."

"Hey, buddy, come here," rasped the dusted body. "I wanna tell you a secret."

Trixie was already filling the tank when he came out. He took out his phone and called Manuel.

He picked up on the third ring. *"Bueno."* Drowsy, but getting clearer as he added, *"Rory, what's up?"*

"I need help, Manuel."

"No problem, man. What kind of trouble are you in?"

"It's not just me, man. It's the whole fucking city. There's gonna be a war tomorrow, and it's already starting, all over town."

Trixie topped off the tank and sealed the tank. A car peeled out on the street, and she jumped, eyes big and white and pleading with Rory to get moving.

"Manuel, you still there?"

"Yeah, Rory, I'm here, man, but what do you want from me? I'm not a fighter, and I don't hear shooting outside my window. Not more than normal, anyway."

"Listen, man. You know people, right? People inside the joint, people in the Mexican . . . you know, the . . ."

"Mexican Mafia. Is that what you're trying to say? Listen, Rory, if you're into somebody for serious money or something, I'll work until you figure it out, but I don't talk to those guys. My cousin, he's—"

"Tell them something, Manny. It's important somebody knows, who can do something about it."

"All right, I'm listening."

"There's a huge shipment of tainted cocaine being pushed all over town. It's worse than poison. It turns people into . . ." He checked the creeping craziness in his voice, started again. "It brainwashes them, or something. It turns everyone who ingests it into a new gang."

"That's not going to make sense to anybody, man. You need to get some sleep before you go telling anybody anything."

"We can't go home. That's what I'm trying to tell you, Manny. They came into our house and tried to take Trixie. They made me help them drive the stuff down into Watts and Compton—"

"You need somewhere to crash, you're welcome to come over here. Lupe's at her mother's. Don't ask."

"Thanks, man."

"No problem. You helped me out when you didn't have to, didn't even know me. Whatever's wrong, I'm happy to help."

"We'll be there in twenty," Rory said, and hopped on the motorcycle. It occurred to him just then that they didn't have helmets, and could get pulled over. He knew a lot of motorcyclists who bitched about the helmet law like it was designed to treat them like babies. Nobody cared what they did with their heads tonight.

Manuel lived off Pico, in a duplex behind a Catholic girls' school. The guy in the front house fixed up and sold old pinball machines. Rory heard the fruity clang of bells and analogue squeals from his garage as he and Trixie rolled past.

He parked the bike on Manny's porch and helped Trixie get off. Before he knocked on the door, Manny opened up, but he didn't move out of the way to let them in.

"Rory, who are they?"

Rory turned to see three *vatos* in black navy shirts and

chinos cross Manny's yard to hem them in on the porch. They had machine pistols pointed at his wife.

"This the guy?" one of them asked Manny.

Rory started to draw his gun. "I trusted you—"

Manny backed up, but he couldn't look at Rory or Trixie. "You told me to call him, but you didn't say how deep you was involved, *esse*. They know who you are."

Rory put his hands high and let a little guy with acne scars like acid burns take the gun out of his jacket and pat him down. "What d'you guys want?"

"You been served a subpoena, homes. Star Chamber wants to see you." The little guy edged up on his tiptoes to look into Rory's eyes. You the other guy's brother."

He butted his forehead into the target between Rory's eyebrows. Rory stumbled backward into a black hood that dropped over his head and drew tight around his neck.

"Rory, help me!"

Punch-drunk, he tried to put his fist in somebody's face and grab his wife even as he fell to the ground and his world filled with kicking shoes.

The Star Chamber.

Lousy movie, but not a bad idea. If you can't get justice from the system, make your own.

They whipped the hood off and shone a light in his face. It burned right through his eyelids, but he couldn't raise his hands to block it out, because they were tied behind his back.

"You know why you're here. So don't waste our time."

He sat in a metal chair, bound hand and foot to it. "I don't even know who *you* are."

Rory looked around, straining to see past the white light in his face. The darkness behind it was deep, and everywhere he looked, it seemed to be full of people.

"Where's my wife?"

A line of men seated at a table, wearing masks or hoods;

behind them, an audience, filling a brick room that might be a warehouse basement. "Is she a part of this, too?"

"No, she doesn't know anything! Leave her out of this, but I want to see her—"

"Bring her out, Chuy." A huge figure in a hoodie sweat-shirt and a Dia de los Muertos skeleton mask stomped by Rory and rapped on a heavy steel door set in the brick wall. Someone opened it and let the hooded Death go out.

The tall one at the end wore a plain wool ski mask and smoked a pipe like Subcommander Marcos, and he sounded like a college professor. "So, you have our undivided atten-tion. What do you know?"

"It's hard to believe."

Somebody in the darkened gallery laughed. The judge next to the professor wore a gold *luchador* mask with a flaming third eye on its forehead that flashed in the dim light. "You're not talking to the cops, here, Rory Long. We don't care what you did. We just want to know what the fuck is going on."

Everything. He wanted to tell them all of it, if it would wash his hands. But in their eyes, he was a threat to the community, an agent of whatever it was that was taking over L.A. And though these guys were anything but a court of law, it would be a deadly stupid mistake to treat them as anything else. "Don't I get a lawyer?"

"Just tell them the truth, homes," Manny whispered in his ear. "They ain't playin'. That's Tres Ojos."

Even Rory had heard of the gang lord called Three Eyes. According to local legend, he got shot in the head by a cop at age sixteen in a raid on the wrong house. Capitalizing on his legend to become a fiery community activist, he also somehow found time to handle half the Colombian cocaine traffic flowing into Los Angeles from Mexico.

The big steel door grated and slid open and Trixie stag-gered into the room. Her hands were cuffed behind her back.

Rory tried to get up. The chair flexed, but didn't come close to giving.

"I'm okay, baby." She didn't sound okay.

"My brother's in county lockup. He called me tonight about a driving job. I took it. That's all I know."

The professor said, "You just regularly agree to courier massive quantities of narcotics into other people's neighborhoods, Rory?"

"My husband's not a drug dealer—"

"Chuy," said Tres Ojos, "gag the defendant's bitch, please."

"Don't you touch her!"

"I'll be quiet . . ."

Rory rushed into it. "I didn't know what they were doing, but I swear, I had no choice. They had guns. Trust me, those fuckers aren't my friends."

"Richie Long is the top guy."

"Yeah . . . I don't know. I don't know if this is all his idea, or what . . . This isn't a rival gang you're dealing with here. Nobody's in charge of it."

"Oh, I see now." Tres Ojos threw up his hands. "This is nobody's fault. We should just let you go." The audience jeered Rory like he was a bad pro wrestler.

"Listen, man! I tried to warn you about this! I've been running from them all goddamned night. They've got inside the cops, and they probably run the TV and the radio, too. They're locking down the freeways, and as soon as the sun comes up, they're probably going to take over the malls. Somebody has to do something, or this won't be your city for very much longer."

Nobody said anything for a while. Someone coughed. One of the judges was taking a text message and whispering into the ears of his fellow benchwarmers.

Rory squirmed in his chair as the door opened again and a mountain of a black man avalanched into the room. Taking off his bowler and shouldering through his own bodyguards and the Mexicans, he started to cross the room for Rory. "That's the motherfucker who drove their car."

Nobody got in his way.

Rory tried to kick off the floor, backing the chair out of the light. "Hey, I've never seen this guy in my life! I was just a hired driver—"

The black man hauled off and socked Rory in the jaw so hard he rocked back on the chair's hind legs, and tipped over.

The floor knocked the wind out of him. Hands grabbed his feet and yanked him upright, then hit him again. This time, the black guy stood on his feet, so he couldn't fall over.

"That's enough, Stymie."

"Give it up, punk. Who you working for?"

Rory had to spit out blood and a chipped tooth to speak. "House off Laurel Canyon. I went there, burned the place down . . ."

"No shit."

Trixie screamed, "Get off him, you fucking clowns!"

"Stymie," said the professor, "this court doesn't recognize your authority."

"Yo, fuck that kangaroo-court shit, motherfucker. We are at *war*. Maybe you know who's at fault here, and maybe you know who's laughing up their sleeves at us while we cut each other down, but you still pushing us out of South Central block by block."

The silence stretched out long enough for anyone who wanted to deny his charge to break it. Finally, a judge in a scaly green *luchador* mask chuckled and asked, "So why are you here?"

"Because they hit both sides. This thing ain't just dividing us up, it's conquering us overnight. You ain't heard from your boys in Boyle Heights all night, have you?"

The judges knocked heads for a moment. Tres Ojos demanded, "Where else did you go tonight?"

"Boyle Heights, a loft or something on Manitou—"

"Where else?"

"Watts. By Inglewood Cemetery. The bowling alley, I guess you know about. Some place in Commerce. I don't know whose place it was."

"That's it?"

"I wasn't the only driver. I think they covered the whole county. The operation was at that house, but it's gone, but the people who sniffed that shit, they're the threat now."

The impact of his speech sent whispering ripples through the audience. The professor demanded, "What do you mean, exactly? In Spanish, if at all possible."

"They're a disease. The drug just spreads the disease all over town, but the people can infect each other. It grows out of their heads, but it can be passed through spit, and I don't know how else."

The judges conferred among themselves. Clearly, something else had happened that he didn't know about. Something that made them listen, even if they didn't want to believe.

Finally, Tres Ojos stood up and came around the table. He was a short guy, stocky with stooped shoulders. Rory thought he could kick the guy's ass without getting out of this chair, if he wasn't tied to it. "You want us to believe you're just a crazy white boy who used his own product too much. You think we'll just turn you loose when this is all over if you play dumb."

The judge came over to stand before Rory. Stymie backed up, cracking his knuckles.

"I don't know much," Rory said, "but I know that it's not something anybody's ever seen before. It makes people want to spread it around, makes them do anything it needs them to do, even throw away their lives. I swear to God, why would I make something like this up?"

"Because he's *one of them*," Stymie said. "They infiltrated my inner fucking circle. Homies I came up with.

They talk you in circles until you dizzy, then stab you in the back. We ain't never seen shit like this, but we know how to find out who's lying, and who's flying."

Stymie turned and banged on the steel door.

"I'm not one of them, goddamn it," Rory said. "I'm trying to help you. Instead of fucking around with me, you should be out there—"

The door opened and Stymie reached out for something. He turned and led a pair of brawny pit bulls into the room on leashes. The massive fighting dogs sniffed and strained, then started growling.

"We found out something from talking to those boys in Watts. Dogs hated those white kids. Tried to kill this one bitch, half tore her arm off, even when she shot it in the head."

The dogs snarled and leaped to the end of their leashes, dancing on their hind legs to get at the one whose scent drove them insane.

"We ain't never seen shit like this before, but we figure out shit pretty quick down here."

The dogs barked and bared their teeth at Rory.

Stymie dropped their leashes.

Rory took a deep breath and braced himself. There was nothing else he could do. His feet kicked at the floor and threw the chair sideways, and as he fell, he watched the dogs.

Pearl gray pit bulls; litter mates, probably. Identical, like bullets from the same gun.

Standing in the center of the courtroom, they bayed at Rory, their intended target. The whole courtroom leaped to its feet and sucked in a breath to scream for his blood.

But as soon as Stymie shouted, "Sic 'em!" they leaped at the judges.

The professor stood and caught a dog in the chest, which drove him back into the audience.

Rory flopped around in his chair, shouting for Trixie. He

heard her call his name, but he couldn't see her in the flurry of bodies. "Get down, baby!"

The bailiffs drew guns and crashed into Stymie's guards, who threw punches and drew concealed weapons as they tried to retreat to the steel door. The Camera Estrella must have had a metal detector, because everyone seemed to have plastic prison shivs.

The other two judges leaped to their feet and tried to save the professor. Tres Ojos drew a gun and shot the second dog as it leaped onto the table. The audience erupted in a riot. Thrown chairs and screams filled the air.

The professor rolled over on the dog and seized it by the throat. It whipped around in his hands and sank its fangs into his forearm, but he snapped its neck. Dying, its forepaws flailed at his face, shredding his mask. The judge got up, and the whole room fell silent. Frozen.

Staring.

The professor looked around the courtroom with his one staring, intact eye. The other eye bulged and sagged from its socket like a poached egg, weeping curdled milk. His nose was gone long before the dog attacked him. In its place, a ragged, inflamed second mouth slobbered white clods of infected mucus down the front of his fatigue jacket.

His mouth twisted in a sad smile, the judge turned to his colleagues and the bailiffs and made a *what-can-you-do* gesture with his mangled hand. Then he shook with a terrible, hacking cough and vomited in the faces of the front row of the audience.

The crowd of forty or fifty had pressed close to watch the dog attack, but now they trampled one another to get away. Three people doused in the judge's white mischief stumbled and swooned to the floor like they'd been touched by an evangelist.

"*La luz, y la vida,*" wheezed the noseless judge. "*Yo soy el camino del cielo . . .*"

Two bailiffs opened fire on the infected judge. Their high-caliber fire went right through the shambling target and hit fleeing members of the audience. The judge in the silver *technico* mask folded over and sank into the mob.

Tres Ojos jumped onto the table and fired a round into the ceiling. "Everybody shut up and sit the fuck down!" Then he shot the infected judge in the face.

The bloated, overripe face split and slid off. All connective tissue and most of the muscle beneath the skin had dissolved and been replaced with turgid sacs of chunky white fluid, like packets of explosive strapped to the tottering, cackling skeleton.

"*Burn it!*" Rory screamed. "Don't shoot it, *burn it!*"

The infected judge grasped Tres Ojos by one leg and swept him off the table. Bullets slammed into the professor from all sides, but hardly bothered him at all, next to his other problems.

White fibrous fruiting bodies burst out of the cracks in his skull, and out of the holes in his torso. Bladders popped and sprayed white slime everywhere as the judge waded into the crowd.

Stymie's posse pounded on the door, but it was locked from outside. Likewise, the audience of panicked people surged back from the locked exits just as the freshly infected in the crowd climbed to their feet.

The infected judge staggered over toward where Tres Ojos lay stunned against the wall beside the shrine, and where Rory lay hog-tied and helpless on the courtroom floor.

Chupacabron, the judge in the green mask, leaped over the table and planted both size-fourteen feet in the judge's back, driving him into the wall. But the thing recovered with uncanny speed and dragged the *rudo* gang leader to the floor. Driving his mangled hand up to the second knuckles into Chupacabron's neck, he leered at the bailiffs as they shot him.

Manuel broke into the shrine of the Virgin of Guadalupe and grabbed the statue by her sainted neck. The professor turned away from the choking Chupacabron, leaving him to dig the severed digits broken off in his windpipe, and stumbled after Tres Ojos.

Manuel came up behind the professor and chipped the crown of his head off with the Virgin.

The judge stumbled but stayed upright, whirled and reached out to embrace Manuel. Choking up on the statue's neck, Manuel feinted right and, when the judge lurched at him, he swung for the fences.

The statue's base connected solidly with the judge's cheek and jaw, whipping his head around so violently that his jawbone flew out of his slack, slobbering mouth. Looking down at the crack of his own ass, the infected judge still walked, but he was very confused.

Manuel said something perhaps only Rory and the monster heard. "I'm sorry, Uncle."

He jabbed the professor in the chest as hard as he could with the statue, staving in his ribs and driving the judge back into the Virgin's empty shrine. The shambling thing fell on the banks of votive candles and slithered to the floor, upending dozens of hot candles and dousing itself with molten wax and lamp oil.

Roaring flames enshrouded the crawling judge. Even as its tendons and joints blackened and curled, the judge tried to crawl toward Rory, the nearest human body, and spread its infection.

Noxious black fumes filled the room. People gagged and threw up, but nobody spoke as the fire hungrily devoured the shambling corpse, the crackling greenish flames battling the hiss of popping spore-sacs and boiling fluids.

A knife slid between Rory's wrists and cut the nylon rope binding him to the chair. Rory rolled to his knees and grabbed the chair, prepared to throw it. Trixie grabbed him and they fell to the floor together.

Manuel helped Tres Ojos to his feet and led him over to where Rory lay with his wife. Rory tensed up and got his feet under him, reaching to take the knife from Trixie.

"Rory," Manuel said, "I'm sorry about this, man. I told him before he picked you up that he could trust you, but he wouldn't listen."

Tres Ojos peeled off his mask as he offered his hand. Rory felt a momentary twitch of mistrust before he took the judge's hand. Unmasked, he was just another brown face, with a thin mustache and shaved head, sleepy, sly brown eyes, and an alarming scar above his eyebrows that looked like the empty socket of a third eye. All three eyes seemed to bore into Rory's as he said, "Sorry."

"This is my cousin Hector. Hector, this is my boss, Rory Long." Leaning into Rory's ear, he whispered, "Don't give him too much shit, okay? That thing was his father-in-law."

Rory had to bite his lip and wait for the right thing to say. "I'm sorry, too, Hector. A lot of people we care about died tonight. We didn't bring this to your door. But we want to help stop it."

Tres Ojos looked around the courtroom. The judge in the silver mask was helped to his feet by the bailiffs, bleeding but alive and angry.

El Chupacabron lay dead with his hands clamped over the hole in his throat. And the fourth judge was a smoldering pyre in the middle of the room. Stymie and his men were waiting to talk to whoever was left.

"Oh, we're gonna fix their shit," Tres Ojos said. "You want to help?"

"Fuck yeah."

"You can start by telling us where your brother is."

The dawn had broken in sulfurous yellow over a city slowly waking up to find its bed on fire. Traffic snarls turned into gridlock on major streets as pedestrians jumped out in front of cars. The radio was overrun with reports on the spreading fires in the Hollywood Hills, and where evacuees should go.

Manuel drove the van around any sign of trouble, even jumping the curb and taking the sidewalk, where smashed cars blocked the road.

Rory and Trixie sat on the mattress in the back, between a pair of teenage gang soldiers with assault rifles on their knees and bandannas over their faces.

"I'm scared, Rory."

"Me, too, baby. And tired and pissed."

"How could anyone stop this? Even if they can make the city listen, even if it's not too late, they're everywhere already."

"They've got a plan. But now we have one, too." Stymie and Tres Ojos had been a lot more receptive after the courtroom got cleared, and they'd worked out a strategy in less than an hour. Even if only a fraction of it went down, today would make them more than wanted felons. It would probably make them terrorists. But the alternative was unthinkable. Nobody else was ready to believe this was happening, let alone stand up to fight it.

"You saw how quickly it takes people over, and what it can make them do. Can those people be cured, or will they . . . have to be . . . ?" She started to choke up, thinking of all the people she saw, all those lost, cast-off people who acted, for the first time, like they'd been found, like they were really alive.

"It can be cured. We didn't get sick. I've been around it all night, and I didn't get taken over."

"I've been thinking about that, too. Why, do you suppose?"

"I don't know for sure, but I think—" He trailed off, looking at the guards.

"What?"

"We'll talk about it when we get where we're going."

"Tell me now."

He whispered in her ear.

"*No* fucking *way*."

"It's the only thing that makes sense."

"Wherever we're going, there better be a bed. I just want to sleep."

Manuel turned the van up a steep hill somewhere in Hollywood. Sawhorses and police cars marked the neighborhood as closed and evacuated, but nobody manned the barricades.

Less than a mile away, the vast brown columnar clouds of a wildfire reared up out of Vermont Canyon, just east of Griffith Park. Rory felt a fresh stab of guilt, but it probably wasn't his fire. The radio said copycat fires had sprung up in Hollywood and the mountains north of the San Fernando Valley.

Fire was more than just L.A.'s perennial natural disaster. It was a gun to the city's head that could go off whenever the weather was just right, or some asshole decided to make himself important, and often enough, for no earthly fucking reason at all. Whether or not the infected mobs were behind it, the unrest had tipped the city into a free fall it might not survive, even if the plague was stopped.

The van gratefully lurched to a stop near the top of the hill. Manuel jumped out and came around to open the back door.

Rory and Trixie stumbled out. Fatigue made them both shaky, almost drunk on the dregs of multiple waves of adrenaline. Trixie clung to Rory as he shook hands with Manuel.

"You sure this guy's all right? Maybe we should come in with you." Manuel looked sideways at his two new friends, who shrugged and cocked their rifles.

"Absolutely not. This guy's the craziest bastard I know, which is saying something. But he's my friend, and if anybody would know how to get a handle on this shit, and how to fight it, my money's on him to get it first."

Manuel shut the van and looked up and down the street like a very old soldier. His hand on the gun in his pocket was steady, but totally ready. Amazing, how some people just reflexively locked their shit down, the minute trouble came knocking. "Okay, but stay in touch. If anybody but me calls you from the Syndicate, assume they're dusted."

Rory scanned the steep front yard, so densely forested in trees and untrimmed shrubbery that he could see no sign of the house they'd come to seeking refuge and help.

"If you hear from me before I've had a good long fucking nap," Rory said, "you better believe I'm dusted. And you better come kill me."

"Rory!" Trixie punched him in the ribs.

"Okay. You better come kill both of us."

TWENTY-EIGHT

Euclid Byorik was a lot harder to convince than Rory thought he was going to be.

He buzzed them in the front gate as soon as he heard Rory's voice, without listening to what he had to say. But his eye peeping at them through the bolt hole in the front door was anything but welcoming. Impatient with Rory's thumbnail sketch of the night's events, he left them standing in his courtyard.

"This was already a pretty strange day before you showed up, kids." A chunky pause stretched out as Euclid hit a bong. The oily smoke he coughed out could fell a charging elephant. "But you see the position I'm in. If what you're saying is true, you could still be infected, and lying about it. And then there's the very real possibility that you've just cracked and caught the L.A. disease."

Rory sank onto the porch beside Trixie, who ran her fingers over the surface of the murky pond that took up most of the courtyard, teasing something huge and pop-eyed that may have been a gigantic black koi, so big it could only flop around in the shallow green water.

She twitched every time a car passed on the street. "This was a mistake," she said.

Sunlight only managed to peer into the narrow space between the rambling wings of Euclid's massive neo-Victorian firetrap for about an hour a day, but the creeping ivy that covered the ground thrived in the shade. A big black tomcat strutted out into the yard and flopped on the brickwork to groom itself.

Rory pulled his hair and rocked until inspiration struck. "If I wanted to trick you into letting me in, would I even bother with a crazy story? I'd just ask to buy an ounce of grass."

"And I probably would've let you in, and I'd be fucked, too." Euclid took another hit off the bong and coughed thoughtfully. "Shit, might as well let you in, then."

Four bolts turned and the huge red front door swung open. He held a gun in one big, mocha-colored hand. "Is that a black cat?"

Trixie looked over her shoulder. "He's got white on his belly."

Euclid heaved a sigh of relief and eased back the hammer on his revolver. "Come on in."

"You know why cocaine invented people?"

Rory had heard this particular Euclidism before, but shook his head. He sipped his coffee and took a seat at the bar to watch Euclid whip up an omelet.

"So it could go to parties and listen to itself talk all night. You like mushrooms in yours?"

"Fuck no."

Trixie lay prone on the colossal suede couch in the next room, having inhaled her breakfast and passed out in mid–thank you. Most mornings, some totally shady character or three would be crashed on the couch; a bearded Grizzly Adams type in a buckskin jacket, or a dwarf bodybuilder. Today, a ravishing skinny redhead in a furry white bikini and go-go boots slept curled up in an egg chair in the far corner of the living room, where a floor-to-ceiling window looked out on the city.

"So, what do you think? Do you believe me, or not?"

Euclid slid a fat vegetarian omelet onto a plate and garnished it with guacamole, salsa, and sour cream before putting it in front of Rory. "I'm sorry and all, but you know, if people are crazy or lying, they usually freak out on you or make up a better story. What you're saying sounds like so much paranoid bullshit, but it explains everything else I'm seeing and hearing today."

Rory looked around for the stereo system among the jumble of bookshelves and record crates. Blaring from speakers secreted in every corner of every room in the house, Dr. Kitch lamented that the size of his needle had frightened another patient. Given what happened to Trixie tonight, the shit would give her nightmares. "Hey, how do you turn this shit down?"

Casting a dirty look at Rory, Euclid hit a button on a remote in his bathrobe pocket and skipped to the honeyed, easy-skanking tones of "007 (Shantytown)."

"You got a problem with Desmond Dekker?"

"Answer the question. Why would I lie to you?"

Euclid took a moment to weigh his answer, cracked a half dozen eggs into the skillet. A heavyset black guy, if not quite truly fat, Euclid hid behind his huge, unkempt Afro, muttonchops, and big, blind-guy sunglasses, but Rory had learned to read volumes in his nervous gestures. "It wouldn't be your fault, man. Everybody who tries to live here succumbs, eventually. Every time and place has its own special mental illness, the unique way it breaks a human brain. And our insanity is so special, it's our principal export. It's our whole economy."

"You're talking about TV and movies? I'm talking about a disease that's taking over the city."

"It's the same thing, man." Tossing shredded cheese, onions, mushrooms, and bell peppers into the eggs, he took a hit off a joint and held it until smoke leaked out of one of his ears. "Check it out. What makes action movies exciting? One man against a corrupt system, or the end of the world, or some such shit, or he's being chased, because he's the only one who knows the truth. That's what Hollywood sells. Not all those bullshit stories, those are just an excuse.

"They find ways to make people feel not just special, but like the *hero*: the most important person in the whole world. The only *real* person, so whatever they do is necessary and important, with a triumphant theme song, and all that."

"Now's really not the time for the Hollywood lecture, man—"

"Relax, it's all going somewhere. Solipsism's what we sell, but it's also how we deal with each other. Everybody in L.A. is the star of the movie they make in their heads every day. Even if they don't want to be in the movies, they dream, all of them, of being that important. It's how everybody deals with the traffic and the crowds and the rudeness of everybody else. But it's also why some people just go off sometimes, and set fires, or shoot off guns on the freeway, or go all *Taxi Driver* on people they just *know* are monsters in disguise . . . Am I getting relevant yet?"

Rory lost his appetite halfway through his omelet. "I haven't lost my mind. I know what I saw. Turn on the fucking TV if you don't believe me—"

"Every channel is telling a different story. Civil unrest, brushfires, traffic and car accidents. It's not even unusual for a weekday, let alone a holiday. Most of the city isn't even awake yet, and they're probably not going to wake up with a big line of coke."

"It's not about the drug, dumbass! The drug was a vehicle for getting thousands of people infected overnight. They have enough people all over the city to infect millions, before tomorrow."

Euclid took Rory's plate away and dumped his food in the trash. "Don't eat my food and call me names in my own house, man."

Rory felt bad for all kinds of reasons, but not for avoiding the food. Euclid's days of dosing his houseguests with liquid LSD were not so far behind him. "I'm sorry, but you're trying my fucking patience, Euclid. I came to you because you're the only person I know who could think this through."

"That may or may not have been a huge waste of your time, and mine."

"Well, what would you do if you believed us?"

"I'd need proof."

"Like what?"

"Like these spores you say they're pushing. I'd have to see them."

"Be my guest. Where's my jacket?"

Euclid shoveled his own omelet onto a plate and took it out of the kitchen, waving for Rory to follow. "I took the liberty of scraping your jacket when you dropped your story on me. It was all over your sleeves and collar. Trixie had some on her shirt, but it was in some kind of fluid—"

Eating all the way, Euclid led Rory down a hall filled with comic-book boxes to a door with a rubber seal around it.

Setting down the empty plate, he handed Rory some paper slippers. "Take off your shoes, and put these on. And don't touch anything. My babies are insanely susceptible to fungal infections."

Rory did as he was told and then entered Euclid's laboratory.

Euclid Byorik had three master's degrees and over forty published articles on botany, biology, and genetics, but he quit academic research to pursue his first love, which was cultivating arcane new subspecies of marijuana. If you ever read about that gene-spliced marijuana at UCLA that glowed in the dark, or if you ever smoked a single joint that made you black out and give away your car, you can thank Euclid.

After winning two Cannabis Cup trophies and four *High Times* centerfolds, Euclid had moved into regions even his fellow growers considered insane. He earnestly claimed that his prized Green Jesus strain would, with a little more tweaking, cure at least three varieties of blindness.

The lab was lined with plastic, and contained cells with varying degrees of humidity and carefully controlled temperature. Along one wall, partitioned from the hydroponic cells by heavy plastic curtains, a countertop with incubators, scales, and a stereo microscope.

Euclid took a look into the eyepieces, adjusted the focus, then stepped aside. "Take a look."

Rory bent to the lenses. He blinked and squinted a bit before getting the hang of it, but what he saw was just a cluster of spiky white orbs, like the burrs that stuck in your socks when you walked in wild grass. "That's it?"

"That's your diabolical mastermind, buddy."

"That can't be right." Rory looked again. If he expected them to move or grow before his eyes, he was disappointed. "They're just seeds, dude."

"No, no, no. They're spores."

"Whatever."

"There's a world of difference. Spores don't always have to be fertilized. They can carry the genetic material of one parent organism—clones—effectively. It's not just a new species here. It's all one individual fungus."

"Well, that's all good, but what the hell do we do about it?"

Euclid turned to the big silver incubator on the end of the counter. "You can kill fungus with the right chemicals. It's just a question of how far gone the host is . . . ah, fuck!"

Rory looked at the incubator and pushed Euclid away from it. "Don't open that!"

The porthole in the door of the incubator was coated with white fibers and bloated, fleshy bulbs that quivered and sprayed little clouds of spores with every vibration of the door handle.

"Fucking hell," Euclid said. "I only put those fucking spores in there a half hour ago."

"You see what that shit can do. It's not just a fungus, Euclid. It warps people's minds so they'll do anything for it, but it teaches them . . . It uses their intelligence, but it has a master plan. It has the whole system figured out. And everybody who did that shit knew who Richie was. They knew who I was . . ."

"It's not as weird as it sounds if you'd watched more nature shows on basic cable."

"What?" Distracted, Rory watched the probing white roots grow up the inside of the glass like milk spilling upward, seeking a way out.

"Parasites have been around for as long as there've been living things. They push more and faster evolutionary changes than any other environmental threat. Parasites have to overcome all kinds of immune system barriers to get into a host and reproduce. Complicated shit, but without brains of their own, they figure out how to defeat it, because if they didn't, they wouldn't get to breed.

"Our society, if you look at it from far enough away, is no different from any other host organism. If you see L.A. as one big body, with downtown for a heart and the hills for a head, you've got hundreds of square miles of exurban guts, muscle, and fat fed by a scrawny, clogged-up circulatory system.

"Our immune system is the cops, and not much else, because nobody's looking out for anybody but themselves. Our individual cells all think they're the only important cell in the body, and they all go crazy every day, trying to live the fantasy.

"Our system might all seem pretty complicated to you, but to a parasite, it's not that hard to figure our shit out. It's just the biggest host body of all time, begging to be taken over."

Rory rubbed his eyes. "I think my head's going to explode."

Euclid sat on a stool with his hands tucked in his armpits. He looked like he was going to jump out of his skin, his anxious excitement so overt that, if Rory didn't know better, he'd think Euclid was infected. "You should get some sleep."

"I don't know if I can, but I definitely do need to lie down." Rory headed for the door.

Euclid turned away to change the slide under the microscope. "Sure, sure. Take Trixie and go crash in the front guest bedroom. The one with the aquarium. I'm just gonna play around with this stuff, and, uh . . . call a few people."

PART SIX

Nine Circles

TWENTY-NINE

The sun rose red over Los Angeles.

By the time Rory closed his eyes at last, settled into deep and dreamless slumber, the city was just awakening to air thick with smoke and ash, the smell of doom and radical transformation.

The night shift had sown the nocturnal seeds far and wide and deep.

Now it was time for the day shift to kick in.

"This is Dwight Simmons from the KCAL Nine traffic chopper, and the only word to describe the view from up here is apocalyptic.

"As you can see from this shot of the 101, it is gridlocked for miles in either direction. Not slow-moving traffic, but absolute gridlock. Some of these cars have been here for hours, and word is that many of them have been literally abandoned."

"How is this even possible, Dwight?" cut in Brett Hedges at the KCAL news desk.

"I have no idea. Here's the seventeen-car pileup that initially blocked the westbound lanes by the Spring Street exit. But as we move east, you can see an equally epic pileup just above the Silver Lake exit, up ahead. It's almost as if they're mirror images of each other.

"And we've got reports of similar incidents dotting the 2, the 5, the 10, the 110, the 134, the 210, the 405, the PCH, and on

and on and on. Every major artery in and out of the greater Los Angeles area is totally blocked."

"And where are the police, and the DMV?"

"Completely overwhelmed. Tow trucks can't get within miles of the actual incidents. And as you can see in the background, the Hollywood Hills are on fire. Griffith Park is on fire. Malibu is on fire. It's a [bleep]ing nightmare out here."

"Thank you, Dwight. Please keep us up-to-date. Meanwhile, the governor has declared a state of emergency, and has mobilized area National Guard units to restore order. The Department of Homeland Security is investigating the possibility of a terrorist attack . . ."

From the air, the city's troubles seemed so simple, so unmistakable. The broken, burning body of Los Angeles thrust out columns of smoke to the sky like the arms of a drowning man. Unseen from the air, the sickness pulled back to regroup, and initiate a new phase of infection.

Long after sunrise, the wide streets and gated alleyways of downtown's Robinson Hill remained in cool yellow shadows cast by the spires of the banking titans. The citadels of wealth were locked down and staffed with well-armed security, but they'd withdrawn into their towers, and ceded the streets to the staggering armies of the infected.

At the base of Two California Plaza, an Asian woman in tattered rags knelt before the forty-two-story glass and steel skyscraper as if bowing to a god. Filthy enough to pass for one of the countless transients who prowled the city center, she owned two stores in the Garment District and had a merchant account with the very bank encased in this tower, but all that was behind her.

She gagged, coughing and choking up a torrent of white slime, which she caught in her hands. The sticky, viscous mucus made a perfect seal when she slapped her palms on the glass, and bore her wasted weight easily as she began to crawl up the window.

While a security guard in the lobby tapped impotently on the inside of the glass, she hauled herself up the wall past the first floor. Her tiny bare feet kicked at the slick glass until they found purchase in the slime from her hands, and she began to climb in earnest.

Her arthritic limbs quivered and threatened to fail, but the last buried reserves in her body were laid bare and consumed for this, her ultimate purpose. She was a seed on its final journey to fertilization, to become something unimaginable. To become new life.

By the time she reached the twentieth story, the whipping, smoky winds had pinned her to the glass, and her sinuses were exhausted and dry.

But more of her kind had found her snail trail and followed her up the wall. Silently, they crawled over her and added new rungs to the ladder of slime, until they formed an unbroken human chain like a column of army ants, inching ever closer to the summit of the tower.

"Isn't it remarkable, my friends, how no matter what problems the rest of the country faces, the president will always rush to save California from itself, always jump like a trained dog, whenever his masters in Hollywood jerk his leash?

"News wires are clogged with all kinds of crazy stories coming out of Los Angeles, but if you read between the lines, the story is pretty clear. Drugs. Rampant street crime. Tolerance of deviant lifestyle choices. Police so hog-tied by the trial lawyers and victims' rights lobbies that they can't do their jobs.

"The governor out there has asked the feds to step in and declare a state of emergency, and Congress is dropping everything to debate the appropriate response. They're going to take a couple hours to do it, but we can settle that debate right here and now.

"You made your bed, California. Fix it yourselves, or lie in it and die, with the best wishes of real Americans everywhere."

"Take it easy, sweetie," her partner said. "Nobody's shooting at us. Yet."

Officer Monikah Robinson goosed the cruiser's sirens as they sped south down Budlong, whipped a left against the red at the Faith Dome, and slalomed between abandoned cars in the street around the old Pepperdine campus.

"Yes, sir," she bristled, but checked her speed turning onto Vermont. Only a month out of the academy, her first day driving the car, and the city was tearing itself apart. The police force at war with itself.

Pulling into the minimall, she took note of the people waiting out in front of the Rumpus Room, and her heart sank. Big T lounged in his wheelchair with the Reverend Tentman and a couple girls from high school with kids at home who had no business hanging out at a bar at eight in the morning.

"This is just another day," Russ reminded her. "People still got problems, they still get up to mischief."

Robinson didn't argue. Sergeant Russ Theisiger didn't do arguments. She figured he never took off the badge when he went home to his family in Simi Valley, never stopped being the hard-ass cop. But she could tell he was at least as frightened as she was.

The morning briefing was like being hit in the head, over and over. Nine cops killed last night. Five more missing. Fourteen cars wrecked. And another list, that Captain Giordano only hinted at, because IA was handling it: cops with reports pending against them, who may have lost their minds out there last night, then come back to work smiling.

But that wasn't their detail. Their next call was a simple assault. The woman who called 911 said her husband was out all night and she tracked him down this morning to the Rumpus Room, which was notorious for staying open all night for its regulars. She hit him, but when he attacked her, the bar patrons joined in, trying to stop her leaving. The victim, one Shaniqua Green of Morningside Park, had placed the call while running east on Gage.

"Take the statements out here," Russ grunted as he slid out of the car. She radioed in their position and watched him lumber over to the Rumpus Room and haul open the big door. He treated her like a kid and she still wasn't sure he wasn't a secret bigot, but Russ was a good teacher. What she needed right now, to show her how to turn off her humanity and be a cop.

Big T and the Reverend rolled up on her as she crossed the lot, all shrugs and shit-eating grins. The neighborhood girls shrank back, wall-eyed and tweaking bad.

"Check you out, Mo," the Reverend said. All decked out in his finest black suit like when he still had a church. "They send you to shake us down? I'd of thought your masters had bigger things on their minds today."

Lots of them talked to her like this. Friends of her family, neighborhood folks, tried to play her like this. Like she was the enemy, but also like the badge was just a Halloween costume. "Morning, Mr. Tentman, Mr. Morris. Did you witness the incident?"

"Oh, we witnesses, all right," Big T drawled. "Saw the miracle. You want to see it, too, y'feelin' me?"

The Reverend took her arm, bracing her shoulder in a fatherly way that she didn't resist until it was too late.

His nose ran, streaming milky snot into his yellow dentures. "You got to come see it right now, girl."

Robinson stepped back and tried to shake off his skinny arm, but his fingers dug into her, and she couldn't quite draw her stick on him. "Don't touch me, or—"

"Or what, *Officer?*" Big T levered himself out of his wheelchair and butted his forehead into hers. Hit her so hard, she blacked out for a second. "It's all good, Mo."

Robinson shouted for assistance. Her feet kicked in the air. Big T slipped her gun out of its holster and tucked it in his sweatpants. His legs were wobbly and his feet dragged, but they worked pretty good for not having carried him in almost ten years.

A *miracle*. She screamed, but nobody came to help her, which was no miracle at all.

The Reverend opened the door for Big T to carry her into the bar. It was so dark inside that all she could see was green and black and the lurid blue glow of a TV tuned to static and the neon beer signs.

The bar was full of regulars, but nothing else about the scene was regular. No music played. Everybody looked happy, if not downright ecstatic. And they were all drinking water.

Russ was lying on his back just inside the door. White powder and blood-flecked foam covered his mustache and chin. One hand clutched his chest, while his feet kicked at the brass rail on the bar.

Big T dropped her on a stool. "I know just what you need," said the bartender.

White shit oozed out of his nose, which had been whittled down to a nub of naked bone Michael Jackson would've envied. Above his bulging yellow eyes, the flesh and bone of his skull had split open like a flowerpot burst by an overgrown tree. An arm-thick white stalk sprouted from his forehead like a unicorn's horn made of cauliflower. Throbbing sacs at the business end of it spurted white dust into the air as he came closer and leaned over the bar.

"*Get the fuck back!*" The force made her keep her nails a sensible length and shade, but she raked Big T's face hard enough to grate on bone.

She kicked at the bar and flipped back off the stool. Surprised more than hurt, Big T let her fall to the floor.

The crowd closed in over her. Many of them had weird white horns cracking through their skulls. She covered her eyes as white dust and stinking jelly rained down on her.

She was hiding her eyes when they came in.

The front door slammed into the wall. "Yo, last call, dustheads."

Machine guns opened up on the bar.

Screams and wails as the bar patrons rushed the door, wading into the shooters' field for fire. Bodies exploded and flew apart as the shooters played the sprays of bullets up and down the tiny barroom. Blood and curdled, bitter milk sluiced the floor.

Robinson had never faced fire as a police officer, but she'd gone to sleep with gunfire echoing outside her window often enough not to let it freeze her up. Rolling into a booth, she reached for her gun.

It winked at her from Big T's sweatpants. He sat against the bar with his chest split open and grabby white tendrils like the roots of some crazy crackhead plant growing out of it.

Robinson steadied her hand and then reached for her gun the moment the shooting stopped.

She grabbed it and popped up from cover, shouted, "LAPD! Freeze—"

Three Crip foot soldiers stood in the open doorway, slapping fresh clips into their HK assault rifles. Their eyes got real big over their blue bandannas when they saw her gun, but then they all started laughing.

"Oh, baby, give it a rest," one of them said. "Don't you know it's Opposite Day?"

She risked a quick look around the Rumpus Room in the dull yellow light that spilled in the door. Everyone in the place lay dead or dying. The Reverend tried to crawl out the door past the Crips, trailing yards of bloodless guts behind him, but a kid who couldn't be sixteen yet put a high-top sneaker on his neck and blew his brains out, then high-fived his friends.

"Drop your guns! You're all under arrest!" She stepped over piles of bodies to get to the door.

They just looked at one another and turned to go. "You're welcome," one of them said over his shoulder.

Robinson knelt beside her partner and checked his pulse. Russ was dead, probably from a heart attack, upon inhaling whatever they gave him. Whatever it was that changed them.

Officer Robinson stepped outside and put away her gun.

The Crips climbed into the back of a convertible Cadillac with three more soldiers in Raiders jackets and blue ski masks. One of them had a bipod-mounted sniper rifle; another had a belt-fed M60 machine gun. A digital scanner on the dashboard bleeped and burbled with overlapping emergency calls. She recognized the dispatcher's voice calling an all units down on the roller rink on Normandie.

"Take the day off, baby," the driver said, and threw her a Rollin '70s salute. "We got this shit."

"—The governor's press secretary refused to comment on the president's conversation with the governor, and he likewise deflected questions about rumors being broadcast on local Spanish-speaking news, with their unfounded claims that the civil unrest and mass hysteria are being driven by a viral infection or new designer drug.

"With the California National Guard already overcommitted abroad, there is little hope of maintaining an effective quarantine of the greater Los Angeles area without federal assistance. The Department of Homeland Security issued a brief statement calling on the citizens of Los Angeles to defend their own neighborhoods until order can be restored . . ."

Life in the Arroyo Estates was always intense. Today just brought into sharper relief what they'd always been fighting for.

Terry Hartung went over to Marty Finkelstein's house as soon as he'd caught the morning news. As a committee-man on the HOA's security council and the neighborhood watch block warden, Marty would know what to do.

Marty was up on his roof with binoculars and a rifle. "Come on up, Terry!" he shouted down. "Ladder's around back. Bring your own rifle, though."

Marty sounded pretty worked up, so Terry got his .220 Remington with the Ertl scope, a cooler of beer, and a couple boxes of lemon cooler cookies, and joined his friend on the roof.

"You see the news?"

"KCAL had a special report about the fires and the traf-fic, but—"

"Not that bullshit. The real news." Marty handed Terry his heavy Zeiss binoculars and pointed down the long, gentle slope that cradled their development. Rolling hills furry with lush coastal scrub rambled over a quarter mile down to the bottom of the canyon where the nearest traf-fic light blinked like the border of civilization, the start of everything they'd fought to leave behind.

Only when he saw the traffic light did he track back upslope and take in the graded planes gouged out of the breast of the land; the armada of bright yellow construc-tion machines parked in formation like an invasion force from the planet Sprawl; the scabs of poured foundations and gimcrack pinewood skeletons of adjoined two-bedroom homes; the hastily paved web of roads and parking lots feeding into the lonely two-lane road that was once their private driveway. On a clear day, you could see Pasadena at the bottom of the valley, but today, the haze was so thick he could barely read the garish orange sign that proclaimed their virgin meadow the FUTURE SITE OF ARROYO GRANITO: CITY-CLOSE COUNTRY LIVING FROM THE LOW 400,000's.

"I'm not too worried, Marty. The winds are blowing the fire west—"

"You believe that? You think it's just one fire? The have-nots are on the march, buddy boy. Some new kind of drug is making them crazy and superstrong. They tore up their own neighborhoods after Rodney King, but they won't be so stupid this time."

"You want some Girl Scout cookies?"

Marty took a box and gobbled a fistful of lemon coolers, sniffing the powdered sugar on his fingers and wiping them off on his golf shirt. "These been in the freezer for a while, or something?"

Terry popped the top off an Arrogant Bastard IPA and sat in one of the lawn chairs Marty kept on a special deck he'd installed on the tiled roof of his garage. Code committee raised hell over it, but Marty got the security committee to override their decision. His neighbor sat up here most nights, providing "air support" for the foot patrols.

"Dude," Terry moaned, "settle down. Have a beer. So the city's tearing its own ass out again. So what? Nobody's coming out here to loot, and nobody's going to set fire to the Estates. This is why we moved out here. This is why we work so hard. Relax." He handed Marty a beer and turned the binoculars on the street.

Terry's daughter strolled down the walkway of the Mattinglys' place, towing her Radio Flyer wagon loaded with Girl Scout cookies. He waved to her, and she waved back.

Marty took a pull off his beer, pissed off the edge of the roof. "Those fuckers who're bulldozing the rest of the valley, they've got billions sunk into uncontrolled growth. They don't give a shit about people, or communities. All they care about is money. In all this chaos, man, anything could happen, that's all I'm saying. And if they had to start over . . ."

Terry had heard it all before. The Estates fought Arroyo Granito every step of the way. You had to gild the lily just so, to get by the PC Nazis, but no one had any doubt the 224-unit, FHA-approved development would drag the slums into their pristine valley.

They paid every day to live here, spending three hours in their cars to commute twelve miles to Burbank or downtown. They sent their kids to private schools in Pasadena that were so exclusive, you had to apply for a prospective child before you started dating. They had all watched their equity go to hell in the recession, and now the only value left in their homes was about to turn to shit.

"We gotta do something. Today," Marty said.

Terry sipped his beer. An itch started to bother him in the base of his skull, but with Marty ranting, he couldn't quite scratch it. "What did you have in mind?"

"Those unfinished houses down there are a firetrap. We should get some guys we can trust and go patrol it, make sure the construction site is . . . secure. If you know what I mean."

Terry got up and watched his daughter crossing the street to the Singhs' house. She waved to him again and blew him a kiss. Everybody was getting free cookies today.

"How're you feeling, Marty?"

"I'm fine. I mean, I had that flu everybody's crying about on the news, but we had these antibiotics left over from that thing I caught in Mexico, so I've been taking those. Why?"

He turned around just then, which was unfortunate. Terry's rifle butt smashed into his forehead, just above his right eye. He sputtered and spat beer and cookie crumbs, then toppled off his roof to fall headfirst in the paved dog run between his yard and the Mattinglys'.

Old Man Mattingly was out back watering his lawn. He waved to Terry. "Thanks for the cookies," he said.

"Thanks for being a good neighbor," Terry shouted back, and looked through Marty's binoculars as he finished Marty's box of dusted cookies.

It was too bad about Marty, but he was right about one thing. You had to draw a line around what you loved, and be willing to fight anything that crossed it.

* * *

The Channel Five News Center had just completed another special report and punted back to the regularly scheduled *Ellen Show* rerun, when the studio doors flew open and five men in *luchador* masks barged in, pointing guns.

Rod Landon, the midday anchor, had just sat down to begin taping the bumpers for his eleven thirty report. He was deep in correcting his script copy until his hairdresser yanked on his bangs as she screamed, "Terrorists!"

The gunmen fanned out to cover the cameramen and storm the control booth, while a short guy in a Mexican soccer team tracksuit shouldered his rifle and jumped up on Rod's desk.

"Get this shit back on the air, yo," he said. His mask had a blazing third eye on its forehead, and his air of command was almost as strong as his cologne.

"What the hell is this? Do you idiots have any idea—"

"We found some of those unfounded rumors you were talking about, Rod Landon, and we wanted to help you share them with your viewing audience." He dropped a bloody Adidas satchel on the desk, right on top of Rod's script. "You want to show people what's up, then you put that shit on the air."

The Napoleonic terrorist jumped down off the desk and shouted in Spanish at the control booth. "*Arriba*, Chuy!"

A huge terrorist in a skull mask tapped the glass with his gun barrel and squawked over the intercom, "*Es en vivo, Tres.*"

Rod Landon blinked at the camera. Sweat squirted out of his forehead and streamed into his eyes. "Um . . ."

Tres Ojos shooed Rod out of the chair and sat down behind the desk, stretching black leather gloves on his heavily tattooed hands. "Good morning, L.A. This is a *muy especial* report. We're sorry to have to interrupt Ellen again, but we have some extremely too-fucked-up shit that you need to see . . ."

He unzipped the Adidas bag and reached into it, hissing

in disgust as he peeled the bag back to reveal a pile of severed human heads, grown together into a knotty, oozing mass by thick nets of squirming white fibers. Knurled horns of dusty white fruiting bodies wilted under the blazing studio lights. Every mouth flapped and dripped spore-infested saliva. Every eye blinked away white tears as they rolled to stare blankly into the camera.

"This is what's out there trying to push your shit in, *mijos*. It's not gangs running wild, or race riots, or terrorists, or none of that shit. So stop being so stupid, okay?"

Islam Al-Harari had really fought it for a long time, before giving in and admitting that he hated America.

It was not a warm day, but it was sweltering in the tollbooth of the parking garage at the Sherman Oaks Galleria. His Greek boss thought it was funny. "You're used to desert, aren't you?"

Almost no cars were coming in, which was nice, but it made the day drag. The Galleria wasn't a full-service shopping mall. Catering to a certain type of client, it had only shoe stores, overpriced theme restaurants, a snobby Arclight movie theater, a hairstyling academy, a gym, and a plastic surgery clinic.

In short, it was one-stop shopping for aging American whores.

Islam came to America when he was twelve, at the beginning of the second Gulf War. He watched only American movies, bought only American music. Lost his accent. Dialed his cologne use back to a subtle hint of musk, and waxed the hair off his back. Stopped reading the Koran.

And yet, if he were made out of shit and used condoms, he still would have gotten laid more often than he did.

He pecked at his iPhone, but the Internet was all fucked up, and the tiny TV on the counter was worse than nothing. Islam looked longingly out the driveway onto Sepulveda Boulevard. *Where are you, whores?*

He was looking out on the street when the orange city bus stopped across the street and let people off. Strange, because the nearest stops were one block south or two blocks north.

Islam was riding the bus to work while his brand-new silver Range Rover was parked up on P-Three (Lavender), waiting for him to scrape up fifty thousand dollars to buy it.

Fuck this country. Even on a dead day like today, the garage was a quarter full, with two hundred unsold Range Rovers from some Jewish dealership in Van Nuys. With the economy in the shitter and nobody buying gas-guzzling SUVs, the dealer paid to dump them here, where they would sit and rot while hardworking, honest Islam took the fucking bus.

About thirty people got off the bus. No, not people. Bums. Staggering like epileptic drunks, wearing filthy cast-off clothes, drooling on themselves. Each and every one of them probably got more blow jobs than Islam.

With boredom turning slowly to concern and then alarm, Islam watched the filthy horde make its woozy way across Sepulveda and up the driveway of the parking garage. He paged security, but nobody upstairs picked up the phone after eight rings. And by then, they were on him.

"No pedestrians!" he shouted, but they just flowed around the booth and into the garage. A palpable wave of moldy stench flooded the booth in their wake. "Hey, come back here! I already called the police! You better get out of here—"

Fuck it. Maybe they would piss in the windows of some beautiful American whore's Mercedes, and she would scream at him. Scream until her big fake tits sprang free from her creamy silken top—

He tried to call security again, but still no answer. Flipped through the Girls of West Point issue of *Playboy*. God, they were hot. Maybe he should join the army. But then they'd just send him back to Iraq.

A car pulled up to his booth. Not just a car. A Range Rover. Silver. With the dealer sticker up in the passenger-side window.

Islam leaned out and looked around. Ida was in the other booth, but she had her headphones on, listening to that fat talk show host who warned her about foreigners.

The Range Rover's horn honked. "How much do I owe you?" The man in the driver's seat had no front teeth. His beard had something white and slimy, like rancid mayonnaise, caked in it. A snaky, questing root like the "eye" of a potato came out from under one of his eyes, stretching down his face before curling back up his left nostril.

He held out a ticket.

The Range Rovers were here under a special lease. The ticket had to be a piece of trash the bum must've found on the ground.

But America had made one thing abundantly clear. It was none of Islam's business. He pushed the ticket into the slot and read the total.

"Sixty dollars."

The bum peeled three twenties off a roll of bills, then doubled it. "And a little something for you, buddy."

"*No tips!*" Islam barked, but the Range Rover took off as soon as the barricade lifted.

He pocketed it just as the next Range Rover pulled up. The driver, a dazed-looking housewife with her hair in curlers, gave him a ticket and six twenties, then peeled out, turning north on Sepulveda.

His pockets were overflowing with cash when the next bus pulled up and fifty bums got out. Islam found himself stroking the money and smelling it. The bitter aroma he'd first thought was awful now made him shiver with pleasure. He was sharp enough to suspect that he'd been drugged. Ninety percent of the American currency in circulation had at least traces of cocaine on it, and God knows what else.

When the red Lexus pulled up, he was tempted to tell the driver to eat shit and get their own car out, he was quitting. But then he looked into the car, and saw the whore of his dreams.

With her flawless peaches-and-cream complexion, the blue-eyed platinum blonde looked airbrushed, even in the flesh. Curves that defied gravity and fucked with physics, to say nothing for what they did to her cashmere sweater.

"You've been working here all day, and people have just treated you like a machine, haven't they?"

Islam backed up in the booth and looked around again. Ida appeared to be deep in conversation with a bum in a black Range Rover. She closed her booth, leaving the barricade up, and climbed into the back of the Range Rover just before it sped away.

"Ticket?"

The lovely blonde whore tossed her blonde ringlets and giggled at him, reaching out to teasingly grab the end of his tie and pull him close. "But I didn't want to leave, just yet . . ."

Islam knew this had to be some kind of reality show joke, but he was too far gone to try to stop it. Maybe, just maybe, God was real and great and did answer prayers, and maybe it was just his turn.

When she pressed her surgically plump lips to his and heaved a bolus of spores and acidic mucus down his throat, he thought for a moment that this must be wrong. This wasn't sexy at all.

But before he could break the embrace, the flood of psychoactive slime backed up into his sinuses and entered his bloodstream. It was nothing like sex. It was so much better.

America's God, Islam thought, *is truly great.*

"No hostages are believed to have been harmed as of yet, but the standoff turned violent when bands of armed and appar-

ently infected civilians attempted to break into the studio and clashed with police.

"The as-yet unidentified leader of the group has used the airwaves to issue increasingly eccentric demands."

"Get yourself a dog, y'know, regardless. The only way to know for sure if your people are still people . . ."

"County animal shelters were closed today, but all twenty-eight ASPCA shelters and countless area pet stores have already been broken into by self-described vigilantes . . ."

Rhonda Landon, Channel Five's weekend weather girl, had finished her Christmas shopping at the Beverly Center before lunchtime, and was waiting for her boys to get their portrait with Santa Claus.

More to the point, she was hovering over the photographer as he tried to get Ty to stop crying and Bryce to stop picking his nose, working as politely as she knew how to extract a promise from him that in the final photographs and Christmas cards, the unsightly moist patch on Santa's lap would be airbrushed out.

For a Westside mall, this place was really slipping. She looked around in vain for seasonal workers to help load her car with the cartload of prewrapped gifts. They couldn't sell her this much crap and expect her to pack it all away herself, could they?

Rhonda was already keyed up before she left the house. She had a big fight with Rod last night about money, and she had to service him before he gave her back the Onyx Amex card. And after an epic battle with the crush of the mall with her boys in tow, she was completely done with her non-Web holiday shopping on the first fucking day of the season.

She was standing there thinking these thoughts when the punk kid climbed up on the railing on the third-floor gallery overlooking Santa's Workshop.

Other people looked up and let out surprised noises, then took to their heels to watch from a safe distance. They all thought, as did Rhonda, that he was about to jump. If he jumped, he would land on Santa, and her two children.

"Somebody do something, damn it!" Rhonda dragged her cart behind her as she approached the big red chair, calling for her babies.

The kid locked his legs in the balcony railings and threw his arms wide. "God bless us, everyone!" he shouted, and then his head exploded.

Rhonda looked up and screamed, but the scream was warped by the upswept pitch of a wordless question. The kid's head seemed to split open and rain down snowflakes on Santa's Workshop.

The drifting white powder settled on everything. People caught it on their tongues and started laughing, singing "Joy to the World." Ty finally stopped crying.

The punk kid still sat on the railing, head bowed, with white snow pouring out of it like torrential dandruff. Weird, but that's what it looked like, even if nobody but she thought anything was wrong with it.

A security guard tried to lift the limp kid off the balcony. The kid was pretty far away, but she thought he must be wearing a mask, because his face was just a white blur when the guard grabbed his arm and he fell over the railing.

Rhonda shoved her cart aside and dove into a planter box filled with poinsettias. People up and down the mall screamed, but the falling boy made no sound, except for a brief, interrupted remark that only Rhonda heard. "It's all goo—"

He hit the floor headfirst. A wet, sickening thud and a tsunami of flying organic matter kept her hunkered down in the red foliage. She stood and leaped from cover, running for Santa, screaming, "Give me my babies!"

But Santa didn't want to cooperate, and neither did her boys. St. Nick tried to grab her by the neck and pull her onto his piss-damp lap. "You're under the mistletoe, ma'am."

"Let's go, boys! Let go of me!" She slapped and punched Santa with one hand while trying to grab her oldest son with the other. Bryce bit her and spit into the bloody gash he made in her wrist. Ty flopped on the floor but just lay there, smirking at her like he knew she was a fraud.

Ungrateful little brats. Ruined her figure, sidelined her career, sabotaged her marriage, and now the chubby little termites were gnawing away at Christmas.

She screamed for a security guard, and one dutifully came right over the third-floor railing, screaming and flailing and pushed by a fresh wave of transients that seemed to have overtaken the top floor of the mall.

Suddenly, everything she cherished had turned on her.

Digging the red can out of her purse, she sprayed Santa Claus with her pepper spray. She yanked Bryce off his lap and clasped him to her bosom, then turned to run for her shopping cart. Her son bit her neck as she ran howling down the mall for the nearest exit doors.

Her blood sang, turned to incandescent gas in her veins. Not since she was voted Miss Modesto had she tasted such satisfaction and validation as she suddenly felt surging through her veins. Something was wrong with her, but something else was finally, totally right.

Nothing could have stopped her just then, short of the thing that happened next.

Just as she reached the doors and threw her cart at them to shove them open, a silver Range Rover jumped the curb outside and plowed through the bus kiosk.

Almost entranced, Rhonda watched shattered steel and glass fly off the SUV's oncoming grill like sea spray when it whipped sideways on the walkway and skidded into the doors, smashing them shut in Rhonda's face.

A stampede of panicked shoppers ran over her to collide

with the sealed doors. People stooped over her as if to help, but then they grabbed gifts out of her cart and took off, crawling through the broken glass and under the Range Rover, where a mob of dusted homeless waited for them.

It was all too much. Rhonda lay on the marble floor of the mall beside her overturned cart, trampled bags and gift baskets spilled out in the wake of Bryce, who leaped to freedom and ambled off without looking back.

She pulled herself to her feet, but let him go. Let it all go.

Everything was ruined. She'd sue this place into the fucking Stone Age, but it wouldn't save Christmas. And still, she itched and prickled with the nagging certainty that she'd forgotten something.

The security bars began to roll down out of the ceiling. The mall was locking them in.

Only then did she remember. She'd left Ty with Santa Claus. Christ, she'd never live that down. Rolling over and rising to walk, she was almost too overloaded, too numb with shock, to respond to the next outrage.

The woman from the flu vaccination kiosk in the food court had Bryce pinned to the floor. He fought like a wolverine, but she was fat and wily as only a nurse can be, in the ways of small children, and deftly pinned both his hands with one of hers and shoved a long needle up his nostril before Rhonda arrived on the scene.

She drove her knee into the woman's face. The big nurse fell back on her bulky haunches and let Bryce curl up into a catatonic ball. A bloodstain mushroomed out on her white surgical mask. "Little help," she said.

A big man grabbed her and sat on her chest. Rhonda shrieked at the top of her raw red lungs, but nobody stopped him as the masked man shone a flashlight in her eyes. "Doesn't look dusted, but . . ."

"But what?"

"Not worth a shot," he said. Clamping one hand over Rhonda's mouth, he sprayed something cold and stingy up her nose. She felt like she was drowning in it. Her will to fight turned belly-up and left her gagging and hurling up foam when the big man finally got off her and tackled someone else.

Rhonda crawled over to lay beside her son, who was dry-heaving and sobbing the way old people sob, at the doctor.

Ty was still somewhere in the mall. She heard him laughing, but when a whooping teenager ran by with her baby boy on her back, she couldn't begin to muster the strength to care, let alone get him back. He'd stopped crying, that was what mattered.

She pressed her hands to her face as if she meant to crush her own eyes. For just a moment, she'd felt free of everything, even all the shit she had to buy to fill the hole. For just a moment the hole was not just filled. There was no hole. It was only just starting to become more than a feeling, to tell her what her purpose in life really was, when that fat bitch poisoned her.

"I saw God, Mommy . . ." Bryce whined.

"Hush, honey," Rhonda cooed.

"But Mommy, I *was* God. But now he's gone. Now, I'm nothing."

"No, baby, no . . . I know, baby . . . it's okay . . . it's okay." But she didn't know anything anymore, except that it would never be okay, ever again.

The beaches stretched blank and bright and almost empty from Malibu to Hermosa, but for a few packs of die-hard surfers and joggers pacing along the lazy, lackluster waves. The Ferris wheel and the carousel turned on Santa Monica Pier, but the police had set up barricades, and people stayed away, even if the police had long since moved on.

The shore in the lee of the pier was packed with a crowd that covered the sand in ecstatic, shouting bodies from the grass verge to the low-tide line. La Luz De Cristo evangelical ministry staged one of its perennial revivals on the shore.

Padre Juan Salazar waded in up to his waist, his spotless white cassock flowing out around his ponderous bulk in the grimy foam, shouting into his bullhorn at all the sinners in Santa Monica to come down to the water to be baptized.

And unlike every morning before, today, they came.

The first sinner to come bounding naked down the beach was in the full flower of his corruption. Great white antlers sprouted from the oozing fissures in the crown of his skull, and his eyes were weeping cavities stuffed with trembling roots that perked up and homed in on the priest's amplified voice. He careened into one sturdy praying woman after another, stumbling in the sand. The spore-bodies from his head were spent and twitching, his body devoured from the inside out to leave little more than a spastic skeleton, but he expelled gouts of bloody white slime as he reeled through the prayerful crowd.

A trio of deacons surrounded the naked sinner and, taking his arms, dragged him into the surf toward Padre Juan.

The priest invoked the Trinity as he took hold of the sinner's skull, split open like an overripe rose, and dunked him into the sea. The sinner tried to bite him, but Padre Juan was wise in the ways of the devil and of crazy drug addicts. He swept the sinner off his feet and held him beneath the waves.

The demon inside him reacted immediately, withering and flowing out of him in explosive gusts. His hideous white horns puckered and shrank into themselves like snails stung with salt.

He only held the sinner under the waves for ten seconds, but when he lifted him up to glory, his soul burst forth from his mouth and broken skull like a dove and flew up into the sky.

They all saw it. Even Padre Juan was struck mute by the miracle, but with the shock of his bullhorn short-circuiting as he dropped it into the water, he knew what God wanted them to do.

Rising from their knees, they left the beach and went into the streets, searching for sinners.

You could see almost anything on Hollywood Boulevard, but thousands of tourists every day discovered that if they wanted to see movie stars, they had to settle for the Movieland Wax Museum or the wannabes in cheap costumes posed for photos in front of Mann Chinese Theatre.

Despite—or perhaps, no certainly, because of—the chaos and violence sweeping the city, hordes of Japanese and European tour groups still wandered the tacky star-studded sidewalks, snapping shots of Walk of Fame favorites and waiting for something magical to happen.

And then it did.

The limousine pulled up in front of the shrine of famous hand- and footprints, but from the moment he got out and someone shouted, "*It's him!*" they dropped everything and rushed to the curb. To take his picture. To pose for a picture with him. To breathe his air and hear his voice. To touch him.

He smiled and waved and moved among them, like something out of a dream. This was what they had been promised, what they'd been cheated of, all their lives.

And then he reached back into the limousine and helped *her* step out.

For a moment, he was completely forgotten. Their hunger to possess her was far more powerful than their lust to be him. They smiled and posed and pressed the flesh, even kissing those bold enough to request it.

Walking down Hollywood Boulevard without bodyguards, without handlers or hangers-on just like mere mortals, as the mob suckling at the teats of their beauty swelled to become an army. They needed no protection from haters, but the adoration of this crowd was so potent, that without some barrier, it would love them to death and eat their remains.

The milky tears that dripped from underneath their Dior mirror shades and the sticky resin they left on the faces and hands of everyone they passed got licked up or rubbed into weeping eyes with frenzied abandon. They left a trail of bodies in their wake, moaning, stoned into oblivion on the spores of the rich and famous.

"My wife and I have come down here to your studio today to talk about something really important, and we brought all our best friends—isn't that right, everybody?"

"YEAH!!!"

"And we all came down here to tell the world not to buy into the hysteria you're seeing on your TV screens. These are people with an agenda, selling you an act. Los Angeles is a beautiful city, and today, it's better than ever . . . are you feeling me!?"

"IT'S ALL GOOD!!!"

Time spent anywhere you didn't want to be was only as bad as you let it be. That was the message Richie Long had taken from Hamlet. Never mind all that skull-clutching, navel-gazing existential bullshit. In a nutshell, you really could become a king of infinite space, but he hadn't come to really believe it, until just lately.

Richie sat in the dayroom at the center of Cell Block D in the medium-security holding annex of the L.A. County jail, watching the news. Usually, even among these non-violent offenders and first-timers segregated from the lifers and gangbangers for whom prison was finishing school, the fight for the remote control was fierce, but all that had changed. So much had changed in the last week . . .

Richie heard the inmates' hearty laughter at the aerial footage of the demolition derby on the 405, and he could almost see it through their eyes. He joined in their laughter at the comical sight of cars piling into the flaming mountain of wreckage choking the Sepulveda Pass from Sunset to Sherman Oaks. Though he had gone blind sometime last night, Richie didn't miss it, so long as he was close to his new family.

It was really damned funny when he thought about it: the chain of stupid decisions and divine grace that put him in this jail at this time. It was so stupid, what he'd done and what he'd planned to do, but if he hadn't been so stupid, he would never have found himself here.

Arrested for simple possession while driving a client from Burbank Airport, he'd taken the fall for the passenger because Richie was the guy's client, not the other way around. And Richie could only suppose the judge had held him without bail and stiff-armed his lawyer because his so-called professional had talked about how he'd been hired to kill Richie's ex-wife.

Oh well. You live and learn, and if you're lucky, you grow and change.

And right now, Richie wouldn't trade places with anyone on earth.

He was not the first to find it, but he had been the one to recognize its potential, and in him, it had found the vision necessary to give it what it needed.

His cell mates found the mushrooms growing in a corner of the showers, and being desperately in need of anything like a high, they ate them. They both got violently ill that night, but in their death throes, they filled the cell with spores.

Richie woke up to find his brain racing with dreams and visions. It was like a conversation in his brain, the endless unfolding of questions and revelations in his own voice, the euphoria and the freedom from bodily concerns. Water was all he needed now. Water and allies.

Within two days, he'd collected enough fungi to turn on

the whole cell block. By that night, they had the guards. The next morning, the staff and the trustees. By lunchtime, they had all three hundred sixty inmates, forty-eight guards, and twelve staff.

It was a new day, a remarkable first in American penal history. Instant, total rehabilitation. The cells were opened up. Details went to work, harvesting spores from the ones who overindulged and ripened too quickly, and digging tunnels.

The jail's basement was connected to the storm drains, and crews were sent out to hit drug couriers all over L.A. County. But by then, most of the inmates were too ripe to handle the next phase of the operation. So Richie had reached out to his brother.

Maybe that was a mistake. Maybe he had failed the family by holding back on ingesting the spores, selfish to try to preserve himself as long as possible. Maybe, if he had done more and let it all happen faster, he wouldn't have been so weak.

The inmates rushed to the windows as a helicopter passed over the jail. Richie reached out and knew before any of them shouted it that it was a news chopper.

He flailed out with his cane and grabbed Sandy, the older female guard, by the bony stick of one desiccated arm. "Turn it to Channel Nine, won't you?"

She tried a garbled reply, but her mouth was choked with thirsty mycelium and fluffy, phallic fruiting bodies, so he had to take it on faith that she obeyed.

A moment later, the TV changed to KCAL's ongoing live coverage, and he felt, more than saw, the fuzzy relayed impressions from Sandy's fuzzy, half-eaten brain.

Dwight Simmons sat in the traffic chopper's suicide seat, leaning out over the 110 freeway's downtown section. The massive concrete gorge was cluttered with wrecks and obscured by smoke, but Dwight had something else to show the folks at home, and urged the pilot to climb.

"—*virtually quarantined downtown area has been inundated with pedestrian traffic and clashes with police have been a huge headache, but where are all these people going? We think we know, but this only raises more questions, Jerry*—"

The inmates came back from the windows and settled down in front of the TV. Richie's second sight grew richer with more eyes added to the pool, the forest of skyscrapers swelling and pivoting as the chopper climbed, buffeted by high winds and wreathed in smoke.

"*What we're trying to show you may be alarming, but we hope that some sense can be made of what we're about to show you*—"

The rooftop of the Chase Tower hove into the frame, and the smoke parted, the camera automatically dilating to focus.

"Not quite yet, Dwight." Richie picked up the cell phone in his lap and hit the Send button. A text message went through. There was no reply. Not on the phone.

But on the screen—

Dwight Simmons was bucking for an Emmy. "*We're what? No way. We're taking fire from the rooftop . . . Take us down, Pete, take us—Jesus Christ! What the fuck was that?*"

The camera mounted under the chopper's nose swiveled dizzily down the skyscraper's awesome seventy-two-story facade to zoom in on Fourth Avenue, where a starburst of flame from the back of a pickup truck traced a line of smoke from the ground straight up to the helicopter's tail rotor.

The panorama went wobbly, then became a whirling blur. The city and sky became one: consumed in fire, then deluged with static snow.

PART SEVEN

Here Comes the Science

THIRTY

For Rory, waking up was like crawling out from under a boulder. And that was on a good day.

This morning, he felt like the boulder had boots on, had spent the night line-dancing all up and down him. When the door creaked open, it hurt to lift his head from the pillow.

Euclid stood in the doorway with two steaming mugs of coffee big enough to drown a cat in. He'd dressed up for the occasion, wearing a black kimono and a T-shirt with Jesus riding a T-Rex on it that said HERE COMES THE SCIENCE.

"You guys sleep okay? I hope my friends didn't keep you up."

Trixie groaned and stirred. Rory rolled painfully out of bed and took the coffee. "You got *friends* over now? What kind of friends?"

"What time is it?" Trixie muttered.

"Almost two in the afternoon. I let you sleep in. But you gotta get up now. It's showtime."

"What?"

Rory limped out of the room and down the hall, thinking he'd made a mistake bringing in Euclid. He got told the end of the world was here, he probably decided to throw a potluck.

At least ten very professorial-looking people sat or paced around the living room, most of them working on laptops or talking into cell phones. TVs and computer monitors had been arranged into a ramshackle video wall, showing local and national news, and a few grainy Skype video feeds of empty chairs.

A couple of rugged guys in faded concert T-shirts were setting up a video camera and some sort of teleconferencing hub. The atmosphere in Euclid's house had turned into some weird hybrid of hacker convention and university faculty lounge, except that everyone present was smoking a spliff the size of a baby's arm. Loud dub reggae still bounced through the smoke-choked air. Max Romeo was going to put on an iron shirt and chase the devil out of earth.

Trixie caught up, and Euclid led them through the booby-trapped maze of gear to the big suede couch. "After you guys crashed, I called a couple friends." Shoving a huge, dusty seven-volume encyclopedia of fungi and lichens onto the floor, he seated them beside a totally hairless guy in a raincoat who ogled something on his laptop screen with such naked, icky lust that it could only be porn. "And they called two friends, and so on, and so on . . ."

"You found out what this thing is?" Trixie asked. "Can they stop it?"

"We're just setting up for our first real teleconference, to pool what we know, right now. We've had people on the ground trying things, but we just don't have enough boots—"

"Hold up a minute. I got a guy you need to talk to," Rory said, and took out his phone.

As the smashing redhead in the go-go boots, now swaddled in an emerald silk kimono, came round to refill their coffees, Euclid introduced Trixie to the grinning perv in the raincoat. "Trix, Dr. Horace Crawley. UCLA's foremost expert on mycology and fungal diseases."

Trixie took his cold, clammy hand off her knee. "Have you ever seen anything like this, Doctor?"

"No, never," he said, with white foam in the corners of his smile. "It's like Xmas a month early."

Euclid brought over a heavyset black woman who could've been Euclid's mother. She wore a soiled white doctor's coat. "Dr. Mamie Minta, county public health department. She also coordinates the free medical clinics throughout South Central."

Trixie shook her hand. Euclid introduced several more eminent persons who smiled and shook her hand or offered her a toke off a joint. All of these people were very smart, but also very stoned.

Rory stepped back into the room as Tres Ojos finally picked up his phone.

"*Bueno.*"

"You wanted to know what we're dealing with and how to beat it."

"*Hell yes. Hold on, though . . . I need to get one of my engineers in on this shit . . .*"

Engineers? "Where are you right now?"

"*Turn on Channel Five.*"

Rory went to the video wall and changed the big screen to five. Rod Landon sweated like a cheese as he read reports on safe evacuation centers in Burbank and Glendale. Tres Ojos strutted across the set behind the newscaster with his mask on, and waved to the camera.

"No shit, you know *that* guy?" Euclid cackled.

"You have any representatives of L.A.'s organized criminal contingent on the line? Or anybody who controls a TV station?"

"No. We're not too connected with the mainstream media, or the underworld."

"You are now." Euclid gave Rory a number for Tres Ojos to call and patch into the video conference.

Euclid cued the redhead to turn on some lights and hit some switches and the video wall filled with faces.

Dr. Minta stood up before the camera. "Thank you all for tuning in. Especially Chief Magill of the L.A. Fire Department, and Special Agent Bryant. We know you have crises and dire emergencies to deal with and we won't waste your time with formalities. We'll start with a brief rundown on what we know about the pathogen."

Crawley took the floor. "Hullo . . . I assume nobody here knows much about fungi, so a brief—"

"Really brief," Euclid put in.

"—Rundown on fungi is in order." Crawley cued a slide of a diagram showing a mushroom above and below the soil line. "All fungi and molds are remarkably elegant in their simplicity. They eat and reproduce. The mycelium sprout from spores and grow into their preferred dietary substrate, digesting it with secreted enzymes and acids. This activity fuels the growth of the fruiting bodies, which thrust out of the substrate and into the air to disperse spores on the wind, or to be eaten by a scavenger who will sow the seeds with its feces. About four hundred of the fifty thousand known species of fungi prefer a substrate of mammal flesh, and fungi use every conceivable means to spread their spores, so making them a drug that gets inhaled directly into the bloodstream is probably the least incredible feature of our new best friend."

A new slide showed a severely dusted middle-aged man reaching for the camera with a vacant eagerness somehow rendered comical by his being sandwiched between two cars in the middle of an intersection. From crown to jawline, his head was split by a gash like a vertical mouth, with white polyps like clusters of deformed antlers emerging from the cracks, and thick skeins of veiny white worms pulsing just under his sallow skin.

"What we got here is a previously unknown carnivorous basidiomycete that cheats, big-time. Its spores are clones, but it can cross-fertilize itself. The fruiting bodies and feeding modalities are a dead ringer for *Cordyceps*, which is the nastiest living thing on the planet, if you're an ant."

He cued a slide showing the head and thorax of a leaf-cutter ant, blown up until it looked like a tractor. The blunt wedge of the worker ant's head was split open by a cluster of cup-shaped blossoms, which spilled dusty spores into the breeze.

"The spores from our new friend are big fuckers, over twenty micrometers, where most spores are only ten, but they can still aerosolize and travel pretty far from a primary fruiting body."

Crawley flicked through a barrage of slides of spore powder dispersals around the heads of dead, infected bodies. Even in the still images, many of the white fungal intruders were visibly straining to grow out of or escape their spent human hosts.

"Now, psychoactive mushrooms are nothing new, but drugs in the spores themselves? No way. This guy's spores are impregnated with alkaloids that I suspect mimic MDMA in structure and effect. The daughter organism from the spores continues to produce alkaloids to keep the host high, even as the fungus is eating it. But there's a whole lot more in those little spores.

"We don't know the how, or even the what, of it, but the spores can transmit experiential knowledge. Memories. This thing may have no mind of its own, but everyone who ingests the spores seems to instantly and seamlessly join into the conspiracy to spread themselves all over town."

Cross talk and insistent beeping of conference callers punching in rode right over Crawley's reedy voice.

Trixie spoke up. "It's true! We've seen it. People we've known for years suddenly turned on us, trying to get us to join them. And they all seemed to know—"

"My brother," Rory put in. "He's in the private low-security jail annex downtown. I think he was one of the first infected. He sounded like himself, but he was using everything he had to spread the spores in the gang com-munities in South Central." *But mostly just me*, he thought.

On one of the screens, Special Agent Bryant, who looked like his facial features were crudely painted on a brick, ob-jected, "If this thing is so cozy with our biology, it doesn't add up that we've never seen it before."

Euclid answered, "Our best guess is that this is an op-portunistic, subterranean fungus that got pushed up by the falling water-table. It got thirsty and surfaced, stumbled onto us and found us irresistible. That's why the outbreak has been so violent."

"Maybe it used to thrive on us, but it's been isolated," Dr. Minta said. "This city is only a day's flight from any-where in the world."

Crawley leaned off camera and took a monster hit off his joint. "No way. No melanin, for one thing, which makes it vulnerable to ultraviolet light, which means it must have evolved underground. It's almost foreign enough, I could buy that it came in on a meteor, though. The sequencing on this bitch is gonna be a revelation, but if you plot the genomic variation from *Cordyceps* against Perseid meteor showers and comet activity—"

Euclid covered the mic. "Don't try to drag your cosmic diaspora horseshit into this, man."

Crawley winced, but shrugged and moved on. "Okay, then. Moving right along." He pecked at a laptop. "I got these snaps from a fellow traveler who works in the county morgue."

He hit a switch so the image took center stage on the video wall. Trixie and Euclid covered their eyes.

The shot was a close-up of a severed human head, neatly bisected with a radial saw. The inside of the cranial cavity looked like it'd been stirred with a stick. The forward bulk-head of the skull bulged outward and cracked, from the forehead to the temple, as a densely folded cluster of white stalks pressed urgently at the fault line. These stalks occupied the space where a good deal of the cerebrum ought to be.

"Now, similar to *Cordyceps*, the fungus takes over the nervous system, but it seems to infiltrate and partially replace it, as well. The hyphae form in the cranial cavity, then start budding. All the while feeding drugs directly into the host's brain, it starts to eat them from the inside out.

"We found bodies estimated infected no more than twenty-four hours that'd lost forty percent of body mass to the fungus. But an incredible amount of it gets reinvested in mycelium networks that shoot through the whole body. But they're doing a lot more than just eating.

"The mycelia also produce secondary fruiting bodies, mostly in the lungs, throat, and salivary glands. The spores that come from these bodies are stunted and deformed, but they're also encased in a jelly that sticks to everything and is very nutritious and, I hear, pretty delicious. Don't look at me like that.

"As these ripen, the host coughs or vomits them up and they're every bit as infectious as the primaries, but there seems to be a pretty sharp trade-off of quality for quantity. The second wave of infected seem to have poorer motor control, worse brain function, and the fungus eats through them even faster. Which brings me to the pinnacle of my slide show . . ."

A skeleton lay in a pool of human soup in a shopping mall, almost completely consumed by burst white balloons and coils of greedy probing mycelia that bored into the bones and spread across the floor to slurp up the last dregs of its host.

"The primary fruiting bodies mature in less than twelve hours, but most of the cerebrum is either digested or so compressed that lesions form and it drowns on its own blood inside of six. This guy was walking around like this for quite a while before his head cracked open. And this is the part, I don't know whether to laugh or cry."

He pointed to a series of knobby, whorled things like miniature oak galls on the stalks in the bisected skull, underneath the primary hyphae. "Now, these look like a tertiary parasite, don't they? But close-up—"

He keyed a new slide, showing two microscope views of treelike nervous tissue embedded in clusters of pillow-shaped cells. "Now, I may be pretty stoned right now, but if you got me drunk, I probably couldn't tell you which of those is tissue from those weird walnuts on the fungus, and which is human cerebral tissue."

More fierce objections, which Euclid calmed before handing the floor back to Crawley.

"Now, parasites and hosts exchange genetic junk mail all the time, and parasites can rewrite their host's behavior, structure, even its gender. It may or may not mean this fungus has somehow grown brains, which are the most complex organic formation in the known universe. But it does keep people alive long after it's eaten *their* brains, and it seems to keep them alive and ambulatory right up until their heads explode. If you want to call them alive."

Nobody made a Republican or a Scientology joke. Nobody said the Z-word. Good for them.

Special Agent Bryant cut in again. "So, what's their end game? Can we quarantine them until they eat all their current human hosts?"

Euclid replied, "That's exactly what it wants, man. You lock the door on L.A., it'll use up all its people trying to get to the rest. And their end game is a mean motherfucker."

Back to the melted skeleton in the mall. Crawley said, "When the human host is too consumed to think anymore, the same sort of behavior control that *Cordyceps* uses on ants seems to take over. The fungus floods and inflames the host's inner ear canals, inducing what entomologists call summit sickness. Like the ants, the human host is driven to climb . . ."

Back to the infected ant.

". . . to the highest point it can reach to relieve the pain, and then the ascocarp bodies in the head explode, releasing tens of millions of spores each. Think of it this way. Every squirt of semen from a human penis contains hundreds of millions of sperm. Every human host seems to grow, you might say, twelve to twenty penises from his or her unlucky head. Enough to fuck the world."

"Cool it, man." Euclid took the mic. "What my esteemed colleague is trying to say is that, as they get used up, something like ten thousand of these dusted folks are going to climb as high as they can and die together, and when the wind dies down and the temperature falls, they're all going to go off at once, and drop their dust on ten million people. What time's sunset?"

"Four forty-five, dude," somebody at a laptop called out.

"Okay, you've scared us," a gray-haired ER doctor on a Webcam cut in, "but how are we going to stop it?"

An Asian lady in a lab coat punched into the conference and took the floor. "Fortunately, our fungus probably didn't come here on a meteor. Its membranes are regulated by ergosterol, so a suite of fungicides with amphoteracin B out in front should kill it dead."

Dr. Minta added, "Our test cases are responding, if we get them within that six-hour window Horace mentioned. In recently infected subjects, aerosolized Lamisil up the nose seems to stop growth in its tracks. If we act fast, we can still save a lot of these people."

Special Agent Bryant added, "For a brain-eating fungus, this thing seems to know how to run a terrorist operation pretty damned well. We can't spare bodies, but someone needs to watch over the food and water supply—"

"We got it covered," said a dashing bleach-blond guy in a magenta superhero mask, speaking on a Webcam from a dog park in West Hollywood. "The neighborhoods will watch over themselves until the government pulls its head out."

Rory mutely asked Euclid, *Who's that?*

"Captain Fabulous," Euclid whispered, making a *Don't Ask* gesture.

Rory kept poking Euclid until he turned back. "Who's that angry guy on the screen in the corner?" The guy he pointed at was moving his lipless mouth very fast and his eyes bulged like he was yelling at the conference, but his mic was clearly turned off.

Euclid shook his head. "Mayor's office."

The ER doctor punched in. "Amphoteracin is the primary for *Cryptococcus* infections in AIDS patients. We can round up the available supplies from here at Cedar Sinai, Kaiser, and the private clinics. I'll get a list worked up and make some calls."

Trixie whispered in Rory's ear. "Tell them."

He gulped and started to argue, but then tapped Euclid on the shoulder and whispered in his ear.

Euclid boomed, "My friend here has reason to believe that fluconazole in high dosages could work as a stopgap immunization agent."

The Asian scientist asked, "Is your friend a doctor?"

Euclid started to answer, but Rory took over. "No, but my wife and I have been repeatedly exposed to this shi— the spores, and we're not sick. We, uh—that is, my wife, uh, had a serious, uh—"

Trixie added, "*We* had a wicked case of the yeastie beasties, and Monistat couldn't touch it, so we were taking fluconazole. Rory probably stopped taking his as soon as it cleared up, but we feel pretty human and look, no mushrooms."

A long-haired hacker popped up from his laptop. "I'm in the customs database, and I found a freight car filled with industrial fungicide from China. It's on a flatcar in San Pedro."

Minta objected, "You can't spray that stuff on people. It'll kill them, whether they're infected or not."

Euclid retorted, "We won't use it on people we can cure. But take a look at the streets of downtown, buddy. There's no coming back from that."

Somewhere in the living room, a phone rang. Amid the jumble of digital electronics, whirring fans, and beeping battery backups, an antique phone with real bells inside it trilled like a summons from somebody's ancestors.

Euclid bid them continue and went to pick it up.

"Now, as for responses to the pathogen, the center of activity is converging on the downtown skyscrapers, but we're seeing similar patterns along Wilshire in Westwood and in Burbank and Glendale—"

Euclid waved to Rory and handed him the phone. "It's for you," he said.

Rory put the phone to his ear.

The voice on the line was garbled and phlegmy, as if breathing through gravy, but Rory stiffened at the first indrawn wheeze. *"I'm so tired, little man . . ."*

Rory backed out of the room to the extent of the old phone's cable. "You know where I am?"

"It hurts like you wouldn't believe, knowing everything I know. I'm almost done . . . it's almost done with me . . . You know what's weird, it's not the physical shit that drives you up the wall . . . It's all those other people inside your head . . ."

"What do you want, Richie?"

"I still owe you a set of kitchen knives, little man. You did a big-man's job out there. Listen, I gotta cruise, but you want to come with me later . . . it'll be just like old times down at the res."

"Where are you going, Richie? What're you gonna do?"

"Gonna go for a swim . . ."

The line went dead.

Rory hung up and went over to Trixie. "We got our marching orders yet?"

Trixie took him by the shoulders, alarmed. "No *way* are you going down there—"

"Oh, baby, are you shitting me? I can hardly *walk*, much less fight any more."

"Okay, good. But—"

"But I just got off the phone with Richie."

"Oh, no—"

"*Shhhh!*" several people hissed at once.

"I'll tell you in a minute," he whispered in her ear.

Then they listened as the fire chief explained that they couldn't spare a truck for Tres Ojos to take downtown.

"Umm, excuse me? I bet I know where there's a truck," Rory said.

Euclid walked them out to the sidewalk. The redhead walked ten feet ahead of them with a Mossberg pump shotgun.

"Don't worry, but don't go numb either. This is not the end of the world."

Trixie cracked a smile. "I was just about to tell you the same thing."

Euclid threw out his big arms and hugged them both. "See? This thing can't take over L.A. Scratch us hard enough, we're a hive mind already."

Trixie wiped a tear from her eye and let fly a nervous giggle. "I'm all right. It just feels like it's all falling apart."

"This isn't the end of the world. It's not even the end of L.A. It's just an infection. We're growing and turning everything into people and pollution, we're pushing out, so some shit's bound to push back. This isn't the end of anything, it's just a symptom of something else coming. In about ten years, shit like this'll seem normal."

PART EIGHT

At Long Last, Dying

THIRTY-ONE

Manuel didn't get to drive the fire engine, but he got to turn on the siren.

Nobody got out of their way, but that was fine. Most of the abandoned cars strewn across Sunset were lightweight, shitty sedans and hatchbacks that flipped off the pumper rig's grill like empty plastic crates.

As Silver Lake dissolved into Chavez Ravine, the street was empty, the side streets blockaded with cars and trash Dumpsters and patrolled by folks with dogs. People cheered as they rolled through their neighborhoods, but some others shot at them as they passed. They didn't look dusted.

The truck seemed to rise up on its right-side wheels as the driver, a retired firefighter named Reggie Porter, took the rig around the sharp turn onto Elysian Parkway.

The day had not worked out at all like Manuel expected. After dropping Rory and Trixie off at their friend's house, he'd run from one end of the city to the other on errands—raiding medical supply houses and dropping off teams of armed killers at shopping malls and evacuation centers. When his cousin called from the TV station and told him to bust into Paramount Studios to steal their fire engine, Manuel was too wrapped up in the day's weirdness to stop and catch his breath.

The Bronson gate of Paramount Studios stood open and unguarded. The pumper rig and paramedic van parked in the studio's firehouse, right where Rory said they would be, but they were not unprotected.

The white-haired, drunken old man sat in the driver's seat of the pumper rig with an unfiltered Winston in his lipless mouth and a Colt Desert Eagle pointed at Manuel's face. "Goldbrickin' sonsabitches. Whole damned city's on fire, and nobody showed up for work."

Manuel put up his hands and told the grizzled fireman what they wanted to do with his rig.

Tres Ojos had sent nine *vatos* in two trucks to the rail yards to plunder a freight car full of Chinese industrial fungicide. Five survivors in one truck met them on the lot, with a bed loaded with drums covered in CAUTION and POISON stickers.

Porter showed them how to mix the noxious yellow powder into the pumper rig's thousand gallon water tanks, then cussed them onto the truck and smashed through the wrought iron truck gate to head east on Melrose.

The plan was to meet up at Dodger Stadium parking lot, but Manuel had no idea how many to expect. The sight took his breath away.

A couple hundred soldiers were parked in the lot: Crips and Bloods, Mexicans and blacks shoulder to shoulder, flying their colors as masks over their faces. Such a volatile mixture in one place could only mean Armageddon. They were a loose mob of mobs from sets all over South Central, but their unwillingness to mingle drove them to stand in something like regimented groups. This thing that had attacked their city had made them forget their differences in a day, and become an army.

When the fire engine rolled into the lot, a roar of prison-yard love shook the ravine like nothing the Dodgers ever did there.

Manuel served two tours in Afghanistan to get away from the gangster life. He joined right after his cousin got shot in the head and miraculously survived. Manuel still bristled at the thought of going anywhere with these guys, let alone risking his life, but this was his city, his home. So this was his war.

A big black man in a bowler stood in the turret on an armored personnel carrier. Manuel figured out why half the National Guard armories in L.A. and Orange were empty when the National Guard tried to deploy this morning.

"Can . . . you . . . dig . . . it," Porter rumbled.

General Stymie shouted into a bullhorn. "Now our secret weapon is here, get into your squads and get your shit cocked . . . but one more thing before we roll out."

A teenaged Crip with gold teeth and an Uzi older than his dad rolled up on the fire engine and told Porter to scoot over.

"Fuck you, punk," Porter said, settling his Desert Eagle in the crook of his arm.

Stymie strutted on the roof of the APC. "We are not going down there to fight their war for them. Downtown never did nothing for us, but we do for our own, don't we?"

He let the crowd respond with a forced cheer. "And if they're not stopped, these walking dead honkies are going to spread their disease into our neighborhoods on the evening breeze.

"You might not like it, and they may hate it, but we all living in the same city. Nobody's going nowhere."

"Yo, fuck that shit," Goldie said, pointing his second-hand Uzi. "Eight Tray Crip, buster. Stymie's my uncle."

Manuel tried to be patient. "Tres Ojos is my cousin."

Goldie's face fell.

"You wanna work the hose?"

Goldie lit up. The guys on the back of the truck handed him up onto the rig behind the hose turret.

Stymie jumped back into the turret behind the dual sixty-caliber machine guns. "And if I see any of you mother-fuckers looting, I'll cap you myself. Let's roll out and break 'em off some."

Somebody sounded an air horn. Soldiers whooped and fired their guns into the air. Stymie's APC led a ragtag convoy of a dozen cars and trucks back up Elysian Park to Sunset. Another pack of vehicles took off in their wake, but turned southeast down Stadium Way, to come into downtown on North Hill.

Horns began honking. A pack of El Caminos and Cadillacs lined up behind the fire engine. Goldie shouted, "Thought you bitches knew what you was doing!"

Porter threw the enormous pumper rig into gear and turned it around to leave the lot and return to Sunset.

The hills to the north were engulfed in yellow and black smoke that parted every so often with the fitful wind to reveal advancing skirmish lines of flames like a wall of teeth eating the Santa Monica Mountains.

In the shadows of the skyscrapers of downtown, the pall of smoke cut visibility down to five blocks. Even over the big diesel roar of the fire engine, Manuel heard shots and screams echoing out of the toxic fog, and wondered if he'd not made a horrible mistake.

The first roadblock straddled the Sunset bridge over the Pasadena Freeway. Porter cussed and began to brake, but Manuel shouted, "Go on through! Look at them!"

Four dusted cops stood out in the road between four rows of parked cruisers on the bridgehead, shooting at Stymie's convoy as it detoured south down Custer. The last car in his team swerved and crashed into a parked car, the driver slumped over dead.

The cops opened up on the pumper rig. The windshield starred and flew apart in the cab like stinging ice. Manuel tried to stay low, but he couldn't just run over cops, even if they were shooting at him. He peeked over the dashboard, pumping the brake.

They were white. Way too white. They had no faces at all.

Porter swore and stepped on the gas, let the rig have its

head plowing through the roadblock. Cruisers flew into the railings and over the bridge. The rig's grill was smashed in and shoving a pulverized cop car down the road, but no steam shot out of the radiator.

An infected cop climbed up out of the wreckage impaled on the grill and scuttled across the hood. His legs dragged behind him in a boneless, bloody tangle, but he got halfway through the smashed windshield before Manuel slid the safety off on his MP5.

"Holy fucking shit, junior! Do something!"

Manuel froze. This was not a nightmare, was it? It was the war all over again, but on the streets of L.A., and the cops were monsters and whether it was real or not, it felt real enough when the cop's claws raked his shoulder. White worms wriggled out of oozing holes in his flesh and spurted acid on Manuel's arm. Real enough to hurt, real enough to kill him. He tucked the barrel of the rifle under his chin and blew the cop's head off.

The convoy rolled over the bridge after the fire engine and into the free fire zone of downtown Los Angeles.

Where Sunset turned to Cesar Chavez Avenue, burning cars and gutted storefronts added twisted black trees to the forest of murk, and sporadic automatic-weapons fire rebounded up and down the glass canyons to the south. The cars behind the fire engine sped ahead to engage shambling bands of furry, mindless white humanoids spilling out of Broadway down Bunker Hill like the outflow from a Kings game.

The Crip soldiers in a convertible Cadillac stood up and chopped down the crowds with wild volleys of lead in a textbook drive-by. Finally, their reckless tactics had found a perfect application.

But instead of fleeing in panic, the crowd rushed into the path of the bullets, and blocked the car. The Caddy slammed into one, then a few, then a bunch of dusted bums, and stalled on the pile of bodies. One of the corpses under the Caddy's front end exploded, flinging the big luxury car end over end down Sunset as Manuel barreled through the intersection.

Bodies smashed into the pumper rig and flattened under the hurtling weight, but Porter had the engine hurtling down the avenue too fast to swerve out of their way. "Goddamn me," Porter shouted, "if I didn't always wonder what this would be like."

A squadron of police motorcycles swooped in out of the smoke as they turned south on Alameda and flanked the truck. *Thank God*, Manuel thought. Until he saw what was riding them.

Naked and painted bright orange where they were not shaggy with fungus, the howling bikers tried to fire shotguns at their front tires. They were lousy shots because they had branching beards of white fungus dangling from their eyeholes, but they shot one of Tres Ojos's guys off the truck so he fell under the rear wheels.

Manuel's rearview mirror shattered and flew away on wings of buckshot. He stuck his rifle out the window and returned fire in tight, controlled bursts. He took the head off the rider of a bike so it tumbled in front of two more that crashed and fell behind them. The bikes peeled off and turned down Olvera Street, jumped the curb, and disappeared into the Mexican merchant mall.

Too easy. Manuel heard Porter choke on his cigarette and sputter, "Gawddamn it!"

The fire engine seized up in a squealing fit of brakes. A block ahead of them on Alameda Street, the world-famous spire of Union Station faced the Olvera Street park and bandstand, but they could see none of this, for the wall of marching dusted bodies coming toward them. The men on top of the fire truck opened fire into the crowd, but it was like throwing sand at the ocean. The marching mob wore rags and uniforms and random civilian clothes, but they all wore the same wasted white faces. And even as they closed the gap, something in their midst rose up to block the entire avenue.

"I'm not driving into that," Porter snapped, and brought the fire engine to a halt.

California Plaza was an opulent space with fountains and wide reflective pools that doubled the twin skyscrapers' reflections, where executives and secretaries on lunch breaks could calmly reflect on the wealth and power their labor created.

Stymie liked it a lot more today.

The wreckage of at least three helicopters lay scattered all over Third Street and Grand Avenue, like giant swatted flies. The reflecting pools were choked with bodies and fleshy towers of fungus like termite mounds, siphoning up the last of the ash-scummy water.

Stymie's driver rolled the APC up the wide flight of steps to the top of the plaza, taking the high ground to marshal his forces. What was left of them, anyway.

Hordes of stumbling, staggering fungoids swarmed out of the gutted offices surrounding the plaza for the gangster convoy to mow down like grass. Only a few of them seemed armed and capable of shooting back, but the wild licks of gunfire sent his convoy into disarray.

Stymie tried to follow the frantic chatter on his headset over the thunderous clatter of the M60s. He swept the creeping dusted off the steps and blew up a parked metermaid scooter at the curb. Blood and spores glided through the air in a fine pink mist, speckling the lenses of his gas mask.

In his calculating mind, the loss of more men only forced him to scale back his ambitious plans for the afternoon. He ordered the Eight Tray squad to sweep east and go down Fourth to the Jewelry District. No response at all from the team he sent to bust open the county jail, or the hotheads who thought the time was ripe to firebomb Parker Center.

Stymie could give two shits about the roots of the fungoid plague, but the old jail was on lockdown with a skeleton staff, and a couple dozen friends were inside, plus a few hundred other clowns who would provide perfect cover for their getaway.

But his dogs were undisciplined, crazy with elation at the open nature of the fight, and they were getting clipped left and right for it. Idiots thought they were in a zombie movie, but half the zombies could still think.

Hundreds of them filled the streets. They had already overrun or blown up three of his cars, but they had a hard-on for the skyscrapers. The wall of the nearest tower bore a ladder of slime with human bodies mired in it, stuck to the glass like smashed bugs, and more of the dusted climbed over them, scaling the outside of the tower. A naked skinny white woman shinnied up the glass as he watched, planting her feet in the open mouth of a dead Asian lady to climb to the next rung. The lobby of the other tower had been smashed open by a renegade garbage truck, and people drifted across the plaza and into the smoky opening.

Euclid's science lecture had been boring, but Stymie was glad he'd stayed awake for it. The dusted wanted to get up high before they shot their wad. Stymie fully expected this would mean they'd find downtown deserted, but if they didn't get what they wanted today, nobody would.

"Yo, Dookie!" Stymie shouted into his headset.

"I gotcha back."

"Check out Spider-Man up on the tower, two o'clock."

"That shit is fucked up, chief."

"Put some grenades on their asses, won't you please?"

While Stymie laid down a circle of cover fire, Dookie jumped out of the APC and trained a grenade launcher on the human ladder on the window. The grenade leaped out of the fat barrel and somehow looped like a curveball on its way up to the fourth floor of Two California Plaza. The grenade punched through the glass a split second before it detonated, but Dookie, who never knew when to quit, popped off three more.

Stymie had read somewhere once that in a major earthquake, the streets of downtown and Westside Wilshire would be buried eight feet deep in broken glass from the skyscrapers. Despite his abiding love and respect for all human life on earth, Stymie Rollins dreamed about that shit for weeks. And now it came true.

The bottom four stories of the skyscraper simply popped; dozens of windows blew out and flew out into the dusky sky amid a flurry of shredded human bodies. Shards of glittering glass rained down on the churning mob like a blizzard of razors. Stymie saw a dusted woman neatly bisected from neck to navel by a flying wedge of tempered glass, another so far gone with infection he couldn't tell what it was simply exploded in a huge, roiling cloud of spores when an airborne rod of rebar pinned it to an *L.A. Times* kiosk.

It was fun, fun, fun until the M60s ran dry. Stymie called down for a rifle, but nobody answered him.

A helicopter circled low overhead, sucking the smoke up like lifting a curtain. Stymie looked up and let out a cheer.

The chopper wasn't black and white like the LAPD, and it wasn't a news chopper. It was olive green, with Old Glory and a white legend that said USMC on the nose.

An El Camino screeched around the corner of Grand, coming from the Civic Center. Two guys lay in the bed, pointing rocket launchers straight up. As Stymie kicked Dookie in the head, a rocket blasted out of the street and ripped the tail off the marine chopper where it idled, twenty stories up.

"I'm all right, chief . . . all *right* . . . *It's all good* . . ."

"Give me a goddamned gun, dummy." Stymie started to climb down beside Dookie when he saw his friend had taken off his mask and was rubbing something into his eyes.

Overhead, the chopper spun out of the sky like a broken boomerang and crashed in the L.A. River spillway.

Stymie hooked an M16 by its strap with his boot and climbed out the turret.

The El Camino stopped in the road. A rocket ripped out of the bed and almost instantly slammed into the APC. Stymie leaped into the air and was flung sideways through space.

He landed hard on one leg and rolled on a raft of corpses floating in the drained fountain. Stunned, he scrambled until he had something at his back.

It was a tree of pulpy white fungus, with human heads woven into its monstrous bulk. Stymie sprayed it until the trunk split open and the monstrous tree collapsed.

Slobbering, eyeless fungoids skulked around the edge of the plaza, just barely smart enough to come no closer. The winds picked up into a tornado. Another helicopter dropped out of the sky over the plaza but hovered forty feet above him. A cameraman zoomed in on him and waved.

Stymie banged on his headset, but all he could hear from it was a dull, deep ringing tone.

"Where the fuck are you wetbacks with my motherfucking fire engine?"

Alameda Street shook as the crowd parted and a giant stumbled out of the mob to face them.

Reggie Porter knocked back the last of a fifth of Knob Creek. "Now would be a good time for that secret weapon, youngster."

Manuel banged on the roof, but he could not make his mouth form words. What he was looking at made no goddamned sense at all.

It walked on two legs, and dragged two arms in the street behind it, but it was not a man. It was made of men.

Standing almost twenty feet tall, the behemoth had a roughly humanoid outline, but limbs and heads and bodies in orange jumpsuits stuck out of the tightly coiled white fibrous flesh. It had no head of its own, only a twisted tree of swollen fruiting bodies that stood out from the hollow between its shoulders; but the moaning mouths and un-blinking eyes of all the people engulfed in its hulking mass seemed to see and think and speak for it.

The giant stooped and scooped up a handful of dusted people from the mob and hurled them at the fire truck. One headless body smashed through the windshield and tumbled into Manuel's lap.

Two of his cousin's men jumped off the rig, firing wildly over their heads and running for their lives. Manuel emp-tied a clip into it and slapped in another without even seeing where he'd hit it.

"Hey, punk," Porter shouted, "flip the pressure valve on the turret and hose that sumbitch down!"

The fungoid giant plucked a wrought iron lamppost out of the sidewalk and smashed the cab of the fire truck with it, then thrust one huge paw fingered with huge, acid-dripping white tendrils into the cab.

Manuel ducked, but Reggie Porter shot the thing even as it wrapped its wriggling, dripping fingers around him and melted him in half.

"Cocksucker!" Goldie screamed, over and over again. The whole truck burped and bucked, and an arc of pure force shot out over the cab to spear the white giant in its chest.

The giant swung the lamppost at the blast of water. Its arm fell apart like bread in a downpour. All the giant's mouths howled in mortal agony. Blood and white foam bubbled out of the wound.

The giant turned to drag itself to shelter behind a bus stop, but Goldie played the high-pressure fungicidal shower up and down the monster's length until it split wide-open and melted in the gutter.

"Go, old man, go," Manuel shouted. "Left on Alhambra."

Only then did he realize that Porter was gone, from the waist up.

Closing his eyes, Manuel reached over and opened the driver's-side door to shove Porter's legs and pelvis out onto the road, and slid unwillingly into his seat.

Shoving the unruly truck into gear, Manuel rolled forward into the middle of the crowd while Goldie blazed a path with the hose. The water was already losing its pressure, but the industrial agent in the water lit up the dusted like sulfuric acid and holy water.

Three blocks to the jail. He wasn't fool enough to think that killing this thing at the root would undo all the damage or stop the rest of them in their track, like in vampire movies. But if they stopped it where it started and left it nowhere else to go, they might just kill it.

Stymie and his teams didn't answer their phones. They were either dead, or they were doing their own thing.

As he turned onto Alhambra, a flaming green helicopter hurtled by and crashed into the riverbed. As he crossed the bridge over the river, Manuel saw a kid in a hoodie sweatshirt looking over the edge at the burning wreckage. As they passed, Goldie hosed him in the face and flung him over the bridge railing.

Something was wrong. Manuel felt it as soon as he crossed the bridge and came down in the Warehouse District. None of the businesses around here had names on the front, but they all had elaborate graffiti tags everywhere else. Out here, nothing had changed. There were no signs of life whatsoever.

The jail annex was just another warehouse from the outside; a four-story complex with fences around an acre of open ground facing the riverbed. Narrow, shaded strips of windows, like gills. If you wanted to keep low-risk criminals in boxes and keep the overhead low, you couldn't do better. But leaving the front gates wide-open was a pretty stupid idea.

Manuel pulled into the motor pool lot and looked around before jumping out. His legs quivered under him. He grabbed the open door to hang on to, then threw up on his boots.

Goldie was the only one left on the back of the fire truck. He jumped down and ran up the loading dock to the open sally port. When he came out, he'd traded his fireman's helmet for a riot control helmet with a plastic visor. "Cocksuckers all cleared out, chief! Where to next?"

Manuel sagged against the door. He should call Rory and tell him that his brother was out there, somewhere. He should get that stupid kid back on the truck and get back in the action, or get him back home to his family in Compton, and get himself into a bottle.

"Hey, Goldie," Manuel said.

"My name's Tyrone, bitch-ass," Goldie said.

"Fine, Tyrone. We still got water in the tanks?"

"Quarter pressure, but I can put more that nasty Chinese shit in the mix."

Manuel told him, "Do it." He got a text from Stymie: WHERR D FUK R U⁇

Manuel got into the truck and texted back, ON OUR WAY.

THIRTY-TWO

From the roof of Two California Plaza, you could not see the ground, or any of the city, beyond the neighboring skyscrapers, like islands in a sea of smoke. But you could see the sun setting, and the curve of the earth, the moon, and the first stars in the eastern sky.

If you were one of the family, you could look out from the edge of the forty-two-story tower and see forever.

They crowded the heliport deck and clung to one another atop the air-conditioning hoods and the window-washing rigs, crowded into every inch of space on the roof of the tower. But for once in the human history of Los Angeles, nobody shoved, nobody complained, and nobody acted as if they were all alone in the crowd. Nobody made any vocal noise at all, but if a baby in a dead woman's arms stabbed away at a toy phone that moaned in a low-battery voice, or a man on the edge sawed tunelessly at a violin, nobody else made a big deal out of it.

Some had used themselves completely to make the climb and expired standing in the group. Many dusted dead rested their cracked, wasted hands on a still-vital neighbor's shoulder so their mycelia could penetrate and siphon the critical water they'd need to bloom.

The winds were vicious, rolling up the cooling face of the glass to snatch away the weaker and exhausted pilgrims dangling over the edge. Hands thrust out to grab the falling member; sometimes they pulled him or her back, and

other times, they all fell in a silent white cloud. But the
winds were already beginning to fall off, as night began to
fall over the city.

Pressure in their inner ears had driven them to climb,
but together at the highest point in the city, they found
more than mere relief. As if they stood atop an antenna
that radiated their starving egos into the infinite, and received the bombardment of other fruiting bodies gathered
at great heights all over L.A.

From nearby One California and from the City National,
Wells Fargo, and Ernst & Young towers, they felt the overlapping psychic coronae of their neighbors, their brothers
and sisters on this great journey shedding the last selfish
shells of their old selves. More than marriage or childbirth
or any other achievement for which humans thought they
were made, this gave them total, utter fulfillment. To be
here, to become this, was their reason for being.

As the sun began to set into the miasma of smoke over
the city, they ripened in the wind and opened themselves
up to offer their fruit to the sky. Soon, they would be ready.
Soon, they would be everyone and everything, forever.

From down in the street anywhere in Los Angeles, the view
is always pretty much the same. One end may be richer or
safer than the other, but it just rolls on and on until you
break down and settle wherever you end up.

Stymie found himself thinking that and other stupid
things, as he slipped into shock. Stupid thing, shock. The
body's natural reaction to trauma should be something
better than the normal range of reaction, to get out of
danger. None of this heavy-lidded, clumsy, cold, looking-
at-the-world-down-a-long-dark-tube bullshit.

The dusted fuckers drifted by his corner of the plaza
to climb the wall into the huge hole Dookie had made,
presumably to climb the stairs. He'd just made it easier
for them. Every so often, a silent but very alive human

form tumbled from the roof, flailing and kicking in the wind to smash like bags of wet flour on the plaza's stylish brickwork.

He could probably just walk away, if his femur didn't jut out of his thigh like it did. He only got a couple units on the phone, but they sounded dusted, so he dropped them. No doubt half his squads rabbited back to the ghetto the second they got out of sight, and he didn't blame them. No wonder they did all those push-ups and screaming and shit in the real army.

The jailbreak plan had been an insanely stupid, yet necessary, part of getting the gangs to come down here. The jewelry stores were a less stupid, yet equally tangential element of his plan. In the end, Stymie admitted to himself that he had come downtown because he loved this fucking city.

If the army had ever tried to draft him to go to Afghanistan or somewhere, he would say *fuck that* and light out for somewhere nice, where black people got respect, like France. But nobody needed to call him up to fight for this city, this flat, hellish sorry excuse for a metropolis, that everyone from the first Californio landholders to the fucking Mexicans had tried to drive his people out of.

His phone rang.

"Where you at?"

"Manuel, you yellow dog mother—where the fuck you at?"

He couldn't hear Manuel's answer for the building wail of a siren. It took him a second to catch on and haul himself up on his good leg. He leaned against a brick planter box and slid over the pile of dead fungoids and kept sliding until he reached the stairs. Manuel was waiting for him.

"Jail's empty," Manuel said. "Truck's radiator is shot, and the tanks are empty. They're all up on the rooftops. But there's freshly dusted fuckers coming down Cesar Chavez. We gotta find someplace to hide, homes."

Stymie surveyed the purple-shadowed street, let his tired eyes roll up the glass walls just as the last flash of golden sunlight reflected off the peak of Two California Plaza. The wind would die down soon, and the temperature would fall. That's what they said the fungoids were waiting for.

His gas mask sucked onto his face and stank like ass. The filters must be beat. He took out a blue bandanna and tied it over his face.

Manuel took Stymie's arm. "Come on, we gotta get out of here. I got your nephew Tyrone out in the truck. You're welcome."

"Thank you? I didn't even have one before. I'm an only child." Stymie sat against the fire truck with his broken leg straight out. "I'm fucking beat, Manny. You got any guns?"

"Sure. You got any bullets?"

"Fuck . . . hold up, stop." They froze and looked up at the sky. "You hear that?"

In the distance, they heard shooting, but more and faster, and suddenly, a whole lot louder. But over it a drone that became a dull roar.

And in a few more seconds, it was right on top of them.

Manuel picked up his gun and climbed onto the top of the fire truck. Tyrone cocked his Uzi and sat beside him. "Y'know what really sucks?"

"This does," Manuel said.

Something just around the corner spoke in thunder and the facade of the parking garage across the street collapsed like an accordion. A tank rolled down Third Street and stopped on the corner as a gaggle of Humvees detoured around it and raced up the plaza.

Tyrone fired his gun into the air and crowed, "All the jarheads in the house, say—"

Brak-ak-ak-BOOM!

A salvo of fifty-caliber fire from the Humvees slashed the fire truck.

"Stand down, dummy," Manuel said as he pulled Tyrone down behind the truck. "Don't you know how zombie movies always end?"

"Bring us around and head east!" Fire Chief Gerry Magill shouted at his pilot.

The chopper practically got thrown out of the colossal convection cell of roiling heat and smoke that had formed over the mountain of fire that used to be Griffith Park. The loaded thousand-gallon bucket dangling from their underbelly clipped a huge ham-radio antenna looming over a burning Los Feliz rooftop. The chopper fought for altitude against a riptide wind that greedily sought to suck them back into the fire.

Crazy. The fires in the east Hollywood Hills were zero percent under control, and coming down out of the canyons to feast on neighborhoods. In the dark tonight, the fire would grow and spread over the hill and into the valley.

But they weren't fighting them.

From the fire department's temporary command center on Mulholland Crest, Lieutenant Nozizwe hailed him on his headset. "Chief, that volunteer leader from the Greek Theater break is redlining you, again."

"Tell him to withdraw to the Coldwater break, or he's on his own. We're not dumping over there."

"He refuses to pull back. Says neighborhoods are going up."

Magill knew what he would say, knew what they would all say, tomorrow. Homeowners always blamed the firefighters for letting their houses go up. The blame was understandable, yet almost never merited. But today, he'd decided to take it on faith that if they didn't let the east hills burn, something much, much worse would come tomorrow. He didn't expect anyone else to share his hunch.

"The planes are all going back to Burbank for the night,

after this run. Los Feliz captain is calling for one more hit on the Roosevelt—"

"I'm not letting Griffith Park and Los Feliz burn, just so I can make a dump run on a fucking golf course!"

The Roosevelt fairway passed under their skids. The fertilizer buildup in the soil turned the flames a sickly green.

Turning southeast, the chopper skipped like a stone over the rushing winds, swimming upstream. The pilot, Tak, corrected for the swinging seven-hundred-gallon bucket of reservoir water swinging under them. The chopper, a converted Sea Star, flexed under the strain of climbing into the winds.

"Where's the fire, Chief?" Tak shouted.

Pinpoints of lurid red and yellow light sparkled all over the city beneath them, but Magill ordered them to head for the nearest skyscraper.

They passed over the 110/101 junction and approached the towers atop Bunker Hill. The streets sparkled with tiny firecracker bursts that Magill knew must be heavy automatic-weapons fire. He saw a column of tanks churning up Alameda; then Tak screamed in his ear.

"Holy fuck! Chief, they're shooting at us!"

Something ripped the air and split the sky right in front of their noses. The chopper passed through its smoke trail.

"Climb, goddamn it!" Magill ran up behind Tak's chair. "Get us over the roof!"

"What the hell, this place isn't even on fire . . ."

The chopper cleared the roof of Two California Plaza and Tak blurted out, "They're not riding in my chopper . . ."

The roof was covered in standing bodies. Furry white bodies, with arms linked and with upturned heads split open like night-blooming flowers by bloated white fungi, rooted in place by anchors of white fibers like spiderwebs, they looked more than anything else like a field of giant dandelions.

The roof of One California Plaza was twice as crowded, the bodies piled two and three deep and fused together by nets of white fiber.

The other towers were similarly infested. They were right about that much, at least. Magill had gone along with the insane plan, gambled and lost at least one neighborhood already. His conscience wouldn't let him gamble that the insane plan would work.

"Take us higher!"

None of them had ever felt so in touch with the world, with one another, or with themselves. Misunderstood, underappreciated, muted, and stifled, they finally found a way to express all that had remained trapped inside them, all their lives. They approached the face of Godhead, and it was a mirror.

Swept away on waves of perfect contentment, they learned the final lesson, and bid bittersweet, fond farewell to their bodies.

All at once, their heads exploded.

Like a candle igniting, the tower of One California Plaza was engulfed in a cold white fire that the wind seized and ripped away.

Beneath them, the field of dandelions atop Tower Two shook violently in the wind and a cloud of white erupted like smoke from the rooftop.

"Drop the payload," Magill said. Then, because everyone else was frozen in awe, he did it himself.

The floor of the bucket disengaged. A solid wall of water dropped sixty feet to slam into the midst of the seething tangle of bodies just as the first heads began to ripen and pop.

The wave fanned out from the center of the roof and roared out waist-deep over the infected crowd, sweeping them in helpless heaps onto one another and over the low railing of the roof, and out into empty space.

The chopper surged wildly up and twisted in a corkscrew with the relief of ditching its three-ton payload, but Tak wasn't looking out where they were going. An Apache attack chopper darted in front of them, then punched the roof of the Wells Fargo Tower with Hellfire missiles. "Look out, the cavalry's here!"

Lieutenant Nozizwe was trying to call him. On the ground, he was probably already relieved of duty. At his side, Sergeant Guthrie looked at the human chains of drowned bodies clinging to the rooftop below. "Hey, Chief, what the fuck did we just do?"

Magill pointed at the white clouds of spores spewing from the skyscrapers all around them. "Do you see that?"

Tak nodded. "I don't know what the hell it is, but I see it."

"Get in front of it. Can you do that?"

Tak shook his head. "The winds from the fire are like a tornado, Chief. You know that. It's sucking everything over the whole damned city into it. Getting in front of that shit—"

Magill sat back and punched the button to take Nozizwe's call. "That's what I hoped you'd say."

It rained on California Plaza. Like most rains in Los Angeles, it was a light drizzle and over in minutes, but unlike most rainfall in Los Angeles, it also contained several hundred human bodies.

Manuel, Stymie, and Tyrone rode out the downpour under the fire engine. They fell like dead flowers, tumbling and seeming to float on the wind, until they hit the ground and burst like overripe fruit hard enough to crack pavement and utterly crush parked cars.

On the Westside, the spore-clouds of fruiting bodies on the towers on Wilshire and Ventura were ripped apart by the jet stream feeding the fires ten miles to the east, and the nocturnal winds that chased the sunset, blowing the bulk of the spores out to sea.

The largest concentration of the dusted gathered atop the federal building and released their spores without incident, only to have the cloud blown back into their faces by the prop wash of the Channel Five Newscopter, which authorities had tried unsuccessfully to shoot down after it was used in the escape of the Latino terrorist ringleader Hector "Tres Ojos" Gonzalez from the Channel Five studios.

As night fell on the city, the barking and howling of dogs echoed down streets and up the canyons, as citizen patrols tracked down spores and holdout enclaves of the dusted. Sirens and gunfire rocked the city to sleep.

And though half of it still burned, Los Angeles slipped into the peaceful sleep of a broken fever.

And its dreams were only of itself.

Epilogue

The Measure of Wright and Long

The Silver Lake Reservoir was a lovely oasis of calm—up in the hills, but away from the fires—overlooking the funky sprawl of their homeland, with a clear view of the skyline, and the last aeronautic maneuvers in what would forever be known as the Battle of Downtown L.A.

The two of them sat alone at a picnic table, not talking, just watching the sky—helicopters cutting through the bruised plum and blood-orange colors of sunset—when the prison van blew through the reservoir gate, took the winding road up, then down toward the water's edge.

"Well," Rory said, standing painfully. "So much for that peaceful shit."

"You don't have to do this part, you know," Trixie said, also standing, as did the others. "You've done enough, baby. Everybody knows that."

"Everybody but me," he said, clicking off the safety on the last of Stumbo's guns.

Richie had expected resistance all the way uptown, and particularly at the gate itself. But it never happened.

So he was doubly surprised when—less than a hundred yards from the water—machine gun fire blew the tires to confetti, and the crippled van skidded, careened, then flipped onto its driver's side and skidded to a halt.

Inside, the cargo groaned and howled as one, none more than Richie, who'd come so far to gain so little.

From the outside, Rory and Trixie approached, flanked by gunmen who continued to fire, pockmarking the steel exterior. Blowing holes in whatever was inside.

It didn't take long before the fuel line blew, and sheets of mushroom-white contagion sailed flaming through the air on waves of vehicular shrapnel. Evidently, the van had been packed to the rafters with fruiting bodies.

Rory prayed for closure, waiting for the chunks to stop flying before wading into the horror.

Trixie stayed behind, let him do what he had to do.

And there—in a last burst of overachievement—lay what remained of Richie Long. Eyeless. Gasping. Barely recognizable under the tumorous snarl of fruiting bodies. Crutching forward on six malformed limbs, only two of which used to be his arms, the others inherited from fungoid brothers lost in the infinite merger.

One of the gunmen stepped up beside Rory, aiming, but Rory waved him off.

"That's my brother," he said.

Seven hundred and ninety-five million gallons of squeaky-clean Silver Lake Reservoir water sparkled orange in the sunset's glow. Richie couldn't see it, but he could sense the moisture, feel the dying organism within him reaching out for that which it had craved all along.

"You're never gonna make it," Rory said, stepping close.

"Don't be like that," said Richie's remains. "We can still do this."

"Maybe we could. But it's a really bad idea."

"That's what you always say."

"I maybe should have said it more often."

"Oh, little man," said Richie, so close to the water he could almost taste it. Crawling closer and closer still. "You don't know what you're missing."

"Yeah, actually, I think I do."

"*I will spread,*" Richie said. "I will touch every living soul. And it's gonna be awesome."

"You already lost. I don't know if you know that."

"And you're gonna feel like *such a dunce*. Because you had your shot at the inside track. At being one of the few who still can hear themselves think. And you threw it all away."

"You're not listening, Richie. You never fucking listen."

Rory chambered a shell with an audible clack, aimed the barrel directly at Richie's head.

Richie paused, recognizing the moment. He let out a deep sigh. Rory echoed the gesture.

"I'm sorry," he said, "I didn't bring you any leftovers."

Richie chuckled. "Prick."

"Hey." Wiping a tear. "I said I was sorry."

"It's okay."

"It was really, really good, though."

"I probably couldn't taste it anyway." The Richie-thing horribly grimaced, smacked its lips. "You know what my mouth tastes like right now?"

"No. I shudder to think."

"It's like buttermilk and cotton mouth, with an extra turd thrown in."

Rory laughed, though the tears wouldn't stop. "Mmmm. I can see why you wouldn't want to miss out on that."

"Can I tell you something?" And Richie's head tilted back toward him, as if looking, though see he could not.

"Yeah. Sure. Go ahead."

Richie sighed and began.

"I was always ahead of you. In everything."

"I know."

"I was older than you. I got laid first. I made money first. I got married first. I went to fucking jail first."

"You got paddled first."

"I did *everything* first. And you were always the also-ran. You were the guy I brought in when I already blazed the trail."

"Yeah, you're a trailblazer, all right. Richie, we've been down this road before—"

"And I've succeeded over and over, while you always just plugged along—"

"Are you begging me to shoot you now?"

Richie laughed. "In a minute. In a minute."

Then he vomited up something too dry to call moist, too pathetic to call monstrous, before resuming.

"Excuse me," he continued. "But this is the thing. This is the point I'm trying to make."

"I'm all fucking ears, man."

"Once you met Trixie?" And the question was left to echo off. "Everything changed."

"Yeah, I know. She's my Yoko."

"No, no, no. I'm not doing that joke again. I'm trying to say that—" Clearly, saying it was hard . . .

"When you met her, you pulled ahead."

Rory swallowed hard, turned his gaze back to Trixie, who was standing back. So strong. So beautiful. So wanting to be there, and knowing she couldn't.

Trusting in him.

Believing in him.

"I never had that," Richie said. "I never got what I wanted. What I wanted was always ahead. The next scam. The next blow job. The next paycheck. The next negotiation. The next fucking thing that would make me happy. The next win."

"I know. Of course I know."

"So are you *feelin'* me, then?"

"Oh, please, don't ever say that again. I hate that fucking expression."

"Sorry, man. They're the only words I got. Sorry . . ."

"Not from you, man. Please."

"This is Richie. This is not—"

And Richie paused, sniffing the water.

But this was not Richie.

It was the thing that lived in him, and it knew what it wanted. And it was tired of talking.

And tired of feeling.

Life had been so much simpler, waiting under the ground. Dreaming only of moisture and new habitats, with only its own simple appetites to feed. The absence of heads, and their yammering minds, had been a paradise, it now realized, too late.

Oh, to be like that again . . .

But the water was right there in front of it. And with it, the promise of forever expansion. Sharing the bounty that was its form. Sharing the glory that was its vision.

It could not help but press forward, in that moment.

Rory pulled the trigger, and blew half its arms off.

Richie's mouth screamed, but his forearms were strong, as the last of him scuttled toward the reservoir's edge.

"SHOOT THAT THING!" yelled one of the men.

"No. It's okay. Let him have what he wants."

Rory followed closely behind it.

Until the thing hit the water.

And it was not Richie who screamed and dissolved, foaming like an Alka-Seltzer tablet, or an open, infected wound under hydrogen peroxide.

It was the pestilence that screamed, and thrashed, and came apart in burbling curds.

Soaking in the antifungal agents they'd poured into the reservoir, an hour before.

Rory watched as a miniature rainbow formed in the air above his brother: a little miracle of physics, moisture condensing into spray and struck at precisely the right angle by the sun.

He liked to think it was Richie's soul.

But that wasn't science.

That was only hope.

And now, for Trixie, came the hardest part. The thing she dreaded most.

It was time to go home.

Rory didn't seem to want to talk yet, and that was hard,

but she understood, and was reluctantly grateful. In fact, she was terrified by her own need to talk, terrified that she would say the wrong thing, push the wrong button, open the door to her own deepest fears and let them come pouring out uncensored, insensitive, selfish, and hurtful.

But as she drove, the streets were a blur, fogged by the tears she couldn't hold back and the memories that wouldn't stop coming.

And then they were on Hyperion, and the road was mercifully clear, all the familiar landmarks almost entirely the same, save for occasional piles of burning bodies.

Both of them were crying by the time they reached Fernwood. Her hand went out for his, and he held it, clutched it, almost hard enough to hurt.

"I don't know if I can do this," she said.

"We need to—" he started to say, then left it at that. "We need to."

The corner of Fernwood and Hyperion was blocked by a flatbed truck. Behind it stood a couple dozen of their neighbors, some of whom they actually recognized. If they didn't have guns, they had baseball bats. If they didn't have those, they had dogs on leashes.

There were easily a hundred dogs, most of them running free. And all of them barking, as Trixie pulled up slowly in front of the truck, Rory rolling down the passenger-side window and holding up his hands.

"WE'RE COOL!" he yelled. "We're on your side! We're copacetic!" As all the guns aimed at his face, and a dozen large dogs jumped up to the window.

And instantly started licking his hands.

Rory laughed, and Trixie laughed, too, though she didn't know how that was possible. "Damn slobberin' mutts! Get offa my car!"

Trixie opened her door and stepped outside, holding her hands up. A pair of German shepherds came barreling around the front of the car, ran up to her. She recognized them at once.

And they recognized her, too: jumping up to kiss and kiss and kiss her, like they couldn't possibly kiss her enough.

She felt her heart begin to lighten.

But her dread was still so huge.

And then they were passing the truck, coming up on Rory's garage, where the lights were on, and all the doors were open. There were a couple of guys up there, scraping the floor of bay number three with shovels. One of them waved as they passed.

Trixie felt her knees go weak, and almost collapsed before somebody caught her. She didn't know who. Suddenly, there was a wave of people surrounding her, surrounding them, helping her back to her feet and washing them toward their house.

And people were asking questions, but they all ran together, and she didn't know where to start. It was all so overwhelming that she could barely even hear her own frightened voice, going numb with long-overdue shock.

Up ahead, she saw the crazy dog lady, who didn't look nearly so crazy anymore. She looked like the head of the local neighborhood watch, from the way people nodded and responded when she spoke.

The crazy dog lady yelled, "OH, THANK GOD!" as she spotted Trixie, came running forward and swept her up in a hug. She smelled awful, like she hadn't bathed in weeks.

But she also smelled human.

It was a beautiful thing.

Trixie tried to say thank you, thanks for saving my life, but she couldn't get the words out. She was crying too hard.

The crazy dog lady said, "No, no, thank YOU . . . !"

And then Rory was there, peeling her away, walking her slowly up the steps to their house, their home. And the front door was open. And the lights were still on. Just as she'd left them.

And she couldn't bear to look.

So her eyes were closed as she stepped through the doorway, but her nostrils were assailed by Pine-Sol and Lysol, antiseptic smells so concentrated and cloying they belonged in a hospital ward.

It was a slap in the face. A good one. It yanked her eyes open.

Searching for blood that was no longer there.

The crib was gone. The sleeper couch folded up. The throw carpet was gone, and the floorboards beneath it gleamed.

There were no bodies on the floor.

As if the siege had never happened.

And in the corner, on her knees, with a big sponge and a bucketful of sudsy water, a woman was scrubbing and scrubbing away.

The woman turned.

It was Renee.

That was when Trixie collapsed at last, letting go of Rory and embracing the floor. Sniffing it for blood, for ghosts, for spores, for anything left that was poised to rob her of everything she loved, and on which she depended.

Then Renee was cradling her, begging forgiveness, the story pouring out of her faster than time. Her shame at having been so useless. Her shame at having fled the accident. Her horrible, horrible shame at being such a worthless human being, and such a lousy, rotten, pathetic excuse for a friend.

So she had stumbled back from the accident scene, panicking, terrified, thinking only of herself, just trying to get to her rental car and get the fuck out of Dodge forever.

But when she got to the house, and saw what was there, a startling clarity had fallen on her.

If redemption was possible, there was only one thing to do.

So she had cleaned it up. As simple as that. She had

spent hours and hours and hours just cleaning it up. Taking the bodies outside, wrapped in the linen they had slept on. Removing the crib, which was mercifully empty.

Setting it all on fire.

And then scrubbing and scrubbing and scrubbing, till every trace of the slaughter was physically gone. She had mopped the ceiling. She had mopped the walls.

And the floor was almost done.

Trixie kissed the floor, then kissed her friend, then called out for Rory and kissed him, too. He hoisted her up and held her close. Renee piled in, too, and they all stood together.

Giving thanks for all they still had.

"Who wants turkey?" Rory said.

CPSIA information can be obtained at www.ICGtesting.com
Printed in the USA
239412LV00001B/2/P